Abusing His Grace

by

Stephanie A. Gridley

Acknowledgments

First and foremost, I want to give honor to God who gave me the natural writing ability and understanding to write this book, and access to the people and information who have influenced me both to write and to write on this subject matter.

Special thank you to my parents--may my earthly father continue to rest in heaven; thank you to both Stevie and Brenda Smith for introducing me to the wonders of the public library at a young age; emphasizing the importance of a good education; and taking me to New Testament Baptist Church so that I may learn the Word of God and be able to rightfully divide the word of truth.

Finally, thank you to my husband Matt, who, along with our children, provide me with a constant source of ambition toward pursuing my goals. Let's enjoy wherever this endeavor takes us!

CHAPTER ONE

"Fathers, do not provoke your children to anger, but bring them up in the discipline and instruction of the Lord." (Ephesians 6:4)

Grace Hardaway was in a bind.

In her trembling hands she held a letter from GM Financial, the company that had financed the Chevrolet Suburban that she used as her primary vehicle. The payment for the SUV was three months past due. In bold letters, the company was demanding that Dean, her husband, cough up over $1500 to cover the missed payments and applicable late fees or else they would begin the legal process required for repossession. Grace had no idea that Dean hadn't been paying the note or that he was having any type of financial difficulties. It wasn't like he would tell her anyway. She was not privy to information about his money.

It was just one of his many control tactics that led to an overall miserable existence. Under different circumstances, their beautiful house would have been the stuff of her childhood dreams, but her relationship with Dean mirrored that of a warden and his prisoner more than it did a husband and wife. She was barely allowed outside of the home. Grace had given up a lucrative career at Dean's urging to be a housewife. It was the second biggest mistake she'd ever made.

The first was marrying Dean in the first place.

The contents of the letter was only half the problem. The bigger issue was that it was open. Since he made all the money, Dean told Grace she had no business in his financial affairs. Her job was to tend to the house and their children. No bills came to the house in her name, so she had no reason to open any of his mail. If she did she was just being nosy.

Only half an hour previous her day had been going relatively well--as well as a day could go in the Hardaway household. Grace had the same daily routine throughout the week. At six in the morning she woke up, quietly headed downstairs and prepared Dean's breakfast. He ate the same thing every day--two egg whites, wheat toast, turkey bacon and coffee. He even ate everything in the same sequence. The toast first, followed by the egg whites and then the bacon. He usually drank the coffee in one or two gulps. Before he left for work at seven a.m., he walked through the house and made a checklist of things he wanted Grace to take care of before he got home. While he was doing so, she stood by the door in the kitchen that led out to the garage holding his briefcase, lunch, and jacket like a mannequin. Just as he did every day, he took his items from her, handed her the list, and gave her a dry kiss on the cheek. She forced a smile. "Have a great day."

Like a Stepford wife, Grace stood in the door with the fake smile still plastered on her face, waving, as he pulled off and closed the garage. Once he was finally gone she heaved a big sigh of relief, instantly feeling the weight of his presence leave her body. She had about a half an hour to herself. She used this time to pray and read her Bible.

At around eight a.m. she heard the first footsteps above her as her daughters got out of bed and scurried to and fro upstairs. Smiling, she closed her Bible and got the ingredients together for apple-cinnamon pancakes and sausages and listened as the girls ran back and forth from bedroom to bedroom as they got themselves up and ready to eat. They came downstairs quietly in a line--twelve-year-old Eve, six-year-old twins Rebekah and Sarah, and five-year-old twins Abigail and Naomi.

Once they realized their father was gone, the girls dropped the formalities and raced into the kitchen to hug their mother. She returned their affection. Other than God, those little girls were the only thing that kept her going. Grace was their only source of love and attachment. Dean wasn't interested in them--he'd wanted sons. Grace could never forget how embarrassed she was during her ultrasound with Abby and Naomi when the ultrasound technician revealed that she was having two more girls. Grace and the tech were delighted, but the look on Dean's face immediately turned the atmosphere in the room sour. He didn't say a word. His demeanor made the tech uncomfortable, and Grace was extremely embarrassed. During the rest of the scan, Dean sat back in his seat, folded his arms and glared at Grace as though it was her fault. As they drove home from the ultrasound Dean informed her tersely, "I guess we're going to have to try again."

Unfortunately they were unable to do so. During her delivery with Abby and Naomi Grace hemorrhaged heavily and ended up having a hysterectomy. Instead of being concerned about his wife and brand new babies, Dean remained detached, growing visibly angrier with each passing second about the death of his dream to have a son. He barely held either of his new daughters during the first several months of their lives. Even when his sleep-deprived, overworked wife begged him for help, Dean refused, reminding her that tending to the house and the children was *her* responsibility. Dean wasn't a good father to any of his girls. He had grown up with two sisters that he despised and told Grace he didn't find "girl stuff" to be particularly interesting.

Grace and the girls sat down and ate a lively breakfast together. She enjoyed their childish chatter and refreshing innocence. Unfortunately, time was ticking. Grace had to get started on her checklist. The girls were just as used to the routine as their mother, so they knew to clear their breakfast dishes from the table and head downstairs to the play area in the basement once the kitchen clock chimed nine.

Dean was a Marine and used that to excuse his insistence on absolute perfection. Although they rarely entertained guests Dean expected the house to look showroom-new every day. Grace went through the bedrooms, tucking in sheets and smoothing comforters. Dean hated to see wrinkles in the bed coverings. She made sure there were no streaks on the bathroom mirrors or the stainless steel appliances in the kitchen. When she vacuumed she had to make sure the lines weren't crooked in the carpet, because lines drove Dean nuts. Wood furnishings had to be dusted daily.

Grace finished her checklist by lunchtime. She fixed hot ham and cheese subs with fruit for the girls and took it downstairs for them to eat. After lunch it was time for their lessons. Grace made sure the girls were still actively learning throughout the summer but Dean would check by making the girls tell him something they'd learned each day. It wasn't because he actually cared about their education. It was just that smart, well-groomed children were good for his ego and his image. It was also another way of keeping his wife under control. The very thought of Grace having more than ten minutes of time to herself was some type of sacrilege. If Dean wasn't satisfied with his daughters' recitations, Grace paid the price for it.

At three-thirty Grace raced back upstairs to put the finishing touches on the house. While she was back in the kitchen wiping frantically at almost invisible streaks on the refrigerator, the doorbell rang. She froze. Dean forbade her from answering the door, even if it was someone she knew.

In this case, it *was* someone she knew. Curious, Grace stuck her head out of the kitchen and looked down the hallway toward the front door. Her neighbor from next door, Tim Wise, was looking right at her through the skylights on the side of the front door. Grace withdrew her head with a gasp.

Tim had definitely seen her. He rang the bell a few more times, then rapped on the door incessantly.

Grace was extremely put-upon. She could very well stay in the kitchen and wait until Tim left, but why was he knocking like that? Maybe it was an emergency. If it was an emergency, perhaps Dean wouldn't be angry about her opening the door. Sighing, she went to the front door, unlocked it, and opened it about an inch wide.

"Sorry to bother you Grace, but the mailman gave me some of Dean's mail again." Tim foisted an envelope through the cracked door. "I uh… I didn't notice the name on it before I opened it. Both of my cars are financed through GM, so I thought it was for me…I'm sorry it's been opened."

Grace fought to keep the tears from forming in her eyes. Tim thought he was doing his due diligence as a neighbor by personally returning the mail, but Grace wished that he hadn't. She took the envelope and attempted to shut the door.

"Grace?"

"What?" she asked, more sharply than she intended.

"If you need help, you can always ask, you know," Tim said uncomfortably.

"With what?"

"Don't play dumb, Grace. We can hear you and Dean."

Her eyes widened. She tried not to look surprised and forced a laugh. "You mean our arguments? All couples fight, don't they?"

"Not with fists."

Grace dropped her head in shame. It was a humiliating moment. Up until then she hadn't known that her neighbors could hear her being abused. Her secret was out and probably had been for a long time.

"If you need somewhere to go I have a cottage up North…"

"I'm okay, but thanks Tim." She again started to shut the door.

"If I hear it again I'll call the police," Tim warned her before he took the hint and walked away.

With Tim gone, Grace's knees buckled. She crumbled to the floor in a heap, sobbing quietly so as not to alarm her daughters. This piece of mail put her in a quandary. Mentally, Grace ran through possible protective scenarios. She could rip the letter to shreds and pretend nothing had ever happened. But what if Tim saw Dean outside one day and brought it up? Dean would be caught off guard, and he hated that. That would definitely get her beat, worse than if she just went ahead and told the truth.

Grace got up from the floor and went into the kitchen. Only then did the contents of the letter become clear, and she panicked even further. Undoubtedly Tim had read the letter and knew her husband was having problems meeting his financial obligations. Dean wasn't going to deal well with that type of exposure. Grace knew she was going to get it. She began to dry heave and poured herself some water to calm her nerves.

The clock on the stove beeped, jolting her back into reality. Grace had several clocks set throughout the house to go off at multiple intervals during the day so that she would know when the time was nearing for her husband to return. The alarm on the stove meant that it was now four o'clock, and Dean got off work at four-thirty and usually got home a few minutes after five. Grace jumped up and started to prepare dinner. As it was cooking, she raced back downstairs and told the girls, "Time to get ready, sweeties."

The happiness melted off their faces. It was game time. Without a word, the girls cleaned up the play room. There was a place for everything. After all the toys, books, dolls and blocks had made it back to their respective homes and the carpet had been vacuumed, Grace sat the girls in a circle so they could rehearse their lines. "Eve, what are you going to say?"

"I know what I'd like to say," Eve said hotly.

"Eve, please don't." Grace looked into her eldest daughter's face. Out of all her girls, Eve was definitely the most hot-tempered. The others were intimidated by Dean. Eve was not. She often spoke of her hatred for Dean and only complied with him to save her mother from being hurt.

With a heavy sigh, Eve recited her speech. "I practiced solving equations with an unknown for math, learned words for clothing in Spanish, and read more from *The Fault in Our Stars*."

Rebekah and Sarah were next. Much quieter than their older sister, they mumbled their lines and looked to Grace for approval. She nodded and gave them a reassuring smile. Abby excitedly read an entire book from beginning to end. As one of the younger girls, she knew that her home life wasn't like everyone else, but she hadn't yet been completely tarnished by its dysfunction. She also had never been a direct object of Dean's wrath. All Abby knew was that she was happy to learn. Being quizzed didn't bother her. It did, however, bother her twin. Grace looked at Naomi sympathetically. Two tears rolled down her fat cheeks. Naomi was absolutely terrified of Dean.

"Oh, sweetie." Fighting her own tears, Grace patted her lap, signaling for her youngest child to join her. Naomi crawled onto her mother, snuggled her head into Grace's bosom, and cried silently for a few minutes. She wasn't as sharp as her sister, and whenever she stumbled over a word or didn't respond quickly enough to Dean's questions, Naomi would watch in terror as her mother was slapped, punched, or kicked by her father.

Grace cupped Naomi's face with her hands. "Did you like the book Mommy made for you?"

Naomi nodded.

"Can you read that for Daddy, please?"

She nodded again.

Another clock rang out. Everyone froze. It was the last of the brooding alarms, and coincidentally, the loudest and most formidable, coming from Dean's grandfather clock in the den. He was going to walk through the door at any minute.

Grace returned her focus to her terrified youngest daughter. "I know you'll do fine. You're all very smart girls, and Mommy is proud of all of you. Wash up for dinner."

Obediently the girls walked in line formation to the bathroom and took turns washing their hands. They quietly headed upstairs, took their usual places at the dinner table, and waited in total silence as Grace started getting their plates ready. Then came the moment they had all been anticipating. The garage door opened, which meant that Dean was home.

Grace and the girls listened as Dean went through his usual routine. He took his shoes off and put them on the shoe rack in the laundry room. He set his briefcase on the floor next to it and began his walk into the kitchen. Even his steps were menacing, and each one caused Grace's heart to jump. She knew that he was looking around as he approached the dinner table, waiting to see a detail that Grace had missed.

Evidently he found nothing out of place—at least not so far. Grace watched as her husband pulled out his chair at the head of the table and sat down.

"Eve, would you bless the food please?" he instructed his eldest daughter curtly.

Their eyes met for just a second, and Grace's heart raced. Eve often challenged her father, and those challenges meant a spanking for Eve and a punch for Grace. Eve's eyes quickly flitted over to her mother's anguished face, and she said nothing. Instead, she clasped her hands together in front of her. The others did the same.

"Thank you God for blessing us with this food. Please let it be nourishing to us. In the name of Jesus, amen."

The rest of the family chorused "Amen" and began to eat. It was a typical meal. The girls didn't speak unless Dean addressed them first. When he did ask a question of the girls it was only something that required a "yes" or "no" answer.

Part of Grace's job as a dedicated wife was to always show concern about Dean's day, even though he never asked about hers. "How was your day?" she asked brightly.

"Interesting, to say the least. Looks like I'm going to be the project manager for the new electronic health record development at Superior."

Grace was ecstatic. Dean was a software engineer for Innovative Technology Solutions, a company that designed and maintained electronic medical record software and bank software. ITS had won a bid to develop the new electronic health record for the second-largest employer in the area, Superior Heights Health System, the hospital where all five of their children had been born. Superior Heights also employed the doctors the family visited for their health care. It was a considerable undertaking. This was the second major project that Dean would be involved in, and Grace remembered with delight how much overtime Dean worked during the first project. He was rarely at home. Most nights he was gone until nine-thirty, and he often worked Saturdays as well. It was like a vacation for Grace and the girls.

"Dean, that is wonderful! Congratulations!" Maybe this good news would keep him from beating her up when he saw the mail.

The family continued eating in silence. Once the girls were finished, Dean cleared his throat and said, "What did you accomplish today?"

That was the girls' cue. They got up from the table and lined up in front of Dean, oldest to youngest. Grace's nerves were instantly aroused. She hated that Dean always did this after dinner. It was a purposeful move--everything Dean did to terrorize his wife was purposefully done. Grace had a sensitive stomach and emetophobia. Dean knew that hitting her in the stomach after dinner would more than likely trigger at least a gag reflex. If any of the girls messed up badly enough with their speeches or if he wasn't satisfied with their lessons, one quick jab to her tender gut would send Grace running to the nearest bathroom. With the most monotone she could muster, Eve recited her speech first.

"Very good, Eve. You should do just fine in seventh grade."

"Thank you," Eve said in a syrupy-sweet voice, adding a condescending curtsy before returning to her seat. Grace looked at her with wide eyes, then back at Dean, hoping he hadn't noticed Eve's insolence. Luckily for her, he hadn't. He had moved on to the next daughter.

When it was Naomi's turn, Grace's breath caught in her throat. The girls were not allowed to look at Grace when Dean was speaking to them. Dean considered it disrespectful if they failed to look him in the face when he was talking to them. Still, Grace managed to catch her daughter's gaze for a second, enough time to give her a small, encouraging smile.

Naomi acknowledged her mother with a very slight nod, took a deep breath, and flawlessly read the little book Grace had written and illustrated using some of the sight words they had been practicing that week. Dean nodded his approval and even managed a small smile himself, to the surprise of all. He took the book from Naomi and turned it over. Grace had used different colored pieces of card stock, a hole punch, and yarn to make the little book. Apparently, Dean was impressed by her handiwork.

"That was excellent, Naomi."

"Thanks, Daddy." Her voice was barely above a whisper. Head down, she walked quickly back to her seat.

"You girls can go play now."

The girls cleared their places at the dinner table and got out of dodge as quickly as possible. They headed back downstairs, although they couldn't technically "play" the games they wanted. Dean didn't like for them to make much noise when he was home, and they assuredly didn't want to do anything to draw their father's ire, so the most they could do was read books, color, or play a quiet game on their tablets. Even on the rare occasion that they were allowed to go into the backyard and play, Dean still grew irritated if they screamed or laughed too loudly.

"The pork was delicious, Grace. If you don't mind getting me some more?" Dean held out his plate, wiping his mouth with his napkin.

"Of course. I'm happy you liked it." She hurried to the oven and removed the rest of the pork tenderloin. Figuring now was as good a time as any, she put Dean's plate before him and said bravely, "Did you check the mail today?"

Dean looked at her with an eyebrow raised. Already she was taking the chance of being viewed as meddlesome. "Yes," he said testily.

"Well, I know you don't like for me to answer the door, but Tim came by and he was knocking pretty hard, so I thought maybe something was wrong and he saw me from the kitchen so I answered it and he handed me a piece of our mail that had been mistakenly delivered to his house." She was speaking fast even though she knew that annoyed Dean. She just wanted to get it all out; to get it over with, receive her punishment, and go on with her day. Prayerfully, since she had done a good job with the girls, the meal, and the house, he would go easy on her.

Dean pushed his plate away and glared at her. "Where is it." It was a demand, not a question.

Grace retrieved the envelope from the counter. Keeping several feet between herself and her husband, she fully extended her arm and handed it to him. He snatched it from her and flipped it over a few times, examining it. Grace could see his anger growing as he realized what it said.

"It's *open.*"

"Tim opened it before he noticed that it wasn't for him," Grace told him quietly.

"Oh, really?" Dean stood up from his seat and walked toward her. Instinctively, Grace began to back up. Her efforts to maintain space between her and Dean were thwarted by the suddenly intrusive kitchen island.

"Yes," Grace said. The food in her stomach that had once been so delicious wasn't feeling so good right now.

"So you opened up my front door, huh?"

"Yes, but…"

"Did I ask you for an excuse?" Dean sneered, standing over her.

Grace shook her head and folded her arms over her stomach.

"You already messed up when you opened the door, and now I'm supposed to believe you're not the one who opened my mail?"

"I didn't," Grace pleaded. "You can ask Tim. He said he was sorry…"

SLAP!

With the island behind her, there was nowhere to go. Dean's heavy backhand across her face snapped her head back hard enough to cause a sharp pain to go up her neck. He then used one hand to grab her throat and force her to look up into his snarling face.

"Why did you open my door?" With each word, he shook her neck a little.

"I thought he needed help," Grace whimpered.

"It's not your job to decide if someone needs help," Dean informed her coldly. "Your job…your *only* job…is to do what *I* say. Now what if that hadn't been somebody who needed help? What if it had been some kidnapper who pushed you aside and went and got one of the girls? What would you do then? I'll tell you what you would do… *nothing*. You aren't capable of doing *anything*."

His anger placated, Dean released her throat, pushed her aside, and stomped into his place of refuge, the first-floor den that he had converted into his very own man-cave. He closed the French doors. Grace heaved a sigh of relief. It hadn't been as bad as she thought.

As if nothing had happened, Grace fell right back into her routine. The dinner dishes had to be cleaned and put away. The appliances had to be wiped free of streaks again. Dean's clothes for the next day had to be ironed to a crisp. The girls had to be bathed. Grace went downstairs to get them and was not surprised when she couldn't find them.

Each of her daughters had her own place of refuge in the house. Although Grace tried her hardest not to scream, cry or yell during her beatings, the girls always heard what went on between their parents. When Dean was fighting their mother, the girls would tuck themselves into hiding places in the basement in futile attempts to drown out the terror taking place around them. Grace knew if she could get Eve out of her hiding place first the other girls would follow.

She found Eve curled up in a ball with tears streaming down her cheeks in a little storage area beneath the stairs. "It's time for baths and bed, Eve. Can you come out? I need you to come out so that your little sisters will."

Eve stared right through her mother.

It pierced Grace's heart when Eve reacted to her in that manner, because she didn't understand what her daughter was feeling. "It's okay, Eve. Can you come out, please?"

Eve shook her head. She was tired of being the brave, responsible one. It wasn't fair to her, and she was beginning to resent her role. She loved her little sisters--and her mother--but often her burden became too much to bear. Now was one of those times. She hated her father, but Eve also despised her mother for refusing to take her and her sisters and leaving.

Grace had just pleaded with her husband, now it was time to plead with her daughter. Grace sighed. "Eve, I beg you to come out. I have to get all of you in the bed."

Upstairs, Grace heard footsteps. She looked up. Eve recognized the look of panic on her mother's face. Her anger subsided and was replaced by pity. She crawled out of her hiding place and called her sisters to attention. "Let's go, guys."

Naomi ran out first and grabbed Eve's hand. The others followed.

Grace stayed behind and put away the few items the girls had brought out. She went upstairs and was met at the basement door by her husband.

"Is there anything sweet in the kitchen?" he asked her lightly, as though he hadn't just slapped her around less than an hour ago.

"Yes. Strawberries, blueberries, grapes, pineapple, some cantaloupe..."

"Put me a little of all of it into a dish and bring it to me, will you?"

Grace nodded and set to work. Her face and throat were a bit sore, but that did not stop her from arraying the bowl of fruit into a remarkably beautiful spread. It was the inner cook in her coming alive as it always did when she was allowed to use food as her canvas. She took the bowl into the den, where Dean was seated in front of his laptop. He hurriedly lowered the laptop screen when he heard Grace open the French doors. "Looks delicious," Dean said as he received the fruit.

Grace bowed her head humbly and pretended not to notice the pornographic images on the computer screen, which Dean hadn't lowered quite enough. Fighting the urge to shake her head in disgust, Grace backed out of the room, closed the doors behind her, and went upstairs to tend to her children.

The girls were in Eve's room, waiting on Grace to come in, read them a story and pray with them before she dismissed them for the night. The girls took turns picking the nightly bedtime story. Tonight the girls decided that Naomi should pick the book since she had done such a great job working through her nerves to impress their father. Beaming with pride, Naomi went to the room she shared with Abby and returned with *A Pocket for Corduroy.*

After Grace finished reading the story, four girls got on the floor on their knees, preparing to pray.

Eve remained on her bed.

"Eve?" Grace said. "It's time to say our good-night prayers."

Eve gave Grace another of her infamous blank looks.

"What are you thinking, Eve?" Grace prodded.

"I'm thinking that I don't see the point in doing this," Eve burst out.

Grace was dumbfounded. "You don't see the point in praying?" she asked gently.

"No, I don't. I've been asking for the same thing for six years now--to get away from Dean. It hasn't happened yet. Am I supposed to keep asking?"

"Don't call him Dean."

"Why should I call him Dad?" Eve said angrily, her voice getting loud.

Anxious, Grace put her finger to her lips, trying to shush her. "Eve, look…"

"Forget it." Eve got off her bed and threw herself to the floor. "Let's pray. Let's ask God, for the millionth time, to make this a happy home, go to sleep, and wake up in the morning in the exact same miserable house we went to sleep in."

The other girls watched Grace as she tried to calculate a reasonable response to Eve's frustration. She came up empty. Sighing, Grace assumed the same position on her knees as her daughters. Heads bowed, eyes closed, hands clasped together in front of them, Grace led her daughters in supplication to Jesus. Grace kissed each of them and smiled as Abby and Naomi went into their room, turned on their nightlight, and got into their beds, and Sarah and Rebekah did the same, leaving her in the room alone with Eve.

"Eve, it's not right to be angry with God."

Eve, who had been laying down in her bed, sat up straight, her eyes flashing. "Why shouldn't I be?" she retorted. "Isn't God in control of everything? Isn't that what you tell me?"

"To an extent…"

"So it's his fault that we're stuck with Dean," she said, spitting out her father's name like venom.

"People have free will, Eve. It is not God's fault that your Dad behaves the way he does."

"So God could control Dean but he doesn't?"

"Yes…"

"Okay. So why don't you use your free will and leave?"

"Eve, it's not that simple," Grace said helplessly. "I can't just take you five girls and leave. I don't have any money or any place to take you. We'd be homeless."

"So the only reason you put up with Dean is so we can stay here?"

Grace looked at the floor.

Just like earlier, Eve's anger dissipated. More than ever, she felt sorry for her mother. "What a crappy life."

Choking back tears, Grace smiled at Eve. "Not necessarily," she said, her tone of voice brighter than she felt. "I got five beautiful girls out of the deal. I'd say that's a pretty fair trade-off."

Eve's face softened into a smile, and she fell into her mother's open arms. "No it's not, Mom," she said quietly. "Good-night."

Back downstairs, Grace finished her evening chores. Twice Dean called her into the den to ask her for something. She complied wordlessly each time. By ten o'clock she was exhausted but could only go to bed after her husband had fallen asleep, lest he need something. She peeked her head into the den and discovered Dean on the couch, covered up with a heavy blanket, snoring. She thanked God, quietly backed away from the room, and went upstairs. Grace wrapped her medium-length black hair, washed her tender and slightly puffy face, and brushed her teeth. In the master bedroom that adjoined her bathroom, Grace dressed herself in her most comfortable pajamas, got into her bed, and fell asleep before her head even fully hit the pillow. Today had been a good day, all things considered.

CHAPTER TWO

"Therefore I tell you, her sins, which are many, are forgiven—for she loved much. But he who is forgiven little, loves little." (Luke 7:47)

It was a beautiful bright Sunday.

There was always great joy in Grace's heart on the first day of the week. The Hardaways went to church every Sunday, most Saturdays for choir rehearsals or other church activities, and Wednesday evenings for Bible study. Dean was always on his best behavior at church. In addition to her daughters, being a member of Christ First Community Church gave Grace purpose. She was a Sunday school teacher to the children and enjoyed watching her charges grow in their relationship with God.

Dean deserved an Academy Award for the performance he put on at church. He parked the car, hurried over to his wife's passenger side door and opened it with a great flourish, looking to see if any nearby members saw the genteel gesture. He also opened the door to the church as his wife and daughters walked inside and gave each a peck on the cheek as they separated, him going to the Sunday school classroom where the men of the church met and Grace to the children's classroom on the lower floor of the church.

Once she was inside her classroom, Grace forgot all about Dean. The younger girls settled into their desks while Eve helped her mother get the room in order. Knowing that her students were usually tired and groggy, Grace liked to do things that encouraged them to participate and move around. She also made sure that the kids used their Bibles as well as the Sunday school workbooks supplied by the church so they would become familiar with it.

One by one the other children filed in. Grace greeted each of them personally with a hug. The last one to come in was a tall, lanky teenage boy she had never seen. Grace was pleased, as she always was when she got a new student. "Good morning! What's your name?"

"David," he mumbled.

"I'm Miss Grace, David. It's very nice to have you here. Do you want to grab some breakfast before we begin?"

"No, I ate already, thank you."

"Okay," Grace replied. "Here is a book for you, and feel free to sit wherever you want."

Grace opened the class with a prayer, as she typically did, and introduced David to the rest of the class. Without hesitation she began the lesson.

As usual time flew, and before she knew it Deacon Curtis Toole was ringing the bell to announce that class was over. The kids groaned simultaneously, a welcomed sound to Grace—they had enjoyed the class. It had been fun. Not wanting to talk at the kids for an hour, Grace always made sure to ask questions and get the kids involved in discussions applicable to the lesson. They had been in the midst of talking about how the tongue can either destroy a person or build them up, relating that to the bullying epidemic that the kids readily admitted to seeing in their own schools, when the bell rang.

Her regulars gathered their belongings and raced upstairs. Grace's daughters waited for their mother to clean up the room. David lingered as well, unsure what to do.

"Did you enjoy yourself today, David?"

He actually smiled a little. "Yes, I did. Thank you, Miss Grace."

"You're very welcome, David. I must say, I am very impressed with you. A lot of kids don't say a whole lot during their first class, but you were one of my star contributors today."

He gave another small smile.

"It's time to go upstairs now," Eve informed him. "We can drink juice and stuff before church begins."

"You can follow me!" Sarah said as she and the other girls raced out of the room. David shrugged and followed them.

Upstairs the fellowship hall was bustling with activity. It was a room that Grace had helped decorate when the church was renovated ten years ago. Light and airy, with plenty of natural sunshine flowing in from the skylights that Grace had recommended, the fellowship hall was one of her favorite places in the church. In the middle of the large room were two tables for refreshments. On either side of those tables were round tables and chairs where some members were sitting, waiting for Grace and other members of the kitchen crew to put the fruit, bagels, donuts, muffins, juice and coffee out for them to eat.

Always ready to serve, Grace watched as her daughters obediently sat down at one of the round tables and headed into the kitchen that was adjacent to the fellowship hall. She found her kitchen comrades already busy putting food on trays and retrieving paper cups, coffee creamer and other supplies from the cabinets.

"Good morning, ladies!" Grace said cheerily.

"Good morning!" they chorused.

The crew picked up trays and carried them out to the fellowship hall. Grace grabbed the nearest tray and followed suit. Several trips later all of the food and beverages were out on the tables, and everyone was satisfied. The other ladies stayed in the kitchen and began gossiping, cuing Grace to leave. She served her daughters and looked around for Dean. He should have been at the table with the girls, but he wasn't. Shrugging, she fixed a plate for him. She knew he would like a blueberry muffin, banana, and black coffee, no cream or sugar.

As she headed back to the table with Dean's food and drink, Grace spotted him. Dean was at the front of the room with their pastor, Reverend Benny Riley, David, and an impeccably-dressed woman who Grace guessed was his mother. In stark contrast to the boy's unkempt braids, slightly wrinkled red Polo shirt and ill-fitting jeans that hung sloppily off his frame despite being held in place by a brown leather belt, the woman wore an elegant royal blue suit with a matching hat, shoes and handbag. Dean said something that caused the woman to laugh, and only then was Grace able to see her face. She was beautiful, with smooth brown skin and flawless makeup. Grace felt a twinge of jealousy as she watched Dean and the woman laugh. Not because she thought Dean was flirting with the woman—Grace didn't care about that. She was jealous because Dean never made her laugh anymore.

Grace got a bagel, cream cheese, grapes and coffee for herself and sat down with her girls. Dean finally came to their table right before service was about to begin.

"Your coffee is probably cold," Grace informed him. "Would you like for me to get you a fresh cup?"

"No, it's fine," Dean said, sliding into his chair. Within seconds he devoured both the muffin and banana and drank the coffee. "I better get up front."

Grace watched as her husband headed into the sanctuary. His figure became smaller and smaller as he got further inside. He followed several other male members into the pastor's office where they would pray before service began. Grace watched as her daughters cleaned up their messes and took them to the bathroom so they could pee and wash their faces. Once they got back into the sanctuary, where they sat in the third pew from the back—Grace preferred to sit toward the back in case one of the girls grew antsy and needed to be taken out of the sanctuary for a scolding—Dean and the other deacons were already beginning the devotional part of the service.

Yes, *Dean and the other deacons*. Grace's abusive, neglectful husband, Dean, was a deacon at the church.

It was the most hypocritical thing Grace had ever seen. It sickened her each time Dean stood at the front of the church, praying and singing his heart out, emboldened by each "Amen!" or "Hallelujah!" that was shouted out as he did so. Grace had read the entire Bible several times and wondered how her husband had the audacity to stand in front of the congregation each Sunday, to participate in the giving of Communion and to perform all of the other duties ascribed to deacons knowing how he carried himself at home. Although Grace knew it was not her job to determine if one was truly saved or not, she definitely questioned Dean's salvation. A truly saved man would not terrorize his wife.

The members of the church were completely oblivious to the lie Dean and Grace were living. They were often praised as being "the perfect family", a title that Grace strongly detested. She burned with anger inside each time someone praised Dean for being such a good father and husband. They never seemed to notice the icy look he gave her when one of the girls made a noise during service, one that told her she had better take the offending daughter out of the sanctuary or else. It bothered Grace that she rarely got to sit through an entire service uninterrupted—someone always had to go to the bathroom, had a coughing fit, or got tired of sitting. Yet Dean was able to sit up front with the other deacons and hear every word of the sermon, even though it went in one ear and out the other. Grace didn't mind what she had to do as a mother but it offended her that Dean played the role he did in church. Why did he need to listen to anything the preacher said if he wasn't going to...*listen*?

Dean listened to the things that suited him. He was especially interested in Scriptures that could validate his dominance at home. The Christian woman was expected to be submissive to her husband, and per Dean's understanding of submission, that meant he had the only say in everything. Dean believed he had a right to maintain absolute control in his home by any means necessary. If Grace got out of line, he had a Biblical duty to get her back in order.

Ironically, it was Grace who had first introduced Dean to Christ First. She had also encouraged him to be a deacon. Dean was hesitant when he was first offered the opportunity, but Grace, thinking that the training and being around seasoned older deacons would inspire him to be a better husband and father and overall better Christian, urged him to do so. It backfired spectacularly.

Twenty years ago Grace was far from being a Sunday school teacher. She was at a point where she was even questioning the existence of God. She was a disenchanted eighteen-year-old who had just aged out of the foster care system. Her parents had died in a car accident when she was eleven, and when neither of her parents' siblings came forward to claim her Grace was declared a ward of the state. From that day onward what had been an idyllic childhood turned hellish.

Some of the foster homes were okay, but the ones that weren't were *terrible*. There was rampant abuse in the bad homes. Repeatedly she was reminded by her foster parents that she "had better be lucky she was even there" when she complained about having more chores and responsibilities than the couple's biological children. Some of the foster families treated her like their live-in maid or babysitter. However, it was the last foster home that was the worst. She was sixteen years old and had been placed with a couple named the Greens who had two other foster children in addition to their two biological sons. One night when Grace was asleep, she was awakened by Lucas, one of the biological sons, a fifteen-year-old who was twice her size. He was tugging on her pajama pants.

"Wha-?" Before Grace could protest he clamped his hand over her mouth.

"Shut up," he sneered.

But Grace wouldn't shut up. Lucas responded to her efforts with two quick slaps to the face.

Enraged and terrified, Grace struggled as hard as she could, but Lucas was too strong. Grace was saved when they heard the door to her room creak.

Looking horrified, Julia, an eleven-year-old ward, stood paralyzed, trying to process what she was seeing. This was Grace's chance at freedom. She kneed Lucas as hard as she could between his legs, flew off the bed, down the stairs and out of the house. She knew that it was no use telling the Greens what had just happened. They would certainly believe their precious perverted son over her.

Grace was on the streets for a few days before being picked up by the police and put in a group home twenty miles away. There, her basic needs were met, but the atmosphere was cold and it was apparent that the woman in charge of the agency was only there for the money. No love was shown for any of the kids. Once Grace turned eighteen, she was promptly kicked out of the orphanage with little more than the clothes on her back. Grace remembered the friends she had made on the streets after leaving the Greens' house. She went back to them.

Grace was homeless for seven months. In that time, she bonded with other disillusioned youths. Two of them, Jeannie and Wayne, were former foster children like her. The other three, Derrick, Trina and Lola, were runaways. They formed an impenetrable group. During the day they would panhandle, each of them in different areas of the city, and at night they would meet back up, pool their money and buy food, alcohol and drugs. The oldest members of the group, Jeannie and Derrick, showed the others which truck stops had showers they could use and which churches gave out free food and supplies.

Jeannie was a hard-core alcoholic and Wayne was into heroin. Before long, Grace was using both. When she was high she was able to escape her bleak reality. Unfortunately, when she came down from the high, she found herself back in the same pathetic situation—wearing someone's hand-me-down clothes purchased for pennies at the Salvation Army while squatting in an abandoned or empty foreclosed home. She preferred to stay high than deal with her life. In order to stay high she needed money, more than panhandling offered her. One day, desperate to get some more heroin, she ran into JuJu, the dealer who kept Wayne supplied with the heroin the group used.

"I need some," she begged him.

"Where's the money?"

"I don't have it," she wailed. "But I need it, really really bad."

JuJu's lips curled into a demented smile. "You're cute." He dangled a little baggie of heroin in her face. "What will you do for this? Anything?"

"Yes," Grace wailed.

That was the first time Grace prostituted herself for the drug, but not the last. Over the next couple of months Grace would have sex with JuJu or his friends in order to get what she needed. She was living a nightmare.

The darkest period of her life came to an end as abruptly as it began. Drugs, alcohol and the harshness of their lives was driving Grace's group of friends apart and ended up being the undoing of their arrangement. They no longer looked out for each other. As their addictions grew, they were constantly suspicious of one another. Their last encounter occurred when Wayne accused Derrick of stealing his heroin. The argument ended when Derrick savagely punched Wayne in the head, knocking him out. Derrick ran out of the house they were squatting in, leaving the girls there. Soon they heard the wail of a police siren. Someone had heard the ruckus and called the police.

"We gotta get out of here!" Jeannie said, drunkenly stumbling around the room as she tried to collect her belongings. While the others watched, Jeannie attempted to sling her backpack over her shoulder. She tripped over her own foot and fell. When she did, the backpack ended up across the room with some of its contents splayed on the hardwood floor.

"Wait a second," Lola cried, walking over to the backpack. "Is this my silver bracelet I've been looking for? You had it this whole time didn't you, you low-down thief!"

"And there's my earring!" Trina yelled. "What else d'ya have that's mine?"

The three girls began screaming at each other, and before Grace knew what was happening another fist-fight had ensued. In the middle of the fracas Grace saw Wayne's bag of heroin under the backpack, gleaming up at her like a diamond nestled among coal. Grace picked it up and fled the scene just as the police arrived.

That night in the park, Grace injected the entire contents of the bag, more than three times the amount that she typically used, and passed out.

When she woke up, Grace was in a hospital. Confused and almost blinded by the incandescent lights, she tried to sit up, only to find that she was hooked to several machines. She looked to her right, then her left, and saw no one. What in the world had happened?

"You overdosed."

Grace jumped. In the doorway stood a tall, thin Black man, with smooth caramel-colored skin and dark, deep-set eyes, probably around fifty years or so. He had salt-and-pepper hair and a beard to match.

"Who are you?" Grace croaked. Her throat was dry.

The man walked into the room. He picked up a mug that was on the table across from her, stuck a straw in it, and put it up to her lips. Grace looked at him suspiciously. He wasn't wearing scrubs, so he wasn't a hospital employee.

"It's water."

Grace looked at the clear liquid and took a hesitant sip. It *was* water. "Thank you," she said uneasily. "Do I know you?"

"You should," he told her, sitting down in a chair beside her. "My name is Courtney Willows. Does that name ring a bell to you?"

She shook her head no.

He chuckled. "You don't remember me from Macy's?"

Grace furrowed her eyebrows, confused.

"Tell me. How many wallets did you steal that day?"

Grace's eyes opened wide with surprise. It was coming back to her. At Lola's prodding, Grace had gotten into the habit of prowling parks, malls and other places with a lot of people and finding unattended backpacks, jackets and purses. During her last trip to the mall, only hours before she overdosed, she and Lola watched Mr. Willows as he tried on suit coats at Macy's. Lola spotted the familiar bulge in the jacket that he had slung across a nearby chair and nudged Grace. "I'll distract him while you take it."

Lola popped in front of Court and made sure he kept his back turned, flattering him and telling him how good he looked in the coat. As she was offering some suggestions on what might look even better, Grace finagled the wallet from the pocket and sneaked off. She and Lola met up outside the store, laughing as they went to the food court and ate on Court Willows' dime.

"I am so sorry," Grace whispered.

"You should be," he said sternly.

"Why are you here? How did you find me?" Grace asked.

"When you ended up in here, the police searched your belongings and found my wallet. They thought maybe I was your next of kin, so they called me."

"Did you tell them I stole the wallet?"

Court shook his head. "No, I did not."

"Are you going to tell on me now that I am awake? How long have I been here?"

"It has been three days, and no, I do not plan on telling on you under a few conditions."

Grace grew angry. "I am not going to have sex with you or anyone else…"

Court put up his hands in surrender. "Whoa, I was not going to say anything like that!"

Grace quieted down.

"You've had some life, huh?"

Guilty tears began to stream down Grace's face. She nodded slowly.

"I figured as much," Court said. "When the police told me how they had hauled you in here on a stretcher with a needle in your arm, I had to ask myself how a young lady could have ended up in such a situation. Alone and in a park, almost dead. It took awhile for the police to figure out your identity, but once they had your name, I figured out the rest. You were in the system for awhile, weren't you?"

Grace nodded.

"I've had a lot of kids that have been through the system come to my office, and I've never turned them away when they needed help. I don't intend to start now."

"Your office?" Grace asked. "What kind of office?"

It was an interesting turn of events. Court was a licensed psychologist and had extensive experience working with addicts. If Grace would agree to go to the rehab center where he volunteered his services two days a week, he wouldn't press charges. Grace wondered what the fine print was, but there was none. Court sincerely wanted to help. Grace agreed, and two days later she was at New Beginnings Rehab.

The staff at New Beginnings picked up the slack left behind when she aged out of the foster care system. They retrieved Grace's high school transcript and her scores on the ACT and SAT. One of the caseworkers, Molly, was highly impressed. "You were a very good student, Grace. Why didn't you go to college or to a training program of some type? I'm sure you would have done well."

Grace didn't have a good answer for that. It had never crossed her mind to go any further than high school. No one had really taken the time to explore her options with her.

Molly was on the job. "You're a very good cook," she told Grace. "The nights that you cook dinner, all of the staff always stays late or comes in early so they can eat." They both laughed. "Have you ever thought of going into food service?"

Grace shook her head. She had never considered the possibility of a decent future at all. It had never occurred to her that she could cook for a living.

Molly helped Grace get enrolled at Washtenaw Community College where she planned to study Culinary Arts and Hospitality Management and transfer to nearby Eastern Michigan University to complete her Bachelor's degree. Grace got a job working at Bob Evans and was able to get a small apartment with another WCC student, Jade.

Life was as perfect as it possibly could have been during her three years at Washtenaw. Grace excelled in her studies. Cooking was indeed her passion. When she finished her two years and enrolled at Eastern, her life got even better.

At Washtenaw Grace was committed only to herself. She knew it would take a lot of discipline and hard work to make up for time lost. She went to work, school, her new-found church, Christ First Community Church, and that was it. She had no social life and did not care to go to the clubs where Jade and her friends danced every Thursday, Friday and Saturday night away. Grace could often hear Jade stumble into the house in the wee hours of the morning, sometimes accompanied by a random guy she had undoubtedly picked up from the club, and even worse, she could often hear the sounds of Jade and the random guy having sex. It was disgusting and reminded her of her former life. She was totally uninterested in reverting, so even when Jade attempted to involve her roommate in her late night outings, Grace declined. She'd finally found something she enjoyed, something that gave her confidence and a sense of purpose. Nothing pleased her more than to watch people delight in the food that she so diligently prepared.

By the time she started at Eastern Grace had relaxed a little. She was almost finished with her program and had a perfect grade point average. So when a handsome Marine by the name of Solomon expressed interest in her, Grace responded positively to his advances.

One of her first tasks in her program at Eastern happened by surprise. November was approaching and in honor of Veteran's Day, the University wanted to host a special dinner for all of the campus veterans. They invited the Hospitality students and members of the Hospitality Club, of which Grace was a member, to cater the gathering. Grace was surprised and flattered when she was asked to take the lead on the event. She agreed immediately.

It was a major undertaking. Grace had to plan the menu, prepare the budget, assign everyone to their stations, and make sure the kitchen process ran smoothly. To keep herself grounded, she immersed herself in the activities at church and requested for her new church family to pray for her.

Christ First Community Church, then led by Reverend Ronnie Buckley, was strategically located in between EMU's campus and several areas with a large proliferation of EMU students and professors. They had executed a very successful marketing campaign, literally covering the campus with fliers advertising their Sunday services. Grace picked one up one day and decided to go. She had promised Court and Molly that she would find a church home, and up until that time had been doing more church-hopping than anything. So far she had not yet found one that she felt fit her, and decided to give Christ First a try.

As a result of the warmth and hospitality she was shown during her first visit and secondarily because of the powerful message of God's grace that Rev. Buckley preached, Grace was all but sold on her first visit. Yet, she did not join until three Sundays later. It was one of the best decisions she had ever made. Now she had an earthly family.

Christ First ran like a well-oiled machine when Grace first joined. The church had a membership of between 150-200 people, all who contributed regularly, allowing for Christ First to put on numerous programs including one that fed the homeless on Tuesdays. Grace immediately signed up to help. Before long she was involved in several other programs and was given the opportunity to participate in Bible study classes that were offered there through the Moody Bible Institute free of charge. Grace loved her church home, and her love of the Lord grew and grew.

The members of Christ First were more than happy to oblige Grace with prayers, calls and emails containing supportive messages. Over time, Grace revealed her past to them. Their response further encouraged her. No one condemned her. She was urged to use her past to help others, to accept God's forgiveness, and move forward. On the day of the Veteran's Day dinner, the love and kindness she had been shown by her church family and deep prayer kept her nerves in check even when she got to the kitchen at Walker Hall where the dinner was to take place. She found her hospitality colleagues in complete emotional disarray.

"Are you guys nervous?" she asked with a chuckle.

"Of course we are!" exclaimed Allison Hitchcock. "We've never cooked for this many people!"

"Look at it this way," Grace said calmly. "What is the largest number of people you have cooked for?"

"Thirty," Allison replied.

"And at that time, were you nervous? Did you think it was a huge deal to cook for thirty people?"

Allison nodded.

"This is no different. You are still going to use the same techniques and cook the same food as you did then. You will just be making more of it. Let's not focus on the number of people we'll be serving. Let's focus on owning our individual stations, and then focus on each cut of meat, each appetizer, or each side dish or whatever you are preparing at that very moment. The only thing you need to do is put your best into each one so these vets can enjoy their meal. So the first thing I would like for everyone to do is set up their station in whatever way works best for you."

The crew looked at one another in surprise.

"Yep, that's what I want you to do. Demetrius, I know you are left-handed, so you might need to switch some things around at your station. You're going to want your seasonings close to your dominant hand, right? And Marshall, I know you get kind of antsy when things aren't in a specific order." Everyone laughed, and Marshall laughed and nodded as well. "And that's okay. I want you all to go to your stations and take ten minutes or so to make them your own."

Preparing the meal was an unbelievably smooth process thanks to Grace's calm leadership. As the vets came into the dining hall and were being seated, she reminded the crew to focus on the meal and encouraged them to not even look at the crowd as it grew. The members of the Hospitality Club who had not been directly involved with the preparation of the meal waited until every vet had been seated before they began walking out the appetizers. Grace watched as the vets delighted in the appetizers and finally invited the crew to look at their faces.

The tone was set. The crew was even more determined to continue to deliver, and they did just that. The grilled halibut with cilantro butter and steamed mussels were a huge hit, as was the beef wellington and red-skinned potatoes. The selection for the desserts was relatively simple to compensate for the complex appetizers and dinners they had prepared—strawberry shortcake and brownies.

At the end of the meal, the chair of the Hospitality Department and host of the event, Duane Pleasant, went to the microphone at the front of the room. The vets fell silent as he introduced himself.

"First, I want to thank you all, not only for coming here, but more importantly, for your service to this country. You are absolutely invaluable, and this dinner can't even begin to show our appreciation for what you all do."

Thunderous applause followed.

When the claps quieted down, Duane continued. "We are hoping to make this a tradition, but that depends on your overall thoughts about this evening," he informed them. "So you all tell me—did you enjoy yourselves tonight? And how about that food?"

A new series of applause, even more uproarious than the first, caused Duane to chuckle.

"That's all the answer I need," he said, still chuckling. "Well, it took a lot of work to make this evening possible. At this time I'd like to introduce you to the people who put this whole thing together. Kitchen and crew, please come join me."

Grace's eyes flew open. While the others hurriedly left the kitchen to join Duane on the little platform, she hesitated. She looked a hot mess. Grace had expected to be in the kitchen and only in the kitchen and had no desire to be in front of 100 soldiers. Yet, she had no choice. Dutifully, she joined the rest of her comrades on stage and attempted to stand in the back. As the vets applauded, she hoped that would be the end of it. But it wasn't.

"Please join me for a round of applause for Grace Leary, the head chef in the kitchen this evening. The entire menu tonight was of Grace's doing. Step forward, Grace." The thunderous applause grew into a standing ovation as Grace timidly stepped forward, gave the adoring crowd a little wave, and quickly took her place behind Duane.

Luckily, the vets were satisfied with her small gesture and the evening continued. The members of the Hospitality Club that had not cooked graciously offered to take over the clean-up, allowing Grace and the kitchen crew a chance to socialize with the vets—if they so desired. Grace did not. As pleased as she was with her performance that evening, she still lacked the confidence in herself to go and strike up a conversation with such admirable people. She went back into the kitchen and started washing dishes.

By the end of the night, Grace was exhausted and looking forward to going home. As she headed out of Walker Hall accompanied by several club members, she sighed as she slung the strap of her brown leather satchel over her shoulder. "This is about to be the longest walk ever," she groaned.

"Which way do you have to go?" Paige Henderson asked.

"I live on South Adams."

Paige hesitated. "I don't like the idea of you walking by yourself this late." Everyone else in their group lived on campus. They only had to cross a couple streets.

Grace chuckled. "I appreciate your concern Paige, but it's not that far. And it's only ten o'clock."

Paige was unconvinced. As she opened her mouth to protest she was silenced by a deep, rumbling baritone that came out of nowhere.

"I'll walk you home."

Everyone turned. A man stood before them, dressed in camouflage. He was tall, with broad shoulders and an athletic build. Grace could barely make out his face in the dark, but she could tell that he was at least slightly handsome.

He moved a little closer, and the street light showed that he was more than just slightly handsome—he was gorgeous. If Grace were to guess she would have thought he was Native American. He had strong chiseled features and thick black hair. An unfamiliar flutter in her chest took Grace by surprise.

"I figure it's the least I could do to thank you for this full belly," he said, patting what sounded like washboard abs with a super-sexy grin. "I don't think I've eaten that well in my entire life. I'm Solomon." He put forth a hand.

Grace shook cautiously. She looked at her friends with question marks in her eyes, but they were too caught up in Solomon's hotness to see her discomfort. "Umm… well, I have to go to South Adams, so if you live around here that'd be a long way back by yourself…"

"I don't want to come off as arrogant, but I've been in the Marines since I was eighteen. I'm pretty sure I can handle myself if a group of teenagers comes at me."

Grace again cast a glance at her friends. Although they were still entranced, several of them were nodding subtly at her. She could almost hear them encouraging her to go for it. Over the past few weeks, everyone had been asking her why she was so reluctant to date. They assumed she was just shy. That was only the half of it. Her major fear was having to disclose her illicit past to a potential partner and face rejection.

"I wouldn't feel right knowing you walked home alone."

That sealed the deal. Grace wished her friends good-night, agreed to call Paige once she made it home, and kept a safe distance of a few feet between herself and Solomon as they began their trek.

Once they were alone Grace's discomfort heightened. She didn't know if she was supposed to try to make conversation, and if so, what would she talk about? It was at that point that she realized how absolutely boring she was. There was nothing interesting enough about her to make small talk.

Luckily Solomon had the gift of gab, and he first engaged her by complimenting her on the meal and asking her several questions about her background as related to cooking to get her to warm up to him. He was very friendly and funny, and before Grace knew it, they were talking and joking like old friends. The twenty minute walk to South Adams came to an abrupt end, and she was actually disappointed. She had been having a good time.

Apparently, Solomon had enjoyed her company as well. "I'm sure you're tired after all of the work you did today, so I won't keep you," he said.

There was a moment of silence as Grace tried to figure out what she was supposed to do in this situation. She wanted to talk to Solomon again, but was it proper for her to ask for his phone number? Had they even clicked that well enough to where she should feel comfortable asking, or was him walking her home simply a chivalrous gesture?

Just as she was working herself into a nervous frenzy Solomon said, "Can I call you sometime, Grace?"

Thus began Grace's first real relationship. It was one of the happiest and most terrifying times of her life. She liked Solomon instantly, but knew that she couldn't let the relationship go too far. Eventually there would come a time when she would have to tell this decorated Marine that she had once sold her body for drugs. He was a decent, honest person, very proud of his accomplishments, and for good reason. Solomon was very well-respected among his fellow servicemen and on the campus. She kept telling herself time after time to find a reason to break off the relationship but she could not bring herself to do it. She had never felt so special in her life. Solomon was romantic and attentive, albeit a bit arrogant, and she couldn't imagine life without him.

The relationship was fine until April. The campus was preparing for finals, and although Solomon had become increasingly hard to catch in the past couple of weeks, Grace attributed it to his tough academic schedule and other responsibilities. She thought little of it when several of her phone calls went straight to his voicemail. She left messages telling him she missed him, understood that he was busy, and was looking forward to seeing him. However, after four days with absolutely no contact from Solomon, Grace grew concerned and went looking for him.

She knew there was a good possibility he would be in the Rec Center. It was her first stop, and she was right. He was in the weight room, and the phone that she had been calling was sitting right next to him. He looked up briefly when he saw her enter the room, and a scowl crossed his face.

She was confused. Grace did not know much about guys, but she did know that she hadn't personally done anything to cause the scowl. She walked over to him. "Have you been okay? I've been worried."

With a grunt, Solomon got up, slung a towel over his shoulder, picked up his nearby water bottle, and started to walk away from her.

Grace was bewildered. "Solomon? What's wrong?"

"Grace, walk away, okay? Just leave me alone. I can't talk to you right now."

"Is it something I've done?"

He stopped suddenly, causing her to almost run into his backside. When he whirled around, Grace was almost scared by how angry he looked. "I'm afraid so."

"What is it? Tell me so I won't do it anymore. I won't know how I made you angry if you don't tell me."

He shook his head in disgust. "Problem is, there's nothing you can do about what's making me angry. It's already happened, and I've spent the last few days trying to figure out if it's something I can live with or not. I'm thinking more along the lines of...not."

Grace felt sick to her stomach. "What do you mean?" she asked in a small voice.

"I mean, don't you think you should have told me you used to be strung out? You don't think I should have known that you used to whore yourself out for drugs?"

It was quite possibly the most humiliating moment in her entire life. Grace had felt like garbage before, but this took it to another level. There was no need to protest—Solomon's feelings were perfectly understandable. What respectable Marine wanted to explain to his fellow servicemen that his girlfriend was a former heroin-addicted, homeless whore? Grace fled from Solomon, tears streaming down her face.

Back home, she wondered how he figured it out. She got her answer a few days later when Jade left her phone on the living room table while she was in the shower. It was a rare move for her—Jade treated the phone like another appendage. She had gotten especially secretive about it over the past few weeks. When Grace picked it up, intending to take it to the bathroom for her roommate, she saw why.

She recognized the number on the display right away. It was Solomon's.

She pressed the button to answer the phone and said dryly, "Well, Solomon. Isn't this a pleasant surprise."

He hung up.

Infuriated, Grace sat on the couch and waited with the phone in her hand until she heard Jade turn off the water. Jade opened the door and walked out wearing only a towel, dabbing at her damp hair. Grace held the phone up.

"Your phone rang while you were in there. I was going to bring it to you, but then I saw that it was Solomon calling."

All of the color drained from Jade's face.

Grace's frustration could not be suppressed. Jade was one of the first people she had told about her final encounter with Solomon. Jade had patted her back as she cried…and then went out later that night. Now Grace surmised that she had probably went out and met up with him. She couldn't help but blame herself. Sometimes during the day Solomon would come to their place and hang around the apartment while Grace was at class or at work. Undoubtedly he and Jade talked, but Grace had been too naive to suspect anything else. Although she felt culpable in this entire fiasco, that did not detract from Jade's deception. Grace slapped Jade with all of her might—once, twice, and then three times before Jade finally managed to escape Grace's wrath. Sobbing, Jade ran into her room and locked the door.

Grace got another place with a few members of the Hospitality Club. Over the summer she immersed herself in work, school and church, and completely rebuffed any advances from men. She wasn't going to try that anymore. It came as little consolation when fall classes resumed in September and she found out that Solomon and Jade hadn't lasted long as an item.

The incident with Solomon made Grace easy prey for Dean Hardaway. When the annual Vet's Dinner rolled around during her senior year, Grace was again asked to be the chairperson. She agreed and decided within her mind to go out with a bang with an elaborate menu. Once again the food received rave reviews, and once again Grace was exhausted at the end of the night. Luckily, her new home was right off campus, only a five minute walk.

As she was putting the last clean dish back into its home, one of her friends in the club, Cecile Oppenheimer, came into the kitchen. "Grace," she said excitedly. "One of the hot Marines is asking to speak to you."

Grace was completely uninterested. "Please tell him I am very busy."

"Oh, Grace, don't be rude," Cecile insisted. "He's a nice guy. Soft-spoken, maybe a bit shy, but very nice. He really wants to meet you."

Still unmoved, Grace shook her head. "I'm flattered," she said dryly, "but I have things to do."

Shaking her head, Cecile left the kitchen, but only for a moment. When she returned, she had a man with her and a smirk on her face.

"This is the woman who is responsible for tonight's deliciousness," Cecile said proudly. "Grace, this is Dean Hardaway."

Reminding herself to cuss Cecile out later, Grace quickly put on her fakest smile and shook Dean Hardaway's hand. "Very nice to meet you," she said, hoping he couldn't see past her insincerity.

"The pleasure is all mine," he said quietly, cracking a small smile. "Thank you so much for the food. I've never eaten so good. You're quite talented."

"I appreciate that."

"I know you're busy," Dean said, looking around the kitchen at the eight or so club members who were still running back and forth putting leftover food into containers to take home. "I—I won't bother you. I just wanted to thank you personally."

"You're very welcome. Thank you for your service to our country. The least I can do is make sure you all have a good meal at least once a year." That part was sincere.

Dean smiled, nodded at her and Cecile, and left.

Cecile sighed. "Grace, that guy is gorgeous! He's been looking at you all night. What is wrong with you?"

"I am more focused on graduating with honors in May and making the right connections to get a good job somewhere than I am on wasting any of my precious time on some guy," Grace said vehemently.

"Do you plan on being alone for the rest of your life?" Cecile pressed.

"Now is just not the time, Cecile."

Cecile shook her head.

Although Grace had never seen Dean Hardaway before that evening, suddenly he began popping up everywhere on campus over the weeks following the dinner. Each time he engaged Grace in small talk and respectfully left her to her own devices. During their small exchanges she found him to be polite, sometimes reserved. Underneath the reservation was a good sense of humor and a high degree of intelligence and morality. And he was definitely easy on the eyes. He was no ten like Solomon, but his light-skinned baby face was pretty endearing. When she felt attraction to Dean growing, she resolved in her mind to do what she had not done with Solomon—cut him off.

Grace knew Dean was getting close to asking her out on an actual date, and she had a speech prepared. When he finally did just that, she rattled off her lines, her heart heavy.

"I think you're a wonderful guy and I really appreciate our friendship, Dean, but I just can't see it going any further than what it is now."

Dean was undeterred. "Why is that?"

Grace was momentarily stumped. She hadn't expected him to challenge her. She sighed. "I'm not good enough for you, Dean."

"Are you crazy? Of course you are. You're beautiful, smart and kind. What do you mean, 'you're not good enough for me'?"

This was getting uncomfortable. "I've done some things in the past that I am not proud of..."

"Haven't we all?"

She shifted in her seat and refused to meet his probing gaze. "It's not the same. If you really found out the truth about me, I am sure you would run for the hills."

"I could say the same about my past. Why don't you try me?"

Grace shook her head.

"I'm not going to judge you."

"That's hogwash," Grace said quietly. "People are always dogging other people."

"When have you ever heard me dog anyone?"

He made a good point. She had never heard Dean utter a bad word about anyone. Still, she was not comfortable revealing the very secret that had run Solomon off.

"I've killed people," Dean said suddenly. "And sometimes I wonder…sometimes I'm not certain that I didn't accidentally kill people who were innocent."

Grace looked at him. She knew he was referring to being in combat in Afghanistan. Although she wanted to ask a thousand questions, she could tell by the troubled look on his face that now was not the time. She also recognized that he had just entrusted her with a very important confession, and that increased her trust in him. She took a deep breath and told him the sordid story of her life.

When she was done, finally she looked up into his face. She could not read his expression.

"You're disgusted by me, aren't you." It wasn't a question, it was a statement.

"Not at all," he replied. "On the contrary, I'm amazed at how you've managed to turn yourself around."

"I don't believe that you don't have any negative thoughts about me after what I just told you," Grace informed him.

He smiled. "I guess I'll just have to prove you wrong."

After that honest exchange the two became inseparable. If she was not in class, at church or at work, Grace was with Dean. He made good on his promise to prove her wrong, as he was unashamed to tell people they were in a relationship and walk around campus holding her hand or with his arm around her shoulders. Grace thought she could never be as happy as she was with Solomon. Dean took things to another level.

One day in March they were at her apartment studying for finals and eating shrimp tacos when Dean came out of the blue and said quietly, "When this whole college thing is over, I think you should marry me."

Grace laughed and took a bite of her taco.

"I'm serious."

Grace looked at him, and indeed, he was serious. As her stomach flipped and flopped, she put her taco down and turned to face him. "We haven't been together that long."

"How long do people need to be together before they realize they love one another? I already know that I can't live without you."

Deep down, she wasn't sure she was ready for marriage. She did love Dean—well, she *thought* what she felt was love. At the very least she was very attached to him, but there were some things about him she wasn't sure she was ready to deal with forever. Dean would get angry with Grace and expect her to figure out why he was mad, and she didn't appreciate the fishing expeditions she had to go on to determine what had set him off. And it was trivial things that got him going, while she was more easy-going and understood that Dean was not a mind-reader, and sometimes he unintentionally did things that made her angry. To be his age, Dean was pretty intense sometimes, and although he did have moments of comic brilliance, his brooding occasionally put Grace off. He was also a bit possessive and had thrown fits about some of the clothes she wore, insisting that she refrain from wearing them lest some other man take notice of her.

As she was waging an internal war, Dean spoke up and put his hand on top of hers. "I love you, Grace," he said, "and if you're not comfortable with the idea of us getting married, I'll just wait until you are. But in the meantime…"

From his pocket he produced a small black box. Grace inhaled deeply and watched as he opened the box, revealing a small princess cut petite diamond ring.

"It's not much," he said, embarrassed, "but I want you to have it. If you need to think about it, I still want you to wear it." While she sat in stunned silence, he slipped it on her left ring finger.

That night Grace did not sleep. To focus her thoughts, she got out a notebook and wrote the possible benefits of marriage and the consequences of not marrying him. The "yea-marriage" column was significantly longer than the "nay-marriage" column. Grace sighed. She had always wanted to get married and have kids, and this might be her only chance at a respectable life—with a Marine nonetheless. Any other guy she met in the future would probably react the same way Solomon did when they found out about her treacherous past, and she would end up childless and alone. Grace had been alone for years as a ward of the state with no love or stability, and she was not going to allow that to happen ever again. At three-thirty-two in the morning, she called Dean and told him she wanted to marry him.

Looking back with the benefit of hindsight, Grace wished she had put more thought into her decision. Now she was in a position from which there was no easy escape.

Not only was her marriage destructive, Christ First, which she loved, had undergone some very distressing changes over the past few years. The decline of Christ First began when Reverend Buckley became ill with liver cancer. As the sickness began to take its toll on his body, he started to relinquish more and more control to his deacon board, who he obviously thought he could trust to continue to carry out his vision for the church. The deacons saw Rev. Buckley's illness and subsequent absence from the pulpit as their opportunity to do some experimenting with the church. Their first order of business was to shorten the duration of church services, which involved cutting out multiple parts of the program, including the formal welcoming of visitors, one of the choir's songs, and the altar prayer. Church service went from being three hours long to lasting for just over an hour. Apparently, it was a move people liked, because immediately following the change came an influx of new members. This emboldened the deacons, but Rev. Buckley was infuriated when he found out and demanded they return the program to its original script. Unfortunately, he was too ill to come to the church himself and enforce his demands, and the deacons refused to change it back.

Reverend Buckley eventually succumbed to his illness. His family, angered by the deacons' treatment of their patriarch, left Christ First right after his passing. After Rev. Buckley's death, the church immediately began to advertise for another pastor. They sought advice from other pastors in the area, and within a few weeks the congregation had identified two viable candidates. One of them, Reverend Samuel Brown, was well-known in the area. He was a middle-aged man, had been married to his wife for twenty-two years and had three teenaged children. He preached sound doctrine and his life appeared to mirror what he preached. A smaller fraction of the church preferred Rev. Riley, who had seemingly come out of nowhere. Although the area ministers were vaguely familiar with him, Rev. Riley was from a small church in Grand Rapids, which was over a hundred miles away, so the congregation was unable to find any members from his former church to speak with. He had been married to his wife for ten years and they had one daughter.

The deacons played an integral role in getting Rev. Riley approved to pastor the church. Their argument was that Rev. Riley was younger and would be able to lead their church longer than the aging Rev. Brown, who admittedly had several health problems. Although they acknowledged some issues—Rev. Riley was rumored to drink alcohol and had been seen smoking a cigarette as he left the church after his first meeting with the deacons—they were impressed by his energy. The deacons argued that Rev. Buckley was too controlling. Prior to his death, Rev. Buckley had expressed frustration with the deacon board and had even threatened to replace several of them, so Grace could understand why they felt that way. They were looking for a pastor that they could influence and grow the congregation in number. Rev. Brown was firm, and he was not there to put on a show, he was there to teach. Grace preferred his style. However, after hearing Rev. Riley preach, the rest of the members were swayed to agree with the deacons. He could definitely rouse the crowd, and had a dynamic, soul-stirring singing voice, even if his sermons often failed to touch on the Gospel itself.

Now it was apparent that rousing the crowd was Rev. Riley's best pastoral asset. He had no control over the church, nor did he care to. Rev. Riley's father had been a preacher, as had his grandfather and he apparently felt compelled to continue the tradition, although Grace highly doubted Rev. Riley had truly received a call from God to preach. Rumors had been circulating for months that he was sleeping with at least two women in the congregation, and other whispers among church members indicated that the Rileys had left their last church in Grand Rapids because of infidelity on the part of the womanizing reverend. It was a push-and-pull situation in terms of whether the deacons or Rev. Riley controlled the church, and neither seemed to consult God in the process. Everything was out of order, and Christ First had been hemorrhaging members as fast as it had been recruiting them. New members joined all the time, pulled in by the dynamic preaching of Rev. Riley, but once they had a taste of the discord within the four walls of the building, they left as fast as they had come. Grace had been wanting to leave for months, but Dean was happy with his position as a deacon, and happy with Rev. Riley's lax leadership.

When service ended Grace was feeling very uninspired. Rev. Riley had only preached for about ten minutes. He had done more hollering than anything else, and yet most of the church had been on its feet, clapping and hollering right along with him. Grace couldn't even remember the context of the sermon, only that it had come from the book of Romans. She couldn't wait to get home and into her kitchen. She was prepared to cook a slamming Sunday dinner.

Dean caught her by the arm as she was heading to the coat room.

"What were you making for dinner today?" he asked.

"I have a turkey roasting and was going to make some mashed potatoes and fried corn, why do you ask?"

"The deacons are going to come by and watch the game with me. Is there enough for them?"

Grace tried not to look upset. "No…"

"Is there anything there that you can make for them pretty quickly? Aren't there chicken wings in the deep freezer?"

Grace was doing her best to remain calm, but she hated when Dean put her on the spot like this. "Yes…"

"How long would it take you to make them?"

"I'd have to thaw them out…"
"I didn't ask you all that," Dean snapped. "How *long*?"

"Forty minutes, give or take a few."

"Okay," Dean said, not even really talking to her as much as he was talking to himself. "When we get home, thaw the wings. Do some garlic Parmesan, some honey barbecue, some hot. And make sure the house looks nice. Okay?"

Without waiting for her response, Dean walked out of the coat room toward his group of comrades who were standing just outside the room, waiting to hear from him. Her anger building inside her, Grace watched as Dean pulled his coat on and told them, "No, you don't need to bring anything. I'll take care of you guys, you know that!"

Grace said nothing during the ride home. She was frustrated but had no platform to vent. Dean didn't care anyway. At home, she did exactly as she was told. She put the wings in water to thaw, finished cooking the family's dinner, served them all, and ate her own dinner in five minutes. She knew if those guys got there and had to wait too long for the wings she would get it later on. The deacons arrived just as the wings were finished frying. Grace hurried to toss them in their various dressings.

Dean met them at the door, joking and jovial. His cheerfulness toward the men as he herded them into the den was sickening. Of course he was happy--he hadn't prepared eight pounds of wings in addition to a full meal for a family of seven in less than an hour. Once all the men were in the den, Dean came into the kitchen to check on the status of the snack. "Well?"

He didn't know that two of the deacons, Simon Sherman and Andre Benson, had followed him into the kitchen. Before Grace could tell her impatient husband that the food was indeed ready, the men made their presence known by inhaling deeply and loudly.

"You sure know your way around a kitchen!" Andre said. "It smells GOOD up in here!"

Grace smiled. Although she didn't necessarily like how the deacon board operated as a group and how they had wrested control over the church from Rev. Buckley, some of the guys were kind of palatable. Andre was one of them. "I was just finishing up. I hope you'll enjoy them."

Apparently she held her smile toward Andre for too long. Out of the corner of her eye, Grace noticed Dean glaring at her. She quickly dropped her head and began to place the various chicken wings on serving platters, which she adorned with celery and more dressings.

While Grace didn't appreciate that she had been forced to make chicken wings at a moment's notice, the deacons' presence did grant her a much-needed reprieve from Dean. She and the girls were able to relax and play in the basement until it was time for them to go to bed. The guys stayed long after the game went off, and to Grace's delight, Dean again fell asleep in the den after he saw all of them to the door and watched them pull off in their respective vehicles. Before he retired for the night Dean issued a few directives to his wife. "Make sure the kitchen is cleaned up, and pack me two lunches for tomorrow. The Superior Heights project is starting. I'll be late getting home."

Trying not to smile too broadly, Grace nodded her head.

"Good-night." She was dismissed.

Upstairs, Grace dragged herself into her bathroom, opting to take a bubble bath. Every joint in her body ached. She had been in pain for several months, and wondered if it was stress. Or perhaps it was because of her weight. After having five babies including two sets of twins, Grace was far removed from the curvy 150-pound frame she flaunted years ago. As she was also approaching forty her metabolism had slowed greatly, and even though she didn't eat much--the anxiety she suffered due to her lifestyle didn't allow for much of an appetite--she could not lose weight. Dean often reminded her how fat and disgusting she was. It was another reason why she felt trapped. She definitely wasn't as attractive as she used to be. At five-feet-six-inches tall and over two hundred pounds, Dean's deprecating comments were now internalized. He was right. She *was* fat and disgusting. Before she stepped into her bath, Grace looked at the full-length mirror in her bedroom and sighed. She had always been pretty, with smooth brown skin, kind brown eyes, a tiny nose and full lips, but her beauty was overshadowed by the rest of her body which was ravaged by stretch marks and a huge flap of stomach fat that hung over her waist. She turned around and looked behind her, wincing at the skin that protruded from her flanks. Her body was ripe with flaps, folds and cellulite. As if her body wasn't bad enough, her face was beginning to show signs of the tortured life she tried to so badly to hide. Her eyes had lost their sparkle and had noticeable bags underneath. Grace forced a smile, and quickly dropped it. No matter how hard she smiled, her eyes still looked sad.

Well, she thought as she stepped into her bathtub and sat down, sighing contentedly, *they do say the eyes are the window to one's soul…*

CHAPTER THREE

"For the grace of God has appeared, bringing salvation for all people, training us to renounce ungodliness and worldly passions, and to live self-controlled, upright, and godly lives in the present age..." (Titus 2:11-12)

The end of August was both a blessing and a curse for Grace.

On one hand, the end of August meant that all five girls would be in school at Cornerstone Christian Academy where Eve was starting seventh grade, Rebekah and Sarah were going into third grade, and Abby and Naomi were kindergartners. That provided Grace more opportunities to get out of the house. Participating in the girls' school activities was one of the few things outside of the home that got Dean's stamp of approval. The previous year Grace had received a special award based on the sheer number of activities and projects she had participated in and spearheaded. Other mothers expressed admiration that she was so involved in her childrens' education. Unbeknownst to them, it was more than that. It was a chance to temporarily escape her prison.

Unfortunately the end of August also meant Curtis Toole's back-to-school barbecue, a party that Grace absolutely despised. The barbecue was a manifestation of the many problems that had developed at Christ First over the years. As soon as Rev. Riley was installed as pastor, the deacons let him know that he was simply the figurehead for the church. The only thing he really controlled were the words he spoke during his sermons. Other than that, the deacons were in charge of Christ First. As their power grew, they became more elitist. The deacons, as well as the other auxiliaries at the church, operated like a clique. As a result the back-to-school barbecue was only for deacons and their wives—no kids, ironically enough--and a select few members from the church who had kissed enough behind to be invited or had special talents that the deacons wanted to use for their benefit. Jason Allen was a prime example. Curtis had a huge pool in his backyard. Although Jason was not a part of the group, he had secured his invitation to the barbecue by offering to have the employees from his pool-cleaning business clean the pool for free throughout the summer and winterize it when the seasons began to change.

Grace hated the barbecues. They were the same each year. She knew what to expect as soon as Dean excitedly pulled up in front of the Toole's impressive five-bedroom, seven-bathroom ranch that sat on approximately five acres of land.

Curtis had been waiting for his protege. When they pulled up and parked, he came out the front door and approached the car with a huge smile on his face. Dean's smiled mirrored his as he jumped out of the car. Groaning, Grace watched as the two exchanged a brief half-embrace. She put on her best fake smile and got out of the car, holding tight to the spinach artichoke dip and warm tortilla chips she had prepared.

"Grace, come on in, come on in!" Curtis said enthusiastically. "I can't wait to show you and Dean what we've done with the place."

Grace fought the urge to roll her eyes. This was another part of these barbecues that she hated. Each year, right before the barbecue, the Tooles made some grand addition to their house or corral of vehicles that could be shown off to their visitors. They were a very materialistic couple who only wore expensive name-brand clothes, drove luxury vehicles, and owned vacation properties overseas. Curtis's wife, Claudia, employed a personal shopper that she paid hundreds of dollars per hour at the beginning of each of Michigan's four seasons to select a wardrobe for her. She had standing hair, nail and massage appointments at the best facilities in the area. Grace had never seen Claudia without her hair done or a face caked full of makeup. Claudia was also one of the fakest people Grace had ever met.

Curtis led them downstairs to the basement, which had been completely renovated. Formerly one wide-open dwelling, it was now divided into several rooms. One room was a guest bedroom and bathroom, a second area was a fully-stocked kitchenette, and the third area was the piece de resistance: A movie room, complete with acoustic tiles and boards in the walls and ceiling, plush purple carpeting, two rows of massage chairs in lieu of typical armchairs, which were of course too commonplace for the Tooles and their deep-rooted desire to impress, and a 110" flat-screen LED television. Grace sighed inwardly as she watched her husband walk around the room, "oohing" and "aahing" as if it were the most amazing thing he'd ever seen. Curtis stood in the doorway with his arms folded, smiling like a Cheshire cat as he watched Dean slide his hand across the smooth leather of one of the massage chairs before he sat in it. "How much did this run you, Curt?"

"Oh, I probably dropped a good twenty, thirty-thou on it," Curtis said airily. "I'll bet your basement could hold something like this, don't you?"

"You think our basement is big enough?" Dean asked him hopefully.

"Yeah, man, y'all have plenty of space. I can give you the name of my man if you want…"

Grace was subjected to a fifteen-minute demonstration on how everything in the movie room worked. She was annoyed by Dean's excitement. He hadn't made such a fuss when their daughters were born. She was also getting tired of standing there holding the spinach-artichoke dip, but she knew better than to interrupt. So she waited.

After what felt like an eternity Curtis finally remembered Grace and rushed over to her, taking the bowls from her hands. "I am so sorry!" he said. "I know Claudia and the others have been waiting on this. Let's get to the party!"

"Yeah!" Dean said enthusiastically. The two men left the room and raced upstairs, leaving Grace to find her own way. Quietly asking God to help her get through the next several hours, Grace walked through the pristine house into the kitchen and slid open the glass doors that led to the immaculately-landscaped backyard.

"Grace! Hi! So good to see you! Glad you made it!"

Greetings rang out from all sides. Grace again threw on her best fake smile and returned the greetings under Dean's watchful eye. Claudia, always extra, wearing a skimpy metallic-gold bikini, matching heels, sarong and a wide-brimmed hat, skipped over to Grace and embraced her. "Grace, this spinach dip is where it's at!"

"Ah, it's just a little something I threw together," Grace replied nonchalantly.

"Well, I wouldn't mind if you threw it together more often," Claudia said, and the other women, as if on cue, all giggled and nodded.

Sighing, Grace followed as Claudia led her around the backyard. Curtis had made another addition to the backyard—a special area close to the pool had been outfitted with an elaborate bar and a sitting area with another huge flat-screen television. There was food on the bar and two tables in front of it and on the ground in front of the tables were several coolers filled with various expensive wines and alcoholic beverages.

The women settled into the sitting area out of earshot from the men, who were standing around with their various beers and other drinks several feet away talking and laughing. Curtis stood in front of the massive barbecue grill, flipping huge cuts of meat that didn't even need to be flipped. He always had to be doing something to show off. Grace shook her head, trying not to despise his flashiness.

The seats were in a circle. Grace found herself seated between Claudia and Tangi Jacobs. Each woman had a drink, and some even had a bottle next to her seat for quick refills. Grace sighed and waited for the gossip to start.

Not surprisingly, Claudia got the ball rolling. "Do you know that Della had the nerve to ask if she could come today?"

"Whaaaat?" Karla Sherman intoned, as the others laughed. "Who does she think she is?"

Claudia shook her head, lips pursed. "I wish I knew. I only talk to her at church to be polite. Other than that I don't have anything to do with her. Did you see what she had on last Sunday?"

"Oh, my goodness," Tangi said, "she looked terrible. All them fat rolls hanging out all over the place. That woman got more gut than butt!"

"And she got plenty of butt," Lila Pendleton added.

"And do you know that broad claims that she is only thirty-eight?" Claudia continued. "I almost peed myself when she told me that bald-faced lie. Heifer know she at least fifty."

Suddenly, Grace felt eyes on her. She turned, and from across the yard there was Dean, glaring at her, silently telling her to loosen up. The other women noticed their gaze and misinterpreted it.

"Those look like bedroom eyes," Tangi teased.

Grace forced an uncomfortable giggle. "Nothing like that."

"Honey, the two of you are still young. There's nothing wrong with that!" Lila said. "I'm actually jealous. I don't know what's been up with Marlon lately. I know what hasn't been up, though." She shook her head and took another sip of her drink.

"Me and Andre had that problem last year. When's the last time Marlon had his blood pressure checked?" Anna Benson asked. "Maybe he needs to see a doctor. Does he get his annual physicals?"

"I've been telling that fool to take his limp behind to the doctor for months," Lila said witheringly. "He says the problem isn't with him, it's me. But I know there is nothing wrong with me. You want to know how I know?"

"How?" the others, minus Grace, chorused in unison.

"Because that young thang that just joined the church two months ago been telling me so for about a week now!"

As the others roared with laughter, Grace sat back, uncomfortable. In hushed whispers, Lila excitedly told the women about the affair she was having with Trevor Booth, a man twenty years her junior. He had just joined Christ First. Grace thought back to when Trevor attended his first service. He stood and testified to the crowd about how his life had gotten off track and he wanted to do better. Lila was now serving as his stumbling block.

The discussion grew raunchier as the women got more alcohol in their systems. Grace was disheartened to learn that every last one of them was regularly unfaithful to their husbands. Lila had even slept with Rev. Riley. The other women squealed their surprise—and jealousy—as she relayed the details.

"Girl, do you know he has the nerve to be upset about me and Trevor?" she laughed. "It's hilarious!"

"Can you blame the man?" Claudia said. "That wife of his does nothing to make herself look even remotely appealing. I shudder to think what she looks like when she first wakes up."

"I hate that she is on this 'natural hair' kick," Nancy Ogletree chimed in. "Her hair looks like a Brillo pad. I want to slap her with a box of perm every time I see her."

"And she is always up under you, Grace," Mary said.

With that remark attention was shifted to Grace. She knew she was expected to say something negative about Wilma Riley, but she couldn't do it. The woman had done nothing to her. "She tries to be helpful, that's all."

"How do you deal with her bad breath?" Mary continued.

Grace sighed inwardly. It was true that Wilma's breath was often a mixture of stale coffee, garlic and cigarettes. But it didn't make her a bad person. Grace had walked in on Wilma vigorously brushing her teeth in the ladies' room on several occasions and concluded that she possibly had a medical problem that contributed to her breath. "I always have mints on me and whenever I see her coming, I offer her one." The others roared with laughter.

"Grace is such a sweetheart," Claudia said, finishing off her fifth drink. She was beginning to slur her words a bit. "It's like pulling teeth to get her to talk about anybody. And there's nothing wrong with that, Grace. I rather like that about you."

"Me too," Lila said. "You don't find too many honestly decent people anymore."

Yeah, and you guys are living proof of that, Grace thought. Instead, she smiled humbly. "Thanks."

The conversation drifted from sex to more disparaging remarks about other members of Christ First before an inebriated Curtis Toole called to his wife from the pool.

"Bring me that big ol' booty!" he yelled. "I know just what to do with it."

Fully drunk now, Claudia stood up, removed her sarong and tossed it to the side with a great flourish. As she headed to the pool she kicked off her heels. She climbed down into the pool and into her husband's open arms. Grace looked away as they began kissing passionately. The other women, free of Claudia's command, went to their own husbands as well. Grace remained in her seat and watched as the scene unfolded. It was approaching sunset, and everyone, including Dean, was finishing off either a drink or, to Grace's horror, taking puffs from any one of several joints that were circulating around the yard. Sensual music was pumping from a huge sound system. Grace watched as Mary and her husband danced provocatively.

Dean came out of nowhere and plopped heavily on to one of the seats next to her. "Having fun?" he slurred.

"Of course," she lied. "And you?"

"The time of my life," he said. "Let's dance."

Dancing with Dean was humiliating and tiresome. He was too drunk and high to hold up the entirety of his weight, leaving Grace to do so as he groped her breasts and butt in full view of everyone there. She was happy and relieved when he pulled away and took off for the bathroom. When he came back, he wore a drunken smile on his face, telling Curtis, "I almost peed myself, man. What in the world was that drink you gave me?"

Curtis laughed. "That's a special brew," he told him proudly. "It's an old family recipe. It gets you done, doesn't it?"

Three cups later, Dean was beyond done. At two-thirty a.m. everyone else was done too. Claudia had passed out in a patio chair, and Curtis put his wife on top of his shoulders, patting her exposed behind and laughing as he carried her into the house. Dean was also slouched in a chair. Andre and Dallas hoisted him up and helped Grace get him in the car. Grace said her good-byes and drove home. Dean was snoring, and she wondered how she would get him in the house.

He woke up when she pulled into the garage.

"Are you going to be able to make it upstairs okay?" she asked.

His head rolled slightly to the side. "Yeah," he replied.

That was a lie. Grace basically had to drag him upstairs, and by the time they got to their bedroom she was sweating and had hurt one of her arms. To make matters worse, when she got Dean to the bed he pulled her down on top of him and started kissing her neck and pulling on her clothes. She felt sick to her stomach as she realized he was going to try to have sex with her.

They hadn't been intimate in months and when they were there was nothing loving or romantic about it. Nothing about the act was pleasing to her. Dean didn't care, as long as he was satisfied. Usually he would wake her up in the middle of the night after he had gotten himself riled up watching pornography on the Internet. It was disgusting.

As he kissed her roughly on her mouth the taste of marijuana, brandy and the garlicky food he had consumed almost gagged her. Dean rolled over on top of Grace and—promptly fell deeply asleep.

Grace lay there, motionless, for a half an hour. She wanted to make sure Dean was asleep. When she was confident that he was she *slowly* pushed him off and watched as his body rolled and flopped onto the bed. She got up, slowly, *slowly*, and gently picked his feet up off the ground and placed them onto the bed. Then she went into their bathroom, showered, put on her pajamas and wrapped her hair. When she got back to the bedroom, Dean was still sleeping soundly. Grace sighed with relief. He was out like a light. Grace went to her knees and offered up her prayers for the night, asking for God to please have mercy on all who had been at the barbecue, and to please show them a better way. It had been a terrible day, but at least she could get a good night's rest. Dean did not handle alcohol well and would probably sleep until the afternoon and be hung over the next day, which meant the time she would have to spend dealing with him would be minimal—which was perfectly okay with her.

CHAPTER FOUR

"For the lips of a forbidden woman drip honey, and her speech is smoother than oil, but in the end she is bitter as wormwood, sharp as a two-edged sword." (Proverbs 5:3-4)

The past three weeks had been among some of the best in Grace's recent life. The girls adjusted to their school schedules exceptionally well. After dropping them off at school, Grace quickly made her way home. The silence was golden. Dean had just started the EHR project with Superior Heights the previous week. As Grace had hoped, he was gone from seven in the morning until eight at night most evenings, giving her basically the whole day to herself. When he got home, he was usually tired and would go into his den where he would spend the rest of the night, even eating his dinner in there as he browsed the DVR recordings he had set before he left that morning. He didn't even bother to walk through the house to make sure she had completed her checklist items. Grace loved it. She usually stayed at the girls' school all day Mondays, Wednesdays and Fridays, helping out on various projects or in the front office copying worksheets, grading tests and shelving books in the library. Tuesdays and Thursdays were her own. She often found herself humming happily as she danced through the house with her cleaning supplies. She hadn't been so happy in months.

Life wasn't so idyllic for Dean. The EHR project was taking a toll on him. He found it odd when Wesley Han and Mike Kutcher nominated him to be the project manager, as it was a given that Wes, the senior employee in their department, would be awarded the opportunity. When Dean was first hired into ITS Wes and Mike, both Army retirees, had taken him under their wing, feeling it was their duty to welcome a brother from the armed forces into the company. The founders of ITS were strong supporters of the United States military, and Dean's Marine background gave him access to exclusive lunches and banquets where he often stood shoulder-to-shoulder with the CEO of the company and other high-level executives. However, there were other members of the armed forces working for ITS that had never been invited to some of those functions. Wes and Mike had done a lot of networking in the company and it was due to his initial friendship with them that Dean was able to do so much schmoozing. Dean repaid Wes and Mike for their kindness by stabbing them both in the back with the same knife.

Three years into his career with ITS, Dean was on a team working on a software project for Reynold's Dialysis Centers. Wes was the project manager and Mike was his secondhand man. The two had worked on numerous initiatives before with a high success rate. Dean had worked with them before and was usually happy to be a part of their team, but something had changed.

Unfortunately for Wes and Mike their good friend Dean had started an affair with Madeline O'Neal, the estranged daughter of Sheldon O'Neal, the CEO of the company. Madeline, a recovering alcoholic, was looking for a last-ditch opportunity to prove to her father that she was worthy of a job, and more importantly, to be her father's successor for the highly profitable enterprise. She had begged and pleaded with Sheldon O'Neal that he might put her in place to be the project manager for Reynold's. It was a smaller-scale project that she could definitely handle, and if she handled it well her father's trust in her would be restored and she could possibly be given more authority in the company. When the job instead went to Wes, Madeline's scheming began.

She struck up a friendship with Dean after one of the company luncheons that he had been invited to thanks to Wes and Mike. Sheldon announced that the company had won the Reynolds project bid and would begin working on it within two weeks, headed by Wes. After she saw Wes, Mike and Dean with their wives at one of the main tables, Madeline had her mark. The interactions between Dean and his pretty, albeit frumpy, wife were totally disingenuous. It was obvious that there were problems within the Hardaway marriage, whereas Wes and Mike appeared to sincerely love their wives.

As with any project of significant scope, everything did not go smoothly with the Reynolds project. When Madeline overheard through the corporate grapevine that the project was not on schedule, she used Dean to her advantage. It wasn't difficult to coax him into an affair. Madeline had no problem persuading Dean to help her undermine Wes's leadership by feeding her information about the project. Without even realizing what he was doing, Dean began telling Madeline about Wes and Mike's alleged mismanagement of the project and the team. In all reality, Wes and Mike had been hit with several setbacks that were no fault of their own, but Madeline used the information to her advantage, embellishing at her will. Without Wes's knowledge, an upper-level executive began checking his work. He prepared a report about his findings, saying that the quality of the product was substandard at best and that he felt that Wes's laid-back style of leadership was to blame. The report was sent to Sheldon O'Neal. He promptly removed Wes and Mike from their positions and instead put Madeline in charge. They now had to work under her.

Madeline never spoke of her affair with Dean and he never admitted to it, but Wes and Mike weren't dumb. When Madeline told the project team that Dean was her assistant—giving him authority over his old friends—their curiosity was piqued. After watching how Madeline and Dean interacted with each other, it became obvious that the two were involved. Although they were unable to prove it, Wes and Mike put two and two together and knew they had been done in by their so-called friend. It took a year for them to repair their credibility and to be allowed to work together as a team again.

Because of the deception he had committed against them it was a great surprise to Dean when Wes rejected the offer to be the manager for the Superior Heights project and an even greater surprise when Mike and Wes enthusiastically nominated Dean for the job. Now Dean knew why. Sheldon O'Neal was best friends with the CEO of Superior Heights, Alexander Aguanno. As such, Dean was under tremendous pressure to deliver a high-quality product. Of course Sheldon wanted to enhance his bottom line, but this project was also personal. He wanted his friend to be satisfied. This meant that every Monday morning Dean was required to meet with Sheldon, Alexander and Sam Wyatt, the chief IT officer for Superior Heights. It was very intimidating. The three men sat across from Dean with stern looks on their faces, scribbling comments and questions on their notepads as he explained how the project was going. There was always a problem that needed immediate correction, and he faced questions from each of the three men, who were obviously irritated if his answer didn't come fast enough. He received multiple emails and calls throughout the day from Sheldon, relaying messages from Alexander or Sam about some other addition they had just thought up. Dean was on pins and needles all day because of the stress of the project. He had constant headaches and couldn't eat or sleep regularly. Wes and Mike knew it was going to be a tough project and that Dean's job depended upon its success. They had set him up and now there was no way out of it. Even Madeline, who had gotten her upper-level executive position handed to her several months back, wasn't returning his calls for help.

By the time he got home Dean was zapped of all of his energy and barely able to eat his dinner. He usually came in the house, took a quick shower, then settled into the den, where he would eat and watch TV until his family went to bed. Once he was confident that they were asleep, Dean fed one of his newest addictions—Internet pornography. The girls in those films were everything his wife was not—young and in shape, willing to do whatever it took to please their partner. He couldn't get enough. He had recently started perusing Craigslist hoping to find someone with whom he could act out some of his fantasies, but so far none had piqued his interest.

Except Angelica Billups. She'd caught his eye from the very minute she walked into Christ First. Apparently, the feeling was mutual, because ever since that first meeting over a month ago the two had been corresponding regularly by texts and emails. Their relationship began innocently when Angelica saw Dean in the sanctuary testing the overhead projector that displayed the topic of Rev. Riley's sermon.

"Are you an electronics geek for hire or are your talents exclusively for the church?"

Dean whirled around and saw an unfamiliar brown-skinned woman standing at the entrance of the control room. Momentarily taken aback by her beauty and shapeliness, he paused to collect his thoughts before responding. "What do you need?"

"I just moved here and I am having a hard time getting some of my things connected. Nothing is working."

Dean didn't know that Angelica was fishing—not for souls, but for a meal ticket. She had come to Christ First for a purpose: Not to worship God, but to find a man, preferably a married one. When she first walked into the stately brick building that housed Christ First followed by her reluctant son Angelica had one goal for the day—to find suitable prey. As she pretended to take part in the Sunday school lesson,

43

Angelica carefully surveyed her surroundings. She befriended every woman in there and was able to find out who was married to whom. One by one, Angelica weeded out husbands that she hadn't even seen simply based on the personalities of their wives. Certain women were too confident, too brash, too outspoken. They would not go down without a fight. She needed a man who had a meek wife with poor self-esteem. It was always easier to pull men away from wives with little self-confidence, and it was always easier to maintain an affair with a man married to such a woman. Those were the types of women who, in their attempt to salvage their pathetic marriage, would keep their husband's dalliances quiet as long as the family stayed together.

Angelica loathed men. Her hatred of men had long deep roots that traced back to her childhood. Angelica had never known her biological father. Her mother, Shirley, was a sexually promiscuous teen who became impregnated with Angelica on a night when she slept with her high school's entire varsity football team. Embarrassed by her daughter's actions, Angelica's grandmother Lois moved pregnant Shirley from Atlanta, Georgia all the way to Chicago, Illinois, where she had grown up. Only a few months after they relocated to Chicago Lois died unexpectedly. Shirley gave birth to Angelica when she was fifteen and moved into a raggedy apartment with her boyfriend, a twenty-year-old man who Angelica knew only as Buster. Buster was abusive to Shirley, and in turn, Shirley was abusive to Angelica. When Angelica got old enough in Buster's eyes, he turned his abuse toward her—with Shirley's full approval. The two often physically and sexually abused four-year-old Angelica together.

Angelica thought she was saved when Buster was killed in a drug deal gone wrong when she was six years old. Unfortunately, all that meant for her was that Shirley had to go out and find another man to support her. She went right to the streets and brought back another loser named Mickey that treated Angelica worse than Buster had, something she had thought was impossible.

Angelica's childhood was characterized by abuse and instability. She ran away several times, only to be brought back to her mother by the police each time. After being raped by another of Shirley's boyfriends when she was only thirteen Angelica became pregnant. Afraid of what Shirley would do, Angelica hid the pregnancy and was actually relieved when she miscarried. No baby deserved to be born into such a mess. Unfortunately, that was only the first in a series of miscarriages.

Angelica vowed to never be as pathetic as her mother. She got physically ill watching her mother as she begged her abusive boyfriends to stay with her because she had no other means to survive. Shirley had little education and no formal training in any type of trade. Occasionally, in order to persuade the men to stay, she would use Angelica, giving her daughter over to them to satisfy their perverse needs. Angelica learned to lie on her back perfectly still unless she was told to do otherwise. At a young age she learned that there was no enjoyment in sex for a woman. She developed a totally destructive attitude toward sex, using it as a tool for manipulation throughout her life.

Although Angelica had no intentions on becoming like her mother, she picked up some of Shirley's behaviors. Angelica dropped out of high school when she was sixteen and began to use her body to influence gullible men to pay her rent for a small apartment. Unlike her mother Angelica refused to be hit. In one instance her boyfriend at the time hit her in a fit of rage. Angelica responded by grabbing a steak knife and plunging it into his shoulder.

Angelica was beautiful; she had that working in her favor. She had a sophisticated look and aura that belied her true identity. As she got older, she learned to use her looks and hourglass figure to her advantage. She stopped dealing with the roughnecks she had been seeing and began to target men she met at the suburban shopping malls she frequented. Soon she was being lavished with expensive clothing and jewelry and was put up in a better apartment. Her lifestyle was maintained as long as she pretended to care for the supplier and satisfied his sexual needs, which usually wasn't hard.

Shirley was jealous and often tried to compete with Angelica, but Shirley was a rather plain-looking woman, and her rough lifestyle showed on her face. She aged rapidly. The two often got into screaming matches and fistfights. When Shirley grew ill and found out that she had been infected with HIV, she had no choice but to stop sleeping around. With no man in her life, she had no income. When she approached her only child asking for help, Angelica responded by packing up her things and moving to Boston. She was pregnant by her current boyfriend, Joshua, and he had gotten a job there. Joshua wanted his family to be together and Angelica wanted to be rid of Shirley.

Only three months into their new life in Boston, Angelica miscarried a baby girl. Joshua responded to this heartbreak by kicking her out of his home. He was tired of taking care of her. Down but never out, Angelica moved on to the next man… and the next. Over the next several years, Angelica established relationships with multiple men, lived in numerous states, sometimes for only months at a time, and miscarried four more girls. She was convinced that God had cursed her because of her sexual treachery until she became pregnant at the age of 21 and delivered a healthy baby boy. At first, Angelica was not too keen on the idea of having a son, but as soon as she saw David, it was love at first sight.

David's father Simon was a popular married entrepreneur and beloved philanthropist in Philadelphia. He didn't want his wife or his high-society associates to find out about his extramarital affair. Not because he was concerned about the affair itself, as all of his peers had regular illicit sexual escapades of their own, but because an extramarital affair with an uneducated younger Black woman was not a good look for an esteemed White man. In order to keep Angelica silent, Simon made sure that she was well provided for. Angelica was delighted with this arrangement. At the end of the day, she didn't need male companionship. She didn't even really like talking to men or being around them. She could have very well lived without sex. She only did those things because it kept the men—and their money—around. Now she had a new niche. From then on, she exclusively dated married men.

Simon passed away when David was five. In his will he left his wealth to his wife and their children. David wasn't even mentioned. Angelica was not surprised, nor did she care. She had learned to keep several married men at a time at her beck and call. Whenever a man tried to break up with her and she didn't have a good enough supply of men to furnish the lifestyle to which she had become accustomed, she would remind him of the proof of the affair that had she accumulated--hotel and restaurant receipts, letters, texts, screenshots--that she could show his wife and he would rescind the attempt to dissolve the relationship. Angelica wasn't going to give any man the satisfaction of just walking away from her. They had to pay up until she found someone to take his place.

Angelica moved often. As such, David had an unstable childhood. He was always going to different schools and wasn't able to sustain any friendships. There were always different men around him, but Angelica wasn't concerned that any of them would abuse a boy. She was wrong. David was sexually abused by one of her boyfriends. Unlike Shirley, Angelica reacted when she found out by stabbing the perpetrator in his stomach several times and leaving him to bleed to death. Angelica managed to get away with the crime when another man confessed to the murder. Although he eventually recanted and said his confession was coerced, the case was closed and Angelica was never even questioned. It was something Angelica held over her son's head whenever he got upset with her. She would quickly remind him how she had killed someone for him. Because of that, she expected for her son to be loyal and keep her secrets—even the deadly ones.

Before moving to Ypsilanti, Michigan and stumbling upon Christ First, Angelica and David had been living in Las Vegas. David loved it there and would have been content to live there his entire life. Angelica was involved with Joel Perry, a wealthy casino magnate. When he was diagnosed with a rare form of stomach cancer Angelica knew her life of luxury was going to come to an end soon. She was getting older and had less energy to devote to carrying on relationships with multiple men.

Angelica knew that Joel had several life insurance policies and that if she managed to get her name put on just one of them, she'd be set for a very long time. Although Joel's marriage was virtually nonexistent, he still had his wife listed as the sole beneficiary on many of his policies—at least until Angelica cooked up a scheme that turned Joel against her. She paid a handsome young personal trainer named Ivan three thousand dollars to strike up a friendship with Mrs. Perry, who was a fitness buff herself. When they began to have a sexual relationship, Ivan gave Angelica proof in the form of pictures, which she anonymously mailed to Joel. When Joel saw that his wife was sleeping around while he was on his sick bed—although he had been sleeping around himself—he promptly re-wrote his will. When he died the next month, Angelica received half a million dollars. Another several million dollars was divided up among his children, and still other monies went to other charitable organizations and area businesses.

Angelica knew she had to leave town before her dark deed came to light. She took her money and moved to Michigan. It was one of the few states in which she'd never lived. With Joel's insurance money she was able to purchase a well-outfitted home with cash, as well as an SUV. She and David lived a comfortable lifestyle until a few months back when Angelica noticed that her money was dwindling. She was spending too much on clothes, expensive restaurants, and fancy decor for the house. It was time to go hunting again.

Like any skilled hunter, Angelica had developed some tricks of the trade over the years. She knew to go to country clubs, churches, and sporting events at area schools to find married men. The ones at churches were especially valuable because they often paid top dollar to keep their affairs secret. Angelica had visited twelve churches and two country clubs before walking into Christ First that fateful Sunday. Although she knew that Dean wasn't wealthy, that didn't matter. What mattered was how easily he could be manipulated. He had a wife and five daughters and hopefully an insurance policy that could be highly profitable in the right hands. All she had to do was get him into the right situation. Then she could get him to change his policy, as she had done with Joel. If he didn't have one, she could get one.

David knew his mother was on the prowl. After their first Sunday at Christ First, he confronted her. "What good is it for you to take up with that Dean guy? He looks perfectly healthy. How long do you plan on waiting for him to die so you can get your hands on his money?"

Angelica's lips curled into a sinister smile. She had no intentions of waiting for any longer than she absolutely had to. David didn't know, but stomach cancer was only one cause of Joel's death.

Chapter Five

"Beware of practicing your righteousness before other people in order to be seen by them, for then you will have no reward from your Father who is in heaven." (Matthew 6:1)

The pressure at work was steadily building and Dean was reaching his breaking point. Wes and Mike were working a cushy project with a great team. They got off work every day no later than five and had beers at the bar across the street before heading home. They came to work in the mornings well-rested and jovial. It was only a matter of time before Dean snapped and choked the smirk off of one of their faces.

Dean's team was a mess. The project was already turning out to be a monumental disaster. Dean was too narcissistic to have ever acquired any leadership skills, and his pride and dictatorial attitude had sapped his otherwise well-qualified team of any enthusiasm they'd had at the beginning of the project. Dean was sensitive to the fact that two of his team members were new grads from prestigious schools that thought they were more qualified to lead the project than he was, and the others openly expressed to other people within the company that they'd rather have had Wes or Mike as their project leader. Dean simply did not have the ability to inspire, delegate fairly, or communicate professionally. He treated his team with contempt, taking umbrage when one of them merely offered a suggestion.

Several weeks beyond the start date the project was not on track. All of his team members had lodged formal complaints about Dean's totalitarian style of leadership. Other than what they had to do to keep their jobs, none of them were willing to help Dean out with any additional tasks, so when he got one of those last-minute change requests from Sheldon, Alexander or Sam, he often found himself going it alone.

His standing at Christ First was also being threatened, or so he thought. Dean liked most of his fellow deacons just fine, but there were two who were perpetual thorns in his side. One of them, Deacon Allen Chandler, was the oldest deacon in the church. He had been close friends with Reverend Buckley and held fast to his former pastor's teachings. He was usually in the minority when it came to matters of the church, and he and Dean were always at odds. Dean wanted to do things to move the church forward and keep up with the modern times, but Allen always felt Dean's ideas were too secular. Dean could handle Allen only because most of the other deacons, who were closer in age to Dean than Allen, usually supported him, but he still hated being challenged. Over the last few weeks, Allen had argued with Dean over a number of things. Each fall, the church experienced an influx of younger people as the local colleges opened their doors. Dean proposed changing the devotion service to include the young people more. Allen did not think their rap music and suggestive praise dancing was appropriate. Dean reminded Allen how important it was to keep the young people involved. Allen did not think that was the way to do it, but eventually the majority of the other deacons sided with Dean.

The other problem was Deacon Tyler Ware. At thirty-five years of age, Tyler was the youngest deacon, with Dean being the next youngest, at forty-two. He enjoyed a position of high status within Christ First. People sincerely loved and respected Tyler. He was all-around a decent, God-fearing man. Tyler seemed to get everything he wanted in life and Dean resented him for it. Years ago, Tyler had confessed to the deacons that he and his wife Samantha were having fertility issues. Underneath his facade of concern, Dean smirked, then remarked, "I made two sets of twins without even really trying, how hard can it be?"

But the joke was on him. Within months Tyler told them his wife was pregnant, and not only was she pregnant, she was having a boy. Soon after their first son was born, Samantha became pregnant again, and delivered another boy. Shortly after their second son, she became pregnant again. Tyler informed the deacons that he would love a daughter. And he got one.

Tyler had a great family, a great job, and got the love and respect that Dean coveted. He truly was a stand-up guy trying to live a life that pleased the Lord. He and Samantha had come to one of the back to school barbecues. After they saw what it was truly about they politely refused to come to any more. Tyler had gently informed his fellow deacons that the barbecue was in poor taste, but he did it so lovingly that no one took offense. Since he was so beloved, it was totally understandable that Dean absolutely despised him and was always trying to one-up him in church, especially in their deacon's meetings. If Tyler made a suggestion, even if Dean agreed with it internally, he would try to argue it down. Unfortunately, in those situations, the deacons typically sided with Tyler. And that made Dean furious.

Between the pressures of his job and the challenges he perceived within the deacon board, Dean had little respite. Grace bored him. When they were dating he had admired her intelligence and enjoyed conversing with her. Now, she had nothing to talk about but the girls, and honestly, their lives were not interesting. Angelica helped him decompress. Their relationship hadn't gone further than a little peck on the cheek, but Dean was quietly hoping for more. Only days after she had first solicited him for his technological savvy, Dean made his first trip to her house. He had no problems getting her computer and David's laptop connected and he found himself even wondering why the two of them hadn't been able to figure it out themselves. He stopped wondering when he saw Angelica standing in the living room doorway holding a glass of wine.

"You drink?"

He nodded.

It was a smooth red wine, the best he'd ever had. Angelica motioned for him to sit with her, and before he knew it the two of them had talked their way through the entire bottle. Dean found himself pouring his heart out to Angelica about the misery of his life--his lazy, ungrateful wife, his disrespectful daughters, the idiots at his job, the annoying guys on the deacon board who thought they knew everything. Every now and then David would peek out into the living room and scowl, but he said nothing. Angelica acted as though the boy wasn't even in the house. She responded to each of Dean's complaints with a kind, commiserating ear, just what he needed. Every day since then Dean had found a way to see Angelica and his attraction to her was fully cemented. He wanted to know if she felt the same way, and planned to find out soon.

On Sundays they were cordial to each other, never letting on to the other congregants that they had any involvement with each other outside of church. David was used to harboring his mother's secrets, and although he felt guilty walking into Miss Grace's class every Sunday morning knowing that her husband was being unfaithful with his mother, he remained silent as well. It wasn't easy. David had grown to be very fond of Miss Grace. It wasn't a crush or anything. He just saw her for what she was--a genuinely sweet and good person. However, his mom was the only family he had, and their nomadic and deceitful way of life was the only one he knew.

As summer breathed its last and the bright blues, purples and pinks of the Michigan summer foliage began to slowly turn into the browns and golds that signaled autumn, Tyler Ware's wife Samantha unknowingly put Grace in a precarious position and propelled Dean's and Angelica's relationship to the next level. During the worship service, right before the announcements were read, Rev. Riley asked for Samantha to stand. She rose from her seat, holding her fat brown baby girl, blushing slightly.

"Choir, please stand, and come to the front of the pulpit," Rev. Riley motioned with his hand for the choir, seated at the front of the church, to come before him. They obliged.

"I'm sure you all have noticed these beautiful new robes your adult choir is wearing," Rev. Riley said as he descended from the pulpit and joined the choir members at the front of the sanctuary. "If you'll recall, about four months ago we talked about getting new robes. Out with the old and in with the new, right?"

"Amen!" some members chorused.

"Well, what we failed to consider was the talent we have right within this church," Rev. Riley went on. "It was going to cost us an arm and a leg to order brand new robes for twenty people. So Sis. Ware took it upon herself to put her seamstress skills to good use. Ladies and gentlemen, please stand and give Sis. Ware a hand. She made these robes all by herself!"

Impressed, Grace joined the rest of the church and stood to her feet, applauding. Samantha was a lovely young woman, and she and Grace often conferred about various child-rearing issues. Grace yearned to pursue a deeper friendship with Samantha outside of church, but for reasons unbeknownst to her, Dean hated Samantha's husband and didn't want Grace to have much to do with either of them.

Grace stole a look at Dean's face. He was standing, but not clapping. He was glowering at Tyler, who was looking at his wife proudly.

Once the applause died down, Rev. Riley returned to the pulpit. "Before Sis. Woods comes with the announcements, I have one I'd like to make personally." The church quieted down immediately. "As you know, my pastoral anniversary is coming up, and I'd like to know who is going to be in charge of the celebration."

Grace groaned internally. Although Rev. Riley wasn't too keen on many of the duties that came along with responsible and thorough pastoring, he definitely enjoyed a good party. His pastoral anniversary parties involved celebratory services throughout the week and culminated with a big party on Saturday. They were always lavish, over-the-top celebrations, and each individual who planned the anniversary did his or her best to top the one from the previous year. Grace wasn't interested in volunteering for anything related to this party.

Dean had other plans. After seeing how the congregation had just stood and clapped for Samantha for sewing together some flimsy robes he was angry and looking to one-up the Wares. Luckily for him, he had a secret weapon: A wife who was the best cook in the area, hands down. Dean stood up.

"Pastor, I'd be happy to plan your anniversary celebration."

Grace's eyes flew open in shock, but she quickly adjusted her face, hopefully before anyone saw.

Knowing that planning the week-long extravaganza was a major undertaking that few usually volunteered for, the congregation again rose to its feet, providing Dean with the ego boost he desperately craved. Dean shot a menacing look at his wife. She knew right then what had just happened. He was going to use her to outdo his nemesis. And she'd better do a good job, or suffer the consequences.

Grace stewed silently on their way home, but of course she couldn't let Dean know she was angry about having to plan the celebration. At home the girls quietly went to the basement while Grace finished dinner. As she was doing so, Dean came into the kitchen as he was tugging his tie loose from his neck. "I'm going to do most of the planning, you know," he told her. "I really just want you to focus on the cooking. Nobody can mess with your cooking."

"Thanks for the compliment, Dean. I'm sure it's going to turn out fantastic." She didn't bother to turn from the stove. That was a major no-no.

"Care to look at me when you're speaking to me?"

She whirled around and looked him in the eye.

"You got a problem?" he asked her with a snarl. "I already owe you one. Don't think I didn't see your face when I volunteered to do the party!"

He was within slapping distance now, and Grace instinctively braced herself. She didn't bother to refute what he had just said. She *was* mad, and for some reason, didn't care if he hit her. How *dare* he basically volunteer her for such a time consuming effort, for a pastor she barely respected? How dare he diminish her contributions to the house, how she worked tirelessly to make sure the place was spotless, and to take care of those five girls all by herself? Homework, doctor's appointments, choir rehearsal, nightmares, pulling teeth, bandaging bruises, preparing lessons, packing lunches, combing and braiding hair... Had he *any* respect for the energy Grace expended daily simply to keep up with the business of maintaining the home? The more she thought about it, the angrier she grew. If she was going to get hit, she was going to make the best of it. Not even sure of what she was doing, Grace turned her back on Dean and grabbed the pot that held her perfectly cooked beef roast with both hands and turned back around right as Dean was advancing on her. The hot pot hit his belly for a quick second. He recoiled from the heat with a yelp. A small smile crossed Grace's lips as he rushed to the bathroom, pulled up his shirt, and surveyed the microscopic damage done to his golden skin. When he came back in the kitchen, he looked incredulous, wondering if Grace had burned him on purpose. He couldn't read her face.

"Dinner is ready," she said listlessly.

"You thought that was funny, huh?"

Grace wasn't surprised when Dean lunged at her, knocked the pot out of her hands and onto the floor, and unleashed upon her a flurry of fists. She simply curled herself into a protective ball and waited until it was over.

Dean stood over her, his breath coming in mighty huffs and puffs. "Don't you *EVER* try that with me again!" he roared.

He looked up and noticed Eve standing in the doorway to the kitchen. She didn't look scared. She looked angry. He walked toward her.

"What do you think you're looking at? Who do you think you're staring at like that? You better fix your face, little girl!"

As if he wasn't even there, Eve walked around her father as if he were a piece of furniture that was intruding upon her path, went to her mother, leaned down, and tried to hug her. Her insolence infuriated Dean even further. His eldest daughter was now the object of his rage, but he was in for a shock.

Eve saw her father's shadow as he approached her and stood up quickly. The knife Grace had been using to cut the roast was right in front of her. She grabbed it and turned around, wielding it at her father.

"Leave."

Dean stopped dead in his tracks. "Are you crazy?"

"No, you are!" Eve yelled. "Just leave! None of us want you here."

Sensing the worst, Grace pulled herself into a sitting position. Many of the blows had impacted her stomach. Holding her aching belly, she rose to her feet and tried to position herself between her husband and daughter. She knew neither of them would back down, and this situation was dangerous. She couldn't believe what she was seeing. Her daughter, her baby, holding a knife at her father. Doing something she didn't have the courage to do--standing up to Dean.

"Eve...put that down. I'm fine. I'm fine. I'm okay," Grace protested.

"You are not!" Eve shouted. "You are not, and I'm tired of you lying!"

Dean pointed his finger at her. "You are in for such a surprise when you do drop that knife, little girl."

"Oh yeah?" Eve countered. "Do what you want but I'm not like Mom. I'll call the cops on you and they'll come lock you up and everybody will know you're a monster!"

Dean was stunned into submission. He knew that his oldest daughter was fiery, and that she would do exactly what she said she would do. He didn't have the hold over Eve that he had over his wife. Eve was too much like him in terms of her resolve. The situation had gotten out of hand. Without another word, Dean grabbed his car keys and left the house.

Grace grabbed Eve and held her tightly. "What were you thinking?" she asked Eve weakly. "Don't ever put yourself in harm's way like that again, you hear me, Eve?"

Eve didn't respond. Knowing that her mom was in pain, Eve helped Grace up to her room, ran her a warm bath, lit several candles and put on some soothing music. Then she went back downstairs where she was able to salvage the dinner her mother had prepared. Somehow the pot that housed the roast had landed right side up. Eve fixed plates for herself and her sisters and called them out of their hiding places to eat. Once dinner was finished, Eve returned upstairs to her mother with a plate for her to eat in bed. While Grace was struggling to eat through the dull ache in her jaw Eve supervised the other girls as they took their baths. All five girls came into the room with Grace, where they read books to her and put on a finger puppet show that made her laugh. Grace's head was pounding and her ears were ringing. The girls were not surprised when she fell asleep. They knew what to do. They prayed in the room with their sleeping mom, soliciting God for deliverance, brushed their teeth, and went to bed.

Across town, Dean drowned his woes with Angelica. Always the victim, he thoroughly embellished the day's events in a highly effective ploy to get more sympathy as they lay across her big brass bed. It worked. He strategically left out the part where he beat his wife, and instead informed Angelica that Grace had gotten belligerent with him and purposely burned him with a hot cast-iron skillet. As he showed Angelica the barely-there burn on his stomach and talked about his daughter lunging at him with a knife, Angelica rubbed his back soothingly and told him the things he longed to hear. "You don't deserve that!" "I'm so sorry you're dealing with this."

Angelica went into her bathroom and returned with a small vial of aloe. She opened it, put a little on her finger, and dabbed at the tender burn on Dean's abdomen. "I can't believe she did this to you," she fussed. "You should have called the police."

"I know," Dean replied miserably, "but what would people say? To a certain extent, one has to keep what is going on in their house private. I don't want the embarrassment of having the world know what goes on between me and my wife and my kids."

"I guess I can understand that." Smiling serenely, Angelica gently pushed Dean down until he was laying on his back. "Well, you don't have to worry about her tonight. I can take care of you."

As she straddled him and removed her top, Dean's eyebrows raised. "I was going to ask you how you felt about me, but I guess I have my answer."

"You 'guess'? Let me erase any doubts you might have, Dean…"

CHAPTER SIX

"For everything there is a season, and a time for every matter under heaven: A time to be born, and a time die…" (Ecclesiastes 3:1-2)

Dean was trying to plan a party that was fit for a king on a shoestring budget.

The evening upon which he indirectly volunteered his hapless wife to plan the celebration, Dean came home from Angelica's house and stealthily took a shower in the bathroom in the basement to erase the evidence of their lovemaking, hoping that the sounds of the water turning on and off would escape his sleeping wife's sensitive ears. Dean went into the den and put some of his ideas on paper. The trustees had given him a tentative budget based on the amount of money that had been spent during previous anniversary celebrations. Dean felt that it was too small a number. When Grace saw what he wanted to do, she agreed.

He woke Grace from her sleep, excited, holding a yellow legal pad of paper. Completely disregarding her slumber and the pain he had just inflicted upon her several short hours ago, he flipped on the light next to her bed and shook her roughly.

"I changed your checklist for tomorrow," he told her in a rushed voice. "I want you to call a few places and get some prices together. What were you thinking in terms of a menu?"

"What?" Grace asked blankly, rubbing her puffy aching eyes, trying to hide her irritation. "Menu?"

"For Rev. Riley's party, Grace. I couldn't sleep, so I thought I'd write down some ideas. How's your face?"

She sighed. "My face hurts, Dean. So does my stomach, my legs, my back…"

"I get it," he interrupted coldly. "You're in pain. So am I. You burned me with a scalding hot pot. I've decided to let that go. Now shall we move on?"

Years of conditioning prevented Grace from being absolutely incredulous as to the fact that Dean was equating the pain from a minor burn to that of a savage beating.

It was always about Dean; always had been. Without waiting for her response, Dean launched into a monologue about how this pastoral anniversary was going to be the best one Christ First had ever seen and how he intended on making that happen.

"I went ahead and looked up a couple places where we could have it," Dean informed her. "The fact that we're providing the food is going to knock a significant amount off in terms of the location."

"Keep in mind that the food could get pretty costly, depending on what we choose," Grace reminded him gently.

He looked thoughtful. "I guess we should figure that out first," he said slowly. "Do you have any ideas on what you should serve?"

"It kind of depends on the number of people and how much help I have available," Grace said. "How many people are we thinking?"

"Invitations are going out this weekend to the local churches that we typically fellowship with. Based on the last couple of anniversaries, we can probably expect a few hundred people."

Grace sighed.

"I don't expect you to do this alone," Dean told her. "Aren't you going to see if some of the ladies from the kitchen crew at the church can help you?"

Grace inhaled deeply. "I don't mean this to be mean, but if you really want a knock-out meal…"

"I definitely want a knock-out meal," Dean said eagerly.

"…then I'm going to need some professional help. I need people who can make the recipes the way I make them. The ladies at church are good at what they do there, but I don't really think they'd be the best crew for this type of event."

"So what are you suggesting?"

Grace looked him in the eye. "I'd like to see if I can find any of my old colleagues from EMU."

Dean bristled immediately. "Like Duane?" he asked acerbically.

Duane would have definitely been a great help, but Grace knew Dean wouldn't allow it. Duane and his wife were owners of several successful cooking businesses in downtown Ann Arbor. Grace had lost touch with him over the years--mainly because of Dean's jealousy of their friendship--but every now and then there were articles in the paper about his businesses. She could easily get in touch with him if it were allowed, but she knew not to get her hopes up about that.

"I was thinking more along the lines of the team that helped me cater the two Veteran's Day dinners."

Dean gave her a hard look. "Such as who?"

Without hesitation, Grace rattled off a series of names. "I'm not even guaranteed to be able to get in touch with them," she reminded Dean, noting his raised eyebrow.

"I haven't spoken to any of them in over a decade, after all. But if they're around, I know they can help me, if they're willing."

"Well, go ahead and see who you can track down," Dean told her. "Make sure to give them the right date. And I'll let you figure out a menu. You've always been good at that. I'd suggest at least one vegetarian option, though."

"I think that's a good idea." Grace was pretty shocked. She had asked Dean numerous times before if she could try to find her old friends and he always told her no. It became obvious that this dinner was extremely important to him, important enough for him to let his airtight guard down and allow her to actually socialize with people other than himself, the girls and their church family.

"Okay. I'm going to turn in for the night. But here's a list of things I want you to take care of after you drop the girls off in the morning."

As Grace perused the list, her jaw dropped to the floor. A photo booth? A horse and carriage to bring the Rileys to the front of the banquet hall? A DJ? A videographer? "Um, Dean?" she said timidly. "What's the budget for this thing? I mean, how much money am I supposed to spend on the food?"

"Try not to overdo it, but get what you need."

She tried another approach. "It's just that I know some of the things on your list can be get expensive, so I kind of need a ballpark figure that will help me determine my food options."

Dean shrugged. As he leaned back against the pillows with his hands behind his head, his eyes closing, he murmured, "Don't worry about the costs. Let me do that. If we go over budget, I can use some of my bonus money."

"Okay," Grace said, trying to sound more confident than she felt.

The next morning, Grace did as told. She researched the costs of the party list items and emailed her findings to him. They were all outrageous, but Dean quickly sent a reply, telling her to see what she needed to do to secure all of them before someone else did. Everybody wanted deposits and signed contracts. Dean said he would take care of it after work. Shrugging to herself, Grace set about her next task-- trying to find some of her old friends from EMU.

She had some old email addresses; hopefully they were still in use. Fingers crossed, she put together a group email:

"Good morning my former EMU top chefs! It's Grace! I hope all has been well with you and this email reaches you. I do have a huge favor to ask--I apologize, I know it has been well over ten years since I have reached out to you and here I am asking for a favor--but I must. I have been put in charge of catering an extremely large and important event here in the area and I need HELP! If any of you are available Friday, December 4th and Saturday, December 5th (that is the day of the event, it begins at 6pm), please let me know! I would owe you a ton!"

Grace pressed send and uttered a quick prayer. She really needed some of her old friends for this. Her kitchen comrades at Christ First were lovely women, but none of them had much experience with gourmet cooking. And some of them weren't as amenable to instruction as Grace would have liked.

Her prayer was answered just as fast. The very first response came back within minutes from Cecile Oppenheimer--now Cecile Fox. Incidentally, it was Cecile who had urged Grace to meet Dean all those years ago. Cecile lived only twenty minutes away, had just had her third son and was looking forward to getting out of the house. She was definitely on board to help out and had contact information for several other members of their old crew.

Several hours later, Grace received five more emails from other friends agreeing to help. The last one was a total surprise. One of her old friends had contacted the current head of the department of hospitality at EMU and convinced her to send her hospitality students to help in exchange for credit on one of their cooking projects. Grace now had more help than she needed, and it was all accomplished in less than eight hours. She couldn't stop smiling and thanking God as she cleaned the house.

Dean needed the work bonus more than ever, but he was unknowingly sabotaging his own endeavors. The Superior Heights project was still plodding precariously along. Dean had so stifled the ingenuity of his work team that they were putting minimal effort into the project and making novice-level mistakes that Dean would find and fix himself. Thanks to Dean's heavy-handed leadership there was no enthusiasm among them. At the onset of the Superior Heights initiative, everyone was excited about the possibility of having their name attached to a cutting-edge electronic health record for the largest health system in the area. Now they just wanted it to be over so they could enjoy coming to work again.

The team met every Monday morning to establish protocol for the week and Friday to wrap up the week's progress. It was during one of the meetings that Dean's life took yet another unexpected hit.

The meeting wasn't going so well. Several minor issues had come up, and no one wanted to take the initiative to deal with them. As Dean began to assign tasks to team members, they all complained about having to take on more than what they were already doing. As they tried to hand their new assignment off to other team members, arguments erupted. Dean quickly lost control. The arguing only stopped when Amanda, the secretary, opened the door.

"Dean, you have a call. Line three."

Dean frowned. Who would be calling him at work? Grace never did… unless it was a huge emergency. It had to be important for her to call him at work. The call was a welcomed intrusion. Dean hastily excused himself and walked over to the corner of the conference room. He picked up the phone receiver, pressed the number three, and said, "This is Dean."

"It's your father."

Dean froze. He hadn't heard from Darrell Hardaway in years. Even so, he could never forget his father's rumbling baritone. "This…this is some surprise," Dean stammered. "I'm kind of in the middle of an important meeting."

"Fine. I'll keep this brief. I'd like to see my granddaughters. Soon. Call me later." He hung up.

Full of confusion, Dean had no choice but to put the random phone call from his estranged father to the back of his mind and get back to the meeting. No one was talking now; they were all just sitting at the table with their arms folded, scowling at one another. Dean sighed. He was tired of each and every one of them. They were tired of him too.

Dean's schedule was the same for the next several weeks. He spent most of his day at the office, refereeing verbal altercations among his project team, assigning them tasks they didn't want to do, and then having to check to make sure those tasks were completed. In his meetings with Sheldon, Alex and Sam, he often exaggerated his own accomplishments and laid blame for any oversights on his team. His team was aware of this, although Dean didn't know that they were aware that he was throwing them under the bus. Dean's only saving grace was that his project team wanted to keep their jobs. Other than that, they were all on the verge of quitting.

Darrell called the office every day. Dean was afraid to talk to him and kept finding ways to dodge his calls. That is, until one Monday, when Amanda barged into his office without knocking, furious.

"Look," she said, her face red, "I don't know what is going on with you and this Darrell guy, but I *won't* be put in the middle. Either take his flipping calls or tell him to stop calling here! I'm putting him through to your line. Right now." She stalked back to her desk and picked up her phone. With an angry look on her face, Dean read her lips as she said sweetly, "I'm transferring you to Dean now."

When the phone rang, Dean snatched it up quickly, staring coldly at Amanda, who turned her nose up at him and calmly went back to her filing. "This is Dean."

"You're ignoring me like the little coward you always have been, huh?"

"That's a good way to speak to the son you haven't seen in over ten years…"

"Don't come at me with that BS! I haven't seen you in over ten years because of *you*! How many times have me and your mom called and written letters? Huh? Bad enough to deny me, but your own *mother*?"

"What's so important that you decided to call me after all this time? You dying or something?"

"Yes!"

This revelation from his father caught Dean off guard. Instantly he regretted what he had just said. "What?" he said, bewildered.

"I have terminal cancer. It would be nice, before I die, if I could see the little girls that you have kept from me at least ONCE."

Dean swallowed hard. He had kept his parents away from his family for a very calculated reason. Darrell and Pamela Hardaway had only met Grace and Eve once when Eve was a newborn. They'd never met any of the twins.

When Eve was born, Dean and Grace were barely making ends meet and Grace's unplanned pregnancy hadn't exactly been welcomed by her stressed-out husband. Grace was making more money as the kitchen manager at a nearby hotel. When she had to stop working because of preeclampsia their finances took a hit. Dean had to pick up more hours at his job at Best Buy, and he didn't appreciate it. Even so, Dean and Grace were getting along pretty well. There were some things that Grace found disconcerting about Dean's temper and jealousy but she excused his behavior as being the result of stress and trying to figure out his role as a husband. Dean didn't like that more than half of the people Grace supervised were men. Some of them were outwardly flirtatious with her. She would gently but firmly put them in their place each time, but Dean wasn't satisfied. He wanted her to quit, but they needed her income.

Only hours after giving birth to Eve, Grace was awakened from a restful slumber by Dean. He was standing over her with two middle-aged people she had never seen before. After recovering from her initial shock of having them appear so suddenly, Grace quickly figured out who they had to be. She figured they were his parents by the fact that Dean and the man were almost identical.

"Um, hello," she said quietly.

Dean's mumbled,"Grace, I'd like you to meet my parents, Mr. and Mrs. Hardaway." There was no enthusiasm in his voice. It was obvious he was not happy to have them there. Grace felt uncomfortable by the obviously negative family dynamics.

"Nice to meet you both," she managed.

Mrs. Hardaway came forward and embraced Grace with a surprisingly warm hug and a smile. "Please, call me Pam. I've been wanting to meet you," she told her. "Congratulations on the beautiful baby. How are you feeling?"

"Tired and sore," Grace confessed as she tried to put her aching body into a sitting position.
"Let me help." Pam reached behind Grace, fluffed her pillow, and put it right behind the small of her back. "Better?"

"Yes," Grace said gratefully. "Thank you. Dean, do you want me to have the nurse bring Eve from the nursery?"

"I already did."

Eve was wheeled in. Her proud grandparents couldn't get enough of this new, seven pound, eleven ounce bundle of joy. Grace found herself smiling and thinking wistfully of how her parents would probably have reacted the same way if they were alive. The Hardaways fussed and fussed over the baby. Every now and then, Grace stole a glance at Dean. His comportment was baffling. Grace could only wish that her parents were there to share such a special time, and yet Dean looked angry. Why?

In their time together, Dean hadn't said much about his parents or his two sisters. When Grace asked, he informed her that it was a sore subject. He was the black sheep of the family, but he didn't detail why. When he failed to offer any more specifics, Grace left it alone, hoping that maybe as their relationship intensified he would offer more information. He never did. Each time Grace tried to pry he would get tight-lipped and finally angry if she kept trying.

They stayed for two hours, watching *Wheel of Fortune* and *Jeopardy* while eating food from the cafeteria with Grace and Dean. Grace found herself perfectly at ease with the Hardaways as they tried to answer the *Wheel of Fortune* puzzles and come up with the questions to the *Jeopardy* answers. Dean didn't join in, but Grace was having a fantastic time. She was dismayed when Pam stood to her feet and addressed her husband. "Darrell, perhaps we should let these new parents get some rest. I'm sure they're going to have a long first night."

Darrell nodded. "You're right."

Grace, tenderly cradling Eve, was crestfallen. "You're heading back to Illinois?"

Darrell looked out the side of his eyes at his son. "Actually, no. We got a little hotel room up the street. We were kind of hoping to spend a little time with you all. We won't be a bother, I promise."

"You're no bother at all," Grace said happily. She glanced at her husband. He returned her smile with a scowl. She looked away from him, trying to hide her disappointment with him from his parents.

The Hardaways stayed in Michigan for three days. Grace appreciated their presence. They had come with an arsenal of gifts for their granddaughter, and over the next few days, they bought even more stuff. Diapers, wipes, clothes, a bath tub, a special heating pad for Grace, a thermometer-- Grace didn't have much experience with babies and there were so many things she hadn't thought to buy. Pam was a lifesaver. By the time they were set to leave, the small, barren bedroom that had only been inhabited by a second-hand crib, changing table and Sterilite three-drawer tower had been transformed into a fully-furnished nursery complete with a Winnie the Pooh lamp, curtains, crib bedding set, and carpet, as well as an actual set of drawers made of the same red oak finish as the crib, and a rocking chair. The Hardaways went to the grocery store and bought the new parents plenty of ready-made meals. All in all, Grace figured they'd spent well over two thousand dollars during their visit. And the entire time they'd been there, Dean hadn't cracked a single smile or shown an iota of gratitude.

When they left, Dean looked at Eve's room and said disgustedly, "Who picked Winnie the Pooh?"

Grace, seated in the rocking chair with Eve, rocked back and forth gently. She was sick of her husband's insolence. "I did," she said crabbily.

"Hmmph."

His behavior was draining the joy from her and she wanted no parts of it. That night, she made a pallet of blankets on the floor in Eve's nursery and slept there. In the morning, Dean demanded to know why she'd never come to bed.

"Because you were getting on my nerves," she told him as she went into their tiny kitchen, opened the freezer, and took out the frozen pancakes. "Your parents went above and beyond to help us, and you haven't had a single kind word for them."

"I've told you a thousand times our relationship is not good."

"Well, from my perspective, it seems like that is your fault," Grace informed him. "I mean, perhaps this was them holding out the olive branch, so to speak."

"Only because they want to stake their claim to my daughter."

Grace put a plate of frozen pancakes in the microwave and turned to face him. "What's wrong with them wanting to know their granddaughter?"

He sighed and rubbed his hands down his face. "Grace, look. You really want parental figures. I get it. But you don't understand that some things just can't be overlooked. I can't get past years of being treated like crap while my sisters were treated like perfect little princesses. Nothing I ever did was good enough. Now all of a sudden they want my daughter? Nah, it doesn't work like that." He scraped the remnants of his breakfast into the trash, put his plate in the sink, and went into the bedroom.

For the next few months, Pam and Darrell called regularly to check on Grace and Eve. Strangely enough, they rarely asked to speak to their son. During one of her conversations with Pam, Grace felt bold enough to ask her why they had not come to their wedding.

"When was it?" Pam asked.

Grace was dismayed. "We got married on June 7th. It was just at the Justice of the Peace, but…"

"I didn't know anything about it. We found out about it after the fact."

Grace was stunned. "Seriously?"

"Yes, seriously, honey. If I had been invited, I would have come. But we weren't. And we figured we'd never be invited to meet this baby, so that's why we just showed up."

Grace didn't know what to say.

"Dean really hasn't talked about us much, has he?" Pam asked.

"No. It's like pulling teeth trying to get him to say anything about any of you."

"What has he told you?"

Grace was at a crossroads. Her curiosity was definitely getting the best of her but she didn't want to betray Dean's trust. "Not much. Just that there has been some bad blood in the past."

"That's an understatement," Pam said witheringly. "I won't say much, because as you mentioned, the key word there is 'past'. Dean has done some things that have put me and especially his father in very uncomfortable situations. But we're willing to let that go. I was surprised, and very happy, when I heard that he had gotten married. That told me there was going to be some stability in his life, something we hadn't ever seen him establish before, at least not until he enlisted."

Grace wanted to ask for details, but she didn't want to offend Pam by prying. Before she could figure out a way to keep the conversation going, Pam caught her off guard with a very blunt question:

"Is Dean treating you okay?"

Grace felt fortunate that they were conversing over the phone and not in person, because if Pam would have been there, she would have seen Grace recoil from the phone in confusion. Would most mothers ask their daughters-in-law that question, unless there was a reason to ask? Now Grace's curiosity was even more piqued. "Um, yeah. I think the stress of being a new husband and father and some other things get to him sometimes, but…"

"You don't have to lie to me. I won't tell him. I just want to make sure you and that baby are safe."

"Why wouldn't we be?" Grace asked in a small voice. "Is there something about Dean I should know?"

Pam was quiet.

"Mrs. Hardaway?" Grace prompted. "Why did you ask me that?"

Now Pam sounded embarrassed. "Like I said, things happened in the past," she said, flustered. "When Dean was a teenager, he had a situation where a girl he'd been dating said he hit her. Dean was furious when she broke up with him and kind of started stalking her. Darrell had to pay the girl's family to keep them from reporting the stalking and getting Dean locked up, and hire one of his military buddies to baby-sit Dean to make sure he didn't go anywhere near her."

"So do you believe that Dean actually abused the girl?" Grace asked, feeling sick to her stomach.

"Yes, I do. And I tell you, Grace, I don't know where I went wrong. Sometimes as a parent you do everything right and your kid still strays. That's why I asked."

Grace's head was swirling, and her milky breasts were beginning to hurt. She needed to feed Eve. She couldn't believe what she had just heard. Yes, Dean could be intimidating when he was angry, but Grace couldn't believe that he would ever hit her. He wasn't the perfect husband and had been more of a jerk lately than usual, but she had been crabby too. Lack of sleep wasn't doing either of them any good, and they were both bothered by their financial situation. Dean hated working at Best Buy and Grace just missed working. She loved her new baby, of course, but she missed the camaraderie that she had with her co-workers and having the opportunity to go into the kitchen and experiment and create delicious dishes. Simply put, being home with a new baby all day was boring. Since they only had one car that Dean took to work every day, there wasn't much she could do to get out and go anywhere since Dean forbade her from riding the bus. She made a snap decision not to betray her husband.

"Dean's never raised a hand at me," she declared.

"I'm glad to hear it," Pam said, sounding relieved. "I think being in the military grounded him and gave him the discipline he needed."

Grace agreed.

The following week Darrell and Pam sent a package filled with food, clothing and gift cards to their apartment. Grace was delighted; Dean was not. The next month they did the same thing. While Grace was going through it, oohing and aahing and showing Eve her frilly new dresses and playthings, Dean snatched the box out from under her and put it under his arm. Without saying a word, Dean opened the apartment door and walked, almost ran, out to the dumpster. To Grace's shock and horror, he pitched the box right into the trash.

He came back in the apartment, his eyes looking wild. "I don't need their help!" he barked.

Frightened by his loud voice, Eve began to cry. Grace took her into her nursery, managed to calm her and get her to sleep, then closed the door to the nursery and went into the kitchen to confront Dean. He was pacing back and forth with his head in his hands.

"What the heck was that?" she demanded. "What is wrong with you? Why can't you accept a nice gesture?"

"Grace, you don't know *anything*," Dean spat. "And you need to stay out of this. That is *not* a nice gesture. That is Dad saying that I am incapable of taking care of my own family. He's not just being nice."

"If you could get your pride out of the way you would see that we could really use those things…"

Dean stomped past her and toward the front door. "You stay out of it," he repeated. "And stop talking to my mom all the time. Talking about our money problems and giving her and Dad reason to doubt me."

Grace was perplexed. "I've never talked to your mom about our financial problems."

"Yeah, right," Dean muttered under his breath as he left the house, slamming the door behind him. In her room, Eve began to wail again.

From there on out, the packages and calls stopped coming in. Unbeknownst to Grace, when Dean left the house that afternoon, he didn't just go to the local bar to pout and commiserate. He went to a pay phone, called Darrell, and told him in no uncertain terms that he didn't need or want his help and to stop sending boxes to his place.

"I don't need your charity," Dean snarled.

"Number one boy, you better take that bass out your voice before I come down there and put my hands on you," Darrell threatened. "Number two, it ain't about charity. Me and your mom have done a lot of talking and after all the years of you letting us down, we've decided we don't want to keep holding on to that. We want to be done with it. In all your years you've done nothing but cause us pain and we're trying to be nice to you and you got a problem with that? Boy are you crazy?"

"Don't send anything else to my house!"

Darrell hung up on him.

Dean went to the phone company and had a block put on the phone that prevented his parents from calling their apartment. Grace was completely unaware of the conversation between Dean and Darrell and that the phone block had ever occurred. She was depressed when the weekly calls from Pam stopped. That had been her one time of the week where she could enjoy some adult conversation. She had grown accustomed to the boxes of food and gift cards as well. Now, they were back in their typical financial crunch, and Grace was forced to purchase cheap processed food, which made it harder for her to lose the pregnancy pounds. Dean made sure she was aware that her body didn't look as good as it used to. Their verbal spats about her weight grew more frequent and she found herself spending many nights on her pallet of blankets next to Eve's crib crying herself to sleep. Eventually, tired of Dean's verbal abuse, she gave up breastfeeding Eve so she could go on a dangerous crash diet during which she barely ate solid food, took a powerful combination of diet pills and exercised furiously when she should have been resting. She fainted a few times in the beginning stages but kept it up. Dean noticed his wife wasn't eating, but he also noticed when she finally started dropping the weight. He didn't ask any questions. It was the beginning of the decline of their marriage.

The first indication of a second pregnancy was when she experienced a sudden onslaught of ravenous hunger, which she indulged with more food in a sitting than she had eaten for the past couple of years. Her stomach wasn't ready to handle so much after having been deprived of nutrients for so long and she promptly threw it all up. Dean was oblivious to the damage his wife had been doing to her body--all he cared about was her appearance. After Grace announced the pregnancy, he watched everything she put in her mouth and regularly vocalized his disapproval of her weight gain, even after finding out they were having twins.

By then the marriage was even more damaged. Grace was not concerned about having three kids in their two-bedroom apartment. She knew they could make it work, but Dean was frantic. Highly influential people began hinting to Dean that he needed a house. Even though Grace was perfectly content with their affordable home, it bothered Dean that people were looking at him and wondering why he had his wife and soon-to-be three children stuffed inside an apartment. It was during her pregnancy with Rebekah and Sarah that Dean slapped her for the first time.

Dean had been working at ITS for a few months by then and received a signing bonus. Along with money from a first-time homebuyer's program, he had enough for a down payment on a home. He told Grace to look up homes and find ones she liked, and he would do the same. One evening, they sat down to compare notes with their realtor, Barb.

"Okay, you two," Barb said excitedly. "Let's talk about what kind of homes you've been looking at."

Dean went first. The homes he'd picked were big and expensive. Grace was surprised. She knew Dean was making good money at his job, but the houses he liked were much grander than anything Grace had picked. The homes she liked tended to be older, smaller, and more affordable. After going back and forth about their chosen homes and with gentle direction from Barb, Dean asked irritably, "This is my top house. Which one is yours?"

Grace pointed to hers. It was a three-bedroom colonial with an attached two-car garage.

"Why do you like that house so much?" Dean demanded. "It needs a ton of work."

"It just needs a fresh coat of paint and flooring," Grace told him. "That way we can personalize it a bit. Make it our own, you know?"

"It needs more than paint and flooring. Look at the kitchen cabinets. They're terrible. The basement isn't finished…"

"Those things would make good projects for us," Grace insisted.

Dean shook his head. "Yeah right. You really think you're going to be the one painting and pulling up carpet?"

"Dean, my dad owned a company that did floors. I've done it before."

"That was decades ago. I'm sorry, Grace. I just don't like this house."

In the end, of course Dean won. Barb set up a time for the couple to view the house he picked. While they were there the following Saturday, looking around as Barb waited outside, Grace reluctantly admitted to her husband, "This house is beautiful, Dean. But I just don't see how we'll be able to afford it."

Dean whirled around in anger. Grace was used to this particular facial expression, but what she wasn't used to came within seconds of him turning to face her--a sudden, brutal, stinging slap that almost sent her to the ground, had Dean not caught her and used his hand to bring her face close to his.

"I've had enough of you questioning whether I can afford stuff," he snarled, not moved at all by the tears streaming down her face. "I've been taking care of you all this time. Now all of a sudden I can't afford something? Who do you think you are?"

He released her face with a bit of a push and headed to the front door. Shocked and scared by her husband's display of rage, Grace sank to the floor, clutching her stomach. The babies, apparently reacting to the sudden movement, started hopping around in her womb. Barb, who had been standing on the front porch, had no idea what had just happened. "So what did you think?" she asked lightly.

"We loved it," Dean replied listlessly. "Let's start the paperwork."

And so it was. The first time Dean physically assaulted his wife was in the home they were now in. He apologized profusely that evening, and cried as he told her he had no idea why he had hit her and it would never happen again. He showered her with flowers and affection and was on his best behavior for the next few weeks. A month later they moved into the four-bedroom, three-bath, 3,255-square-foot home that had been Grace's beautifully adorned, well-equipped prison ever since.

Darrell Hardaway somehow learned of his son's new address and tried to contact him. Dean again blocked his number and sent back anything his parents mailed to the house along with a note demanding to be left alone. His parents were more interested in a relationship with Grace and the girls, and for Grace, who desperately wanted parents, the feeling was mutual. Dean couldn't let that happen. His parents had too much dirt on him for Dean to allow them to get close. There were certain truths about Dean that Grace was completely unaware of, and he wanted to keep it that way.

On the other end of the phone, Darrell had grown impatient by his son's stunned silence. "As a matter of fact, I'm done asking," he barked. "I'm coming to see them if it's the last thing I do. And for the record, I really couldn't care less if I see *you* or not!" He hung up.

That was the last time Dean would ever hear his father's voice.

For the next two days, Darrell didn't call. Considering the fact that he had been calling everyday without fail for the last few weeks, Dean was confused, but figured that his dad was busy planning his surprise trip down to Michigan. He was wrong. On Halloween, he was in yet another meeting when Amanda came into the room and told him he had a call.

"It's a woman," Amanda said, seeing the look on his face.

"Is it my wife?" Dean asked.

"No."

"Can you find out who it is and ask them if I can call back, please?"

Nodding, Amanda left the room and closed the door. She came back minutes later, looking red and uncomfortable. Dean sighed. "Who was it, Amanda?"

"Can you come out into the hallway, please?" Amanda asked.

Dean was confused. It was out of Amanda's character to be so anxious. Dean sensed that something was wrong. He got up and followed her into the hallway just outside the conference room.

Amanda cleared her throat nervously. "That was your mom on the phone," she informed Dean. "I'm very sorry to tell you this Dean, but your father died."

Dean's eyes flew open in shock. "What?" he asked blankly.

Amanda opened her mouth, but said nothing. She stared at him with wide eyes.

"You're sure it was my mom? Did she give her name?"

Amanda nodded. "She said her name was Pamela Hardaway, and she was trying to reach you to inform you that your father passed away this morning."

Dean dropped his head.

"She also said not to come to his funeral."

Dean's head snapped back up. "Seriously?"

Amanda nodded miserably. She was extremely uncomfortable. Pamela's anger toward her son was evident in her tone of voice over the call. Amanda didn't like Dean, but she hated being the conduit for such sensitive material. "Shall I go and tell your team the remainder of the meeting is canceled?" she asked timidly.

Dean shook his head, his jaw set. "No. Thank you, Amanda."

The team had heard everything that was said between Dean and Amanda but no one wanted to let on that they had been listening. The silence in the conference room spoke volumes. They watched Dean out of the corner of their eyes as he went back to the front of the room, sat in his chair, and picked up his notes. "Where were we?" he said brusquely.

"We're discussing the inefficiency within the patient management component," Abu Singh replied.

"Yes. Thank you."

Just when Dean thought the day couldn't get any worse, Sheldon, Alex and Sam showed up unexpectedly. They were sitting in Dean's office when he finished his meeting. As soon as he saw them, he sighed. His phone was ringing off the hook. When he looked at the caller ID display, he was surprised to see that it was Grace, but figured that maybe she had somehow found out his dad had passed. He wasn't in the mood to talk to her. Wordlessly, he reached over and switched his phone off.

"Dean, we're supposed to have had this thing in the beginning stages of rollout by now. Can you tell me why we're not?" Sheldon asked.

Dean went to his desk and sat down. "One of my team members found some kinks in the billing and patient management systems that he had been working on," he replied, trying to sound more confident and in control than he felt. "I definitely apologize, guys, but isn't it more important that we get it right as opposed to just rushing it through?"

"Your apologies always come with a *but*," Alex informed him. "It's kind of disheartening to see someone who calls himself leader but is completely incapable of taking responsibility for his missteps."

"Dean, your leadership here has been a failure," Sheldon said bluntly. "You're way behind schedule. You have treated your team terribly, and it's led to a decrease in productivity. I've seen the product you're peddling and it's not what it needs to be. Mike's team is wrapping their project on Monday, and they will be finishing up the Superior Heights job along with you and your team. If you were expecting a bonus after this project is over, perhaps you should think again. Your bonus may be disseminated among your team as consolation for being treated like garbage. I just thought I'd come here personally and let you know."

Dean felt his temperature rising as his blood began to boil. He had been putting up with these rich scumbags for long enough and a major part of his brain was telling him to grab one of them--Alex was the closest--by his neck and punch him unconscious. That's what he would have done years ago. He clenched and unclenched his hands, trying to fight the urge to explode. *Why am I putting up with this?* he asked himself. Then he remembered why--good-paying jobs were hard to come by in Michigan, and he had a lifestyle to afford. Also, if he got fired from ITS and had to find another job, there was a good chance that his next potential employer would do a more thorough background check than ITS and find out that Dean was not all that he seemed to be.

Dean needed that bonus money. Although the idea of kissing Sheldon's behind made him want to vomit, he knew that stroking his ego was the best way to smooth things over. "Sir," he said, trying to sound helpless, "I really need that bonus money. I have some things going on with my family…"

Sheldon cut him off. "Bonuses are rewards for a job well done," he spat. "You should be lucky I'm letting you keep your job after this debacle."

The three men got up at the same time. "I expect you won't give Mike and Wes any problems when they bring their team to your Monday morning meeting," Sheldon barked as he led them out of the room.

News traveled fast that Dean had effectively been removed as the project lead. He tried to remain in his office for the rest of the day, but the few times he was forced to leave his office all eyes were on him and he knew it. Some people were kind enough to be embarrassed for him and averted their eyes when he walked by. However, far more of his coworkers were happy to see him receive his just desserts. Dean wasn't well-liked at ITS.

Dean tried to stop by Angelica's after work but she had taken David to a doctor's appointment. Further frustrated from not being able to see the one person who could provide him with mental and physical repose, Dean was in a fury by the time he got home. Without saying a word to his wife or daughters, he stomped around the house, hoping to find something, anything out of place so that he might have an excuse to unleash his fury on Grace. There was no luck--she had been especially diligent that day. That made him even angrier.

As she watched Dean plod through each room of the house, Grace's anxiety grew. She had something to tell him, something she knew was going to drive him into a blind rage. It was his fault, but she knew she would be blamed for it. It was something that could not be hidden. She had to tell him before he discovered it for himself.

She approached him while he was standing in the middle of their bedroom with his arms folded. She watched his eyes as they scanned the floor, making sure the vacuum lines in the carpet were relatively straight. "Dean?" she ventured timidly.

He whirled around to face her, his eyes flashing. "What?" he asked coldly.

A tear slid down her cheek. There was a reason why she had decided to talk to him in their room--except for the dressers, there weren't many things in the bedroom that she could bang her head into when Dean hit her. Basically, the bedroom was the safest room in the house for her to get beat up.

"The finance company repo'd the car today."

"*WHAT?!*"

He started to advance on her, and Grace tried to brace herself for what was sure to come.

"They pulled up behind me as soon as I got home from picking the girls up from school," Grace choked out.

"And you just gave them the keys?"

Grace tried to scoot herself into the corner of the room that had the least amount of furniture. Before she knew it, she had nowhere else to scoot, and Dean was still coming toward her. "I had no choice. They had the police with them."

Dean's fury finally spilled over. The first blow knocked her down, but Dean's anger was not satiated. He roughly pulled her back to her feet, ignoring her cries for mercy, administered hit after hit after hit, some slaps, some punches. When Dean finally let Grace go, it wasn't because the beating was over. It was so that Dean could watch Grace crumple to the ground. He even smirked a little as she curled herself into a ball with her hands over her head, sobbing.

"So you let the entire neighborhood watch as my car got towed away, huh?" He delivered a swift kick to her back.

"There was nothing I could do," she cried.

"That's because you're useless! You don't do anything! I work my behind off to give you this house and that car, and you let some strangers come and take it away?" This pronouncement was followed by three more kicks.

Finally, Dean left the room. Grace listened as he went downstairs and closed the door to the den.

Grace laid on the floor for over an hour. The entire time she did so, her daughters stayed tucked into their various hiding places. The younger girls cried softly, but not Eve. Eve was furious. Eve was sick of living like this. Her hatred for Dean grew exponentially with each beating. She hated Dean for being such a tyrant, but she was mad at Grace too. All the while the girls were in the basement listening to their father terrorize their mother, Eve's mind was racing. She was thinking... thinking of how she would never, not for one minute, allow any stupid boy disrespect her or think he ruled her. Ever.

Grace awoke with a start.

She was still laying on the floor in her bedroom, but someone, probably Eve, had placed a few towels under her head, probably to keep the blood that was seeping from her mouth from staining the carpet. Grace blinked, confused, and just then realized that Naomi was sitting right next to her, holding an ice pack. The girls had been nursing their unconscious mother in shifts. Grace was unaware that she had passed out.

"Hi Mommy," Naomi said quietly.

Without a word, Grace reached for Naomi with both arms. Naomi collapsed into them, crying. The other girls heard Naomi's cries and came out of their rooms. They made a circle around their mother and watched as she struggled to pull her battered body into a sitting position.

"Is it still Halloween?" Grace asked weakly.

They all nodded.

"What time is it?"

"It's five-thirty," Eve told her.

"Oh, no," Grace cried, "We're going to be late. Girls, quickly. Go get your costumes."

That fast, Grace went directly into Mommy mode. She was not going to let Dean ruin one of the girls' favorite celebrations. Each Halloween Christ First held a party with a costume contest, snacks, games and candy. Grace was on the planning committee for this year's party, as she had been the past several years.

Dean was asleep in the den, physically fatigued after the intense ten-minute beating he had inflicted upon Grace. Grace wasn't afraid to go in and wake him up. Surprisingly, Dean enjoyed the costume party. Grace typically picked a theme and sewed costumes for the entire family. The Hardaways had won the costume contest several years in a row. That, of course, brought Dean great satisfaction. This year, the Hardaways were going as characters from *Despicable Me 2*: Dean was Gru, Grace was Lucy, Eve, Sarah and Rebekah were Margo, Agnes and Edith, Abby was a yellow minion, and Naomi was a purple minion. Dean was positively giddy as he put on his Gru costume, completely oblivious to his family's brooding.

Grace did her best to cover up the marks on her face with makeup. Using her fingertips, she tried to dab the foundation onto her face as lightly as possible. It was an exercise in futility. There wasn't a square inch of her face that wasn't tender and painful to the touch. She willed herself not to cry lest one of her tears wash away the makeup that she had so painstakingly applied.

The party was a blur. As soon as they got to Christ First, Grace wasted no time plastering on a smile and going into what she referred to as theatrical auto-pilot--a state of mind she had mastered during her years of marriage to Dean; one in which she was able to temporarily convince herself that she was someone else and that she lived a different, happier life, and to act accordingly without thought. She mingled with other church members, complimented them on costumes, served snacks, drinks and goodie bags, and managed a respectable smile for the camera when the Hardaways again won the costume contest.

On their way home, the tension in the car was impenetrable. Dean reached out and turned down the gospel music. No one said anything or moved. He cleared his throat.

"My father passed away today."

The pain medicine that Grace had swallowed hours before had worn off and her entire faced ached. She had nothing against Darrell Hardaway, but she also had little connection with him, thanks to Dean. Simply out of politeness, she muttered, "Sorry to hear it."

During the party, several members of Christ First had asked Dean about Grace's face and he'd had to quickly come up with a lie: "She tried a new makeup and turns out she is allergic to it!" They bought the excuse, but as Dean stared at Grace under the bright lights of the church fellowship hall, which she had helped decorate for the occasion, he realized he had gone too far and felt uncharacteristically ashamed.

"I lost control today," he said quietly. "I apologize."

Grace didn't say a word.

Back at home, the girls showered and went to bed. Once they were all tucked in Grace returned to her room and was surprised to find Dean running her lavender-scented bubble bath and lighting some candles. Dean was busily arranging a towel and washcloth on the side of the tub when Grace walked in.

"Just try to relax," he told her, his voice full of contrition. "This was the least I could do."

Grace still said nothing. She brushed beside him, removed her clothes, and sank into the tub, inhaling deeply. From nowhere, Dean produced a glass of sparkling apple cider. She took several painful sips. He walked out and closed the door behind him.

As she sat in the bath, Grace felt her body relax. Her muscles loosened; the pain in her joints and on her skin was alleviated. Her mind, on the other hand, was working a mile a minute. In the midst of everything she had done while at the costume party, her eyes were on her daughters the entire time. The beating they had witnessed before the party had taken a toll on them. Most of the time they remained seated at the same table in a corner of the room and barely spoke to anyone. Grace realized that although she was taking the physical brunt of Dean's abuse, the girls were being robbed of their childhood, and she couldn't allow it to continue.

Chapter Seven

"Not many of you should become teachers, my brothers, for you know that we who teach will be judged with greater strictness." (James 3:1)

Grace spent the next few days after Halloween submerged in deep prayer. Her daughters were not themselves, and this infuriated her, but her fear of the unknown and the possibility of disappointing God by flippantly violating her marital vows compelled her to try to find a way to convince Dean to get help. After all, she had no way to provide for her girls if she left Dean and nowhere else to go. She surmised that she should definitely exhaust all of her options before breaking the marital vows that she had made before God. If Dean was not receptive to the idea of counseling she could approach Rev. Riley for advice.

First she had to determine a strategy. Convincing Dean that he had a problem would be no small feat. In order to get Dean to even entertain a concept so abhorrent to a narcissist, she knew she would have to appeal to his fragile but bloated ego. But how?

The untimely death of Sergeant Major Darrell Hardaway compounded with Dean's problems at work provided Grace with exactly what she needed. Dean was highly vulnerable and his compromised emotional state left him amenable to any suggestion. Although it wasn't the most pleasant of events, the timing couldn't have been any more perfect.

The funeral service for Dean's father was held on a Saturday in Northbrook, Illinois, where the senior Hardaways had been living for fifteen years. Already nervous as to how he would be received by his family, Dean took the Friday before the funeral off from work to prepare. Grace was far from pleased to have him in the house with her for a whole day, but he was surprisingly unobtrusive, spending most of the day arranging and rearranging his overnight bag, ironing his black suit so crisply it could stand on its own and attempting to line his facial hair to symmetrical perfection. He even made his own breakfast and lunch.

Left to her own devices, Grace made sure to complete her list of chores and checked and rechecked her bags and those of her daughters. A few times she crossed paths with her husband; they walked past each other like strangers, saying nothing, making little to no eye contact. Although Dean was preoccupied Grace was still on edge. He was obviously highly agitated and could snap at any minute.

Grace was relieved when two-thirty finally rolled around. It was time to leave. Grace found Dean in the den, sitting in his favorite chair with his hands clasped tightly in his lap. "Are you ready to go?" she inquired quietly.

"As ready as I'll ever be," he replied tersely, standing to his feet. "You've packed everything you'll need for yourself and the girls?"

"Yes, Dean."

"Where are the bags?"

"Upstairs. I'll go and start loading the car..."

"No, that's okay," Dean interrupted. "I'll do it." He walked past her and started for the stairs. "Can you just make sure everything is locked and the alarm is set?"

Surprised, Grace obliged. She was even more shocked when Dean told her to leave the cooler that she had packed with sandwiches, fruit, string cheese and juice boxes for the girls.

"We don't need to hurry," Dean explained as they rode toward the girls' school. "Let's stop and get them something before we hit the road. Just bring a few snacks in case they get hungry along the way."

"Okay," Grace said uneasily. All of this behavior--fixing his own food, ironing his own clothes, offering to load the SUV and now allowing his family a meal outside of the house--was completely uncharacteristic of Dean. Part of Grace wanted to enjoy these luxuries, but the bigger part of her wondered if this was the calm before the storm. Totally nonplussed, she sat perfectly still during the ride to the school, said nothing, and barely even looked in Dean's direction.

The girls were equally disconcerted by their father's behavior. They got into the SUV quietly and waited for Dean to acknowledge them before they spoke. Dean's first words to them were a shock:

"Where would you like to eat before we get on the road?"

They exchanged glances. The younger girls were obviously looking to Eve to answer. As usual, she did. "Do you mean a fast-food restaurant or a sit-down place?"

"Since we need to get on the road, preferably a fast-food place," Dean replied.

The girls picked McDonald's. Dean found one close to the expressway, parked, and in they went. The girls glanced longingly at the play area as they ate their Happy Meals in silence. Grace couldn't help but observe the other families in the restaurant. Her girls were the only kids in the entire restaurant who were quiet and visibly uncomfortable. They wanted to go play but were afraid to ask. Grace fought to keep tears from forming in her eyes.

She was unsuccessful, but right before the tears dropped Dean surprised her again. "Girls, if you want, you can go play for ten minutes."

The girls again exchanged looks. Grace nodded at Eve, who got up, pushed her chair in, and quickly but quietly headed toward the play place, followed by her little sisters. Soon they were squealing with delight. She looked at Dean to see if he noticed. He wasn't even looking. He had pulled his phone out of his pocket and was scrolling. Dean and Grace sat in complete silence until Dean stood up, cleared the table, and signaled for the girls to come.

During the ride Dean listened to the uplifting gospel music of 102.7, Grace read from her study Bible, and the girls busied themselves with their tablets. No one said anything during the entire ride. The only noise other than the radio, which eventually lost 102.7's signal, was the GPS as it guided Dean to their destination. Once they reached the Marriott Dean got the key to their fifth-floor room and they headed upstairs. Inside their suite, Dean stretched out on the king-sized bed and sighed. There were two queen-sized beds and a cot. Eve claimed the cot for herself and the twins jumped on the queen beds. Grace busied herself with organizing their things in order to maximize their time in the morning. As she did so, she noticed their bathing suits. Grace had packed them with the hope that there was a pool in the hotel and Dean would allow her to take the girls swimming. It was a long shot, but considering his permissiveness, she thought it was worth a try.

"Would you like to go swimming?" she asked him. "It might help you relax."

"I'm actually pretty tired, Grace," he said. His eyes were closed and his hands clasped underneath his head. "But if you and the girls want to go, I don't care. Just be back within an hour."

Grace quietly summoned the girls to quickly get dressed and exit the room before Dean changed his mind. In the empty pool the girls were finally able to cut loose and act like kids. There were beach balls and pool noodles for them to play with. Grace got in the water with them, delighted to finally be able to interact with her kids like a real mother. The hour went by entirely too fast, but Grace wasn't going to push her luck by being late getting back.

Back in the room, Dean was snoring and did not wake up when his family re-entered the room. Grace ordered a pizza, then made sure each of them showered, got into their pajamas and headed to bed. She did the same. Tomorrow was guaranteed to be an interesting day.

Interesting was an understatement.

Dean was in rare form. Much to Grace's dismay, he woke at five a.m., and he wasn't quiet about it. Grace attempted to go back to sleep but was unable to ignore Dean as he took a long shower, turned on his electric shaver to again line his facial hair, shined his dress shoes, and zipped and unzipped bags for no apparent reason at all. He was a nervous wreck, and because he was, so was Grace. She had no idea what to expect from this type of Dean.

At eight Grace and the girls finally got out of bed, headed downstairs for breakfast, and then came back to the room to get ready for the funeral. Sensing their father's mood, the girls were especially quiet and obedient. None of them wanted to cross his path although he was still being nicer than usual. They knew his mood could change within seconds. Grace's stomach was in knots. More than ever she just wanted to get this day over with and deal with whatever aftermath that was in store for her.

They drove to St. Luke's Baptist Church and found that the parking lot was already full. Dean had to circle the area several times before finding a parking spot. When they were finally situated, Grace went to open her door. Dean grabbed her hand.

She looked at him with wide eyes. "What is it, Dean?"

He swallowed hard. "I don't know about this."

Grace was seeing something she had never seen before--fear. Despite how awful of a person Dean was toward her, Grace couldn't help but feel tenderness toward him. "Why not?" she asked gently.

"I don't think anyone really wants me here," Dean confessed.

"What could have been so bad in the past that they wouldn't expect to see you here for your father's funeral, Dean? I mean, I'm assuming that they knew you would show up."

"I never lived up to my father's expectations," he said miserably. "I was his only son and I let him down. My sisters were his pride and joy. I was nothing. Diana is a doctor, Denise is a lawyer. And what have I done?"

Grace was incredulous. "'What have you done'?" she repeated blankly. "Dean, did you not go fight for our country? Yes, being a doctor is a noble profession--not so sure I can say the same for lawyering, although it is a *distinguished* profession--but there is something to be said for someone who sacrifices his life for the freedoms of people he doesn't even know. You've accomplished as much, if not more, than your sisters, and you have every right to come here and pay your respects to your father."

Although he didn't look convinced, Dean obviously appreciated the pep talk. With a small smile and a heavy sigh, he let go of Grace's hand and opened his door.

The family hour was scheduled to begin at 10 a.m. The family had gathered outside the stately church's formidable entrance, greeting each other, sharing hugs, kisses, tears and sporadic laughs as they readied themselves to say good-bye to their loved one for the last time. Grace was hopeful that they would be distracted enough to where they would not notice her family approaching, but she was not so fortunate. As the black sheep of the family drew closer, the crowd got quieter. Grace grew increasingly uncomfortable as she noticed that all disdainful eyes were on her and her children. Her discomfort quickly turned into irritation. She didn't like how those people were looking at her kids.

"I won't have them looking at my girls like that," Grace told Dean in a rare moment of bravado. The minute she said it, she regretted it. She looked at Dean with wide eyes.

He stared at her with an expression that she could not read, then, to her relief, nodded. "Let's just go the other way."

With their girls in front of them, Grace and Dean turned and began to head toward the back of the crowd of people, away from their hateful gaze. As soon as they did so, they heard a voice. "Well, well. Now you show up. He wanted to see you months ago."

Dean and Grace turned back around. In front of them stood a woman who was undeniably one of Dean's sisters. They looked just alike. Her arms were folded, her lips pursed. She was flanked by a man, probably her husband. The crowd opened up and another woman who also resembled Dean came forward. Dean's other sister. Grace had no idea which sister was which. They looked like twins.

"I didn't come for trouble," Dean mumbled miserably.

"Were you expecting a happy family reunion?" the other sister asked angrily.

"No. I didn't expect anything. I just came to say good-bye!" Dean said, his voice cracking.

Grace looked at him in surprise. He was obviously intimidated by these two. It was another side of him she had never seen before. He was so domineering toward her, it was almost refreshing to see him be inundated by two females--if only the situation was different.

Mrs. Hardaway appeared before them. Impeccably dressed in a simple, no-frills black dress and hat with a pearl necklace and matching earrings, she stood between her son and two daughters. "I will not have any drama at my husband's funeral. We are going to head inside," she told them in a steely voice. "This can be dealt with later." She pushed them back toward the front, looking over her shoulder at Dean as she headed back to the front of the crowd.

Grace patted Dean on the shoulder. He looked hugely dejected, almost as though he was second-guessing being there. Grace knew he needed a prod. "This is an emotional time for everyone, Dean," she reminded him. "Try not to take that personally. Look, we can just go in and sit toward the back if you want."

He nodded wordlessly.

They entered the church at the back of the crowd and waited patiently until it was their turn to view the body. Once they got up there, Grace fought to keep her own emotions from triggering. Luckily, she hadn't had to attend many funerals since her parents passed away, but when she had, she always remembered looking at her parents in their coffins at their double funeral. She remembered the smell of the embalming chemicals that had almost turned her stomach as the church nurses held her hands. It was a memory that was difficult to stifle, but she had to. Before she knew it, they were staring down at a lifeless Darrell Hardaway, dressed in his military uniform.

Grace watched as the corners of Dean's mouth began to twitch as he stared at his father's face. The funeral home had done a remarkable job--he looked as though he were sleeping. It was some solace to Grace years ago that her parents, despite having sustained injuries from the car accident, looked the same as she had always remembered. Despite that, Grace also remembered the major shock she felt when she first viewed her once lively parents deceased. She stole another glance at Dean. One tear rolled down his cheek before he turned and headed toward their seats. The girls stole a quick glance at their grandfather before Grace led them behind their father.

As they walked past the front row on which Mrs. Hardaway, her daughters and their husbands sat, someone grabbed Grace's hand. It was the sister who had first confronted Dean. Grace looked at her in surprise. The sister stood.

"I didn't mean to make you uncomfortable earlier," she said apologetically. "We have some issues in our family and I am having a hard time with this. None of my anger is directed at you or your daughters."

Grace offered a small smile and a comforting squeeze to her hand. "Don't worry about it," she told the sister. "I lost both of my parents at the same time. I know this is difficult for you all."

"I would love to talk to you later," the sister said.

"So would I."

Dean, who had made his way to the back of the room where they were going to sit, had been watching the exchange with a confused look on his face. Once Grace finally made her way to her seat, he asked in a loud whisper, "what did she say?"

"Which sister is that?" Grace asked.

"That's Denise, the lawyer. She's the oldest. What did she say?"

"She apologized for her behavior toward us outside and said she'd love to talk to me later," Grace whispered.

"Why didn't she tell me that?" Dean wondered aloud.

"It was directed toward me and the girls," Grace informed him. His face fell. "But don't worry, Dean. Maybe she'll say something to me that can open up the lines of communication between you all."

Dean faced forward and said nothing for the rest of the family hour. Not a single soul acknowledged him. The funeral began promptly at eleven a.m. It was a well-done, albeit long ceremony, providing Darrell with all of the military honors he deserved, including the 21-gun salute much to the girls' delight. When the obituary was read, Grace was relieved that Dean's name was listed among the surviving relatives. She'd assumed that he would be left out.

At the cemetery, Dean stood toward the back of the crowd as the funeral was concluded. Pam broke down as she watched her husband's silver casket be lowered into the vault. Her daughters and their husbands held her and dabbed at her cheeks with Kleenex. Other family members also lingered, wiping away tears. Grace looked at Dean. He had the same blank expression on his face. She had no idea what he was thinking, and that worried her. After what felt like an eternity, Dean turned and started to walk away, looking over his shoulder at his mother, sisters and brothers-in-law momentarily. Grace breathed a sigh of relief as they walked away from Darrell's burial site toward their SUV.

Once they were buckled in, Dean hesitated to start the car. "I don't think I should go to the repast," he said. "We can go out to eat somewhere else."

Grace didn't bother to hide her disappointment. "Why don't you want to go? Don't you think it's time to try to bury the hatchet?"

Dean shrugged, his face illustrating his dejection. "There are some deep wounds in my family, Grace."

"I understand that," Grace replied slowly, "but do you plan on allowing whatever those wounds are to keep you from your mother and sisters for the rest of your lives? At the end of the day you all are family. And you're all supposed to be Christians! We're not supposed to hold grudges. Especially not against our parents."

He looked almost convinced.

"How did it feel to see your father like that, Dean?" Grace asked him.

He turned his head quickly in her direction. "I'm sure you know that it hurt," he said sharply.

"I know it did. And I'll bet it hurt worse because of your guilt. You know you should have patched things up with your dad years ago, and now it's too late. Don't let the same thing happen with your mother, Dean. None of us know how much time we have left here."

That was all he needed to hear. With a heavy sigh, Dean turned the car on and headed back to St. Luke's.

The fellowship hall was already getting crowded. At the entrance stood two ushers. One of them, an older woman with long, lush silver hair, looked Dean up and down. "Aren't you the son?" she asked.

He cleared his throat. "Yes ma'am."

"Then you should go to the family table," she told him.

Dean looked embarrassed. "If you can accommodate us with another table..." He trailed off.

The two ushers looked at each other, but neither of them said anything. The silver-haired usher motioned for the family to follow her. She led them to a table that was almost smack-dab in the middle of the room. Grace wasn't too happy about that-- people began looking at them and whispering behind cupped hands the minute they walked in the door. Now they were highly visible. Unfortunately, there weren't many tables left that could hold their family.

Pam, her daughters, sons-in-law and their children came into the hall after most of the guests had already arrived. Understandably, they had stayed at the burial site a bit longer and then taken the scenic route during the way back to the church so they could gather their emotions and be ready to mingle with their supporters. They sat at the family table and were served their meals. Grace tried to tune out the people around her and tend to her family. As she was eating, she stole several glances at Denise. At one point, the two caught eyes, and Denise nodded her head toward an exit across the room. That was Grace's cue.

She wiped her mouth with her napkin and stood up. "I'll be right back," she told her family. Dean looked at her with questions in his eyes but said nothing. Grace headed toward the exit, which instead of being an actual exit led her into a storage room, and waited. Minutes later, Denise, Pam and Diana entered the room.

Pam hugged her first.

"I am so sorry about Darrell," Grace said sincerely. "I wish I had been able to spend more time with him. I feel very guilty that he didn't get a chance to know my girls. Very guilty."

She turned to Denise and Diana. "And I absolutely hate that I've never met either of you."

They hugged her too. "So do we," Diana said, "but we know it's not your fault."

"Look, we're going to have to get back out there soon," Denise said quietly, "but we wanted to make sure you were okay."

"Me? Don't worry about me. You're the one who just lost your father."

"I know," Denise replied, "and it hurts. It's always going to hurt. We'll figure out a way to deal with it. But we also want to make sure you know that we're here for you and your daughters, despite what Dean may have told you about us. And I hope that he is not hurting you."

Grace put her head down.
"He is, isn't he." Diana shook her head, her lips pursed. "He is, isn't he."

"If he doesn't get help soon, I'm going to leave," Grace said. It was the first time she had made such a bold statement to anyone. It felt scary to say it, but it also felt good.

"How soon is this going to be?" Denise asked.

"When we get back home," Grace informed her. "He snapped after he found out that Darrell had passed. It got bad. I won't put up with it anymore."

Pam looked concerned, and now Grace was ashamed to be adding to her grief. "Grace," she said, putting her arm around Grace's shoulders, "if you need a place to go or money, all you have to do is let us know. That's all you have to do. You can stay here if you don't want to go back home."

Denise cleared her throat. "It's a great idea, but I don't think it's a wise one," she told her mother. "Dean could say she kidnapped the girls. She would be better off going back home with him and then leaving. Grace, if Dean hits you, if you've never done so, you need to start calling the police and get a paper trail going. That way, when it *is* time to leave, you'll have the law and documentation on your side. I have to get back to my kids."

She gave Grace another quick hug and pressed one of her business cards in her hands. "I hate to say this," she said as she pulled the door open, "but I have no doubt in my mind that you're going to end up having to leave Dean. I really don't know what happened to my brother, Grace, I just don't." She walked out. Diana also offered Grace a brief hug and followed her sister.

Pam lingered. "How bad has it gotten?"

Grace shook her head and sighed deeply. "I don't even know how to answer that question, really."

"Slaps, punches, kicks?"

"All of the above."

Pam's eyes welled up with fresh tears. "I hope you're not angry with me and my husband. I have no idea where we went wrong with Dean. You see that our daughters turned out just fine…but even as a little boy, there was something about Dean. He was a troublemaker. He was never affectionate. He seemed to take pleasure in harming people. He lacked empathy. And I never figured out what I did to make him that way, Grace. Never. I am so sorry."

"Pam, I know it's not your fault, or your husband's. I figured that out the first time I met you two."

Pam wrapped her arms around Grace and hugged her tight. "My husband never hit me," she informed Grace. "He watched his father terrorize his mother, and when he got to be fifteen, my husband worked up the strength to run his father out of their house. His parents divorced shortly after that. Darrell always told me that was why he refused to even raise his voice to me. He saw what a monster his father was, and he refused to be like him." She dug a tissue out of her pocket and dabbed at the corners of her eyes. "I don't understand how Dean learned to be so cruel. He didn't see it at home. Grace, call or email if you need me," she said tearfully as she handed Grace her card. "Anytime, day or night."

Grace nodded and watched as she left the storage room. She waited a few minutes before she made her own exit. Pam's assessment of Dean as a little boy made her blood run cold. What Pam had just described was a psychopath. Was that what she had married?

As the meal wound down, Pam suddenly appeared at their table. She looked stiff as she acknowledged Dean: "Do you mind if I take the girls to go meet their aunts and cousins?"

Dean shook his head.

The girls were eager to escape. At the front of the room, Grace watched them hug their aunts and uncles and cousins. Shy at first, they immediately got comfortable with their extended family members, and Grace and Pam both looked on, smiling, as the kids got loose and started to play with each other.

"We should get on the road," Dean said suddenly.

Nodding, Grace stood and walked to the front table to collect the girls. "We have to head back home," she announced. All five of her daughters groaned, and she smiled.

Denise and Diana were smiling too. "They hit it off right away," Diana remarked.

"Of course they did," said Pam. "They're family."

One of the little girls who appeared to be the same age as the older twins tugged on Denise's sleeve. "Mommy, when can we see them again?"

Denise caught Grace's eye and winked. "Hopefully sooner than later."

"We don't live that far apart, so hopefully we can make that happen."

Everybody turned. Dean was standing there with his hands in his pockets, looking out of place. Out of the corner of her eye, Grace saw both Denise's and Diana's husbands stand up from behind the table and fold their arms simultaneously.

Obviously there was no love lost between Dean and his brothers-in-law, just like there was no love lost between Dean, his sisters, and his parents. Grace wondered if there was anyone in the entire family that liked Dean. No one had talked to him the entire time they were under the church roof.

"Umm…" All eyes were now on Dean, much to his dismay. He rubbed his hands together. "I know it is a lot to ask or expect that you guys would be able to somehow forgive me for the pain I've caused this family, but I think it would be nice for my daughters to know all of you. I will live with the guilt that I kept them from Dad forever."

"You know how to get in touch," Diana said listlessly. "We'll see if you actually do or not."

That was it. No one--not Pam, not Denise nor Diana, not any of the people in the room, even said bye to Dean as he and his family departed the room. Dean tried to hide it, but he cried the entire time as they headed back to Michigan. Grace watched the continuous flow of tears as they left his face ashen and felt bad for him.

This time, the family stopped at a Ryan's for dinner. As they ate, Dean surprised Grace. "I don't want to be like this anymore."

She looked up from her baked potato. "What do you mean?"

"Angry all the time. Ruining my family. I always wanted to be like my dad, and today I couldn't help but think of how much I'm not."

"Dean, you don't have to be like your dad. You just have to be happy. And in order for you to be happy, you have to be living within God's will. Do you think you've been doing that?"

Dean rubbed his face with both hands and exhaled. "No. No, I have not."

"Then it's a simple fix," Grace said encouragingly. This was the conversation she had been wanting. "You've admitted there's a problem. Now let's go fix it. Together. I want a happy family too, Dean."

"You don't want to leave me?"

"Not if I don't have to."

Dean looked surprised. He hadn't considered the possibility of Grace ever leaving him. If she did, that would be counted as yet another failure. All of a sudden, he felt convicted. The look in her eyes conveyed a tenderness that he knew he did not deserve. For as hard as he had made her life, she was still willing to stand beside him. Dean excused himself, went to the bathroom, and cried in the stall.

When he came back out, he cleared his throat. "I want to fix it, but I don't know how," he admitted helplessly. "What do I do?"

"Counseling."

Swallowing hard, he nodded. "Okay. If that's what it takes, I'll go."

There were only a couple weeks left until Rev. Riley's party, and Dean was frantic. None of the area pastors were responding to his requests for their participation in any of the services. It was a toss-up as to who was less popular, him or Rev. Riley himself. Both had earned the reputation of being arrogant and condescending. Rev. Riley's status as a true man of God was also in question in the surrounding area, and for that reason, few pastors wanted to associate with him.

For her part, Grace was doing just fine with her duties. When Dean came to bed one night obviously anxious, she asked him, "What's wrong?"

He put his head in his hands. "I've sent letters and made phone calls basically begging the local pastors to come support Rev. Riley's celebration. I think some of them are avoiding me, and others have flat-out said no. They don't like him. What should I do? We're going to have five days of evening services and no pastors or guest churches. It's going to be a complete flop!"

Grace sighed.

The next day, she made a few phone calls herself. Over the years, she had developed better relationships with the pastors of local churches than had her husband. When Dean returned home from work that evening, Grace had a report that made his heart swell with pride and gratitude.

"I made some calls and got some pastors for the party."

Dean dropped his briefcase and enveloped her in a tight embrace. "How'd you do it? Who'd you get?"

Grace pulled a piece of paper from her pocket and read off the guest pastors and their dates of attendance.

Dean was confused. "I talked to all of those guys and they told me no. Why'd they tell you yes?"

It was because of her approach. Rev. Johnny Milton was the first phone call she'd made. Instead of speaking to his secretary, she asked to speak to the reverend directly. When he got on the phone, she identified herself as being a member of Christ First.

"I remember you. You teach Sunday school there, right?"

"Yes, sir."

"What can I help you with? Are y'all finally looking to leave from there?"

Grace chuckled. "I'm afraid not. I was actually following up on a letter my husband Dean said he sent to you requesting your presence at Pastor Riley's anniversary celebration."

Rev. Milton sighed.

"Sir," Grace said pleadingly, "I understand you're not a huge fan of Pastor Riley. But this celebration has the opportunity to reach people. We always get a ton of people during these services. Who knows… maybe some of them will hear you preach and end up coming to *your* church. That's what it's all about, right? Reaching out to the unsaved? At the end of the day, don't we have to put our personal feelings aside and think of the bigger picture?"

Rev. Milton sighed again. "You are absolutely right. God forgive me. What day do you need me to come?"

She'd used the same script on the other preachers. Some more reluctantly than others, all agreed to come and bring members of their churches with them. Dean had been trying to secure their participation for weeks. Grace got it accomplished in one afternoon.

Dean had been so preoccupied with finding guest preachers that he had neglected other important aspects of the event. Grace took it upon herself to put together a decorations committee, to make sure the choir was prepared to sing at least two songs, and to secure Curtis to be the emcee for the evening. She also talked random members into reading Rev. Riley's biography, making favorable remarks about him, and to put together a picture show. She found a program from past pastoral celebrations and emailed it to Kathryn, the graphic designer at their church who designed their church media. Kathryn would put together the programs for the evening.

Dean was over the moon when Grace informed him that the planning was complete. The next day when he came home from work, he did so with flowers. "I know this is only a drop in the bucket compared to what I owe you," he said earnestly as he presented them to her, "but this can be a start."

Grace accepted the flowers graciously. "It's going to be great, you know," she told him.

"And all because of you," Dean replied.

When the girls came into the kitchen, they were surprised to find their parents in the midst of what appeared to be a very passionate and sincere kiss. It was a sight to which they had grown unaccustomed. Smiling to each other, they backed out of the kitchen quietly, not wanting to ruin the moment.

On most occasions, the drive to Christ First was one of the rare opportunities during which Grace was in close proximity with her husband without being subject to suffocating tension. Even if he did not speak on the way to church, Dean would turn on--and occasionally sing along to--the gospel music station. It was almost like having church before actually having church.

But this ride was different. The Hardaway family was not on their way to church for Sunday morning worship services, Wednesday evening Bible study, a church meeting, or a rehearsal. They were there to meet with Rev. Riley to discuss their marriage. Two weeks had passed since Dean had buried his parents, and Grace had been gently prodding him to keep his promise to attend marital counseling. It was obvious by his constant fidgeting that Dean was a nervous wreck. Grace, however, was the picture of confidence. Rev. Riley definitely had his flaws, but undoubtedly he would condemn the actions of his abusive deacon.

They pulled into the parking lot. Once inside, Dean cleared his throat. "I'll go find Pastor Riley," he said. "Do you want to take the girls downstairs to the classroom?"

Now feeling nervous herself, Grace nodded. This was it. It was game time. Although she was not in the wrong, there was no way Grace could anticipate what

Rev. Riley was going to say to Dean. This would also be the first time Grace told anyone about the abuse that she had been subjected to, the fear that encompassed her daily life. What was Rev. Riley going to say to *her*? How would Dean react? Could this counseling possibly make their marriage *worse?* And what if it did? If this didn't work, was she prepared to pack her girls and go?

Unfortunately, the answer to that last question was still a resounding no. Grace had no other options and no way of making a life away from Dean by herself, let alone with five girls. *The counseling had to work. It just had to.*

Sensing that she was about to work herself into a frenzy, Grace took it upon herself to go into the kitchen and put on a pot of coffee after instructing the girls to behave and entertain themselves in the classroom while she and Daddy spoke to the pastor. Rev. Riley walked in as she was fixing herself a cup.

"Good afternoon, Pastor," Grace said, startled.

"Grace! Hello. You must have read my mind. I start to wind down every day around this time." He retrieved a cup from the cabinet and said,"I'm glad you two came to me. I'm hoping I'll be able to help you."

"Me too," Grace said earnestly. She poured a cup of coffee for Dean and followed Rev. Riley to his office. When they got there, Dean was already there, seated at the table with his hands folded in front of him. Grace walked in and looked around, stunned. It had been awhile since she had been in the pastor's office, and he had done some redecorating.

Rev. Buckley's office was relatively simple, furnished with an L-shaped desk, a reclining chair, a basic black bookcase for his various religious texts, and an armoire that held his robes. There was an adjoining room that Rev. Buckley used as a study, with more bookcases and books and several pieces of office equipment. Having been a pastor for three decades and a man of God his entire life, Rev. Buckley had amassed a pretty impressive collection of theological information. A lot of Rev. Buckley's books and notes had handwritten, supplemental information or was accompanied by personal inscriptions from Christian authors that he had met or otherwise established a relationship with over the years. The simplicity had been replaced with ornate, ostentatious furnishings in typical Rev. Riley style. The new desk was an antique solid wood behemoth that took up almost half of the office, a matching bookcase behind it with more pictures than books, and a plush purple chair fit for a king. The second room now resembled a bedroom more than a pastor's personal study. There was a cot, a couch, a small refrigerator, a microwave, a flat-screen television, and a DVD/CD player.

"Where did the books go?" Her tone was flat and she knew it, but couldn't help it.

Rev. Riley sat down across from Dean at his desk, chuckling. If he had noticed her tone, it hadn't fazed him one bit. "Some of them are in the library, where they belong," he said as he made himself comfy, "and the others have been returned to Pastor Buckley's family."

Grace was disappointed and confused. That study used to house a wealth of religious information. She fought the urge to shake her head. Hopefully, what had been dumped in the library was safe, and his family was putting the remaining material to good use--although Grace highly doubted that Rev. Riley had truly taken steps to return the items to Rev. Buckley's family. He appeared to be doing whatever he could to remove all hints of Rev. Buckley from the church.

As upset as she was, Rev. Riley had the right to do whatever he wished to the office, and Grace had bigger fish to fry. She handed Dean his cup of coffee and sat down next to him.

Rev. Riley cleared his throat. "So I understand the two of you have been having some marital difficulties," he began. "I must admit, I'm surprised to hear it. Who wants to go first?"

Grace timidly raised her hand. "Can we have a word of prayer first? I don't know about you two, but I'm... nervous."

"Oh of course, of course," Rev. Riley said, flustered. He quickly dropped his head and mumbled, "Our heavenly Father, we come before you thanking you for today, asking for you to forgive us for all of our sins, and please help this couple sitting before me. Please allow them to honestly and humbly examine themselves so that this union will be a blessing to them and to you. In the name of Jesus we do pray, Amen."

"Amen," Dean and Grace chorused.
"Now, who wants to go first?"

Grace raised her hand again, this time with more assurance. Rev. Riley nodded.

Grace swallowed past the lump in her throat. "It really embarrasses me to say this, Pastor, but we're here because I want to have a marriage where I don't get beat."

Dean dropped his head. Rev. Riley looked at him with a raised eyebrow. "'Beat'?" he repeated blankly. "Can you elaborate, please?"

That was the ammunition Grace needed. Rev. Riley's initial response and curt tone of voice was strangely empowering, and over the next twenty minutes she talked nonstop about the abuse she had been suffering at the hands of her husband. She told Dean that she knew about his infidelities with various coworkers, a charge that Dean did not deny, although he did look embarrassed. The entire time, neither Dean nor the pastor said a single word. Rev. Riley held up a hand to cut Grace off.

Once she was quiet, Rev. Riley turned his attention to his deacon. "Dean," he said gravely, "is this true? Do you abuse your wife?"

Dean nodded, but would not lift his head. "I have a hard time controlling my anger."

"What is the cause of this anger?" Rev. Riley probed.

Dean sighed and finally looked Rev. Riley in the face. "I just feel so much pressure to maintain our family," he burst out. "Do you know how hard it is to take care of *seven* people? People *do* want to believe we are perfect, and I'd like for them to think that too. And it's hard. It's hard to get mistreated at work every day so that Grace and the girls can have this great lifestyle and then come home and feel--ingratitude."

Grace's eyes flew open. "Ingratitude?" she repeated.

"How so, Dean?" Rev. Riley asked him.

"You act like it's the worst thing in the world that I expect for the house to be clean," Dean said to Grace, his voice getting louder. "Do you expect for me to come home after working eight, ten or twelve hours and do it?"

"Of course not," Grace said, her own voice getting louder, "but your standards of cleanliness are almost impossible, especially when there are five active little girls in that house who are attempting to enjoy their childhood!"

Rev. Riley held up a hand to silence them both. "Okay, okay," he said. "Let him get it out, okay, Grace? We listened to you; now let's hear Dean's side of things."

Dean talked for far more than twenty minutes. Rev. Riley made no efforts to cut him off. And unlike when Grace was speaking, Rev. Riley often nodded or showed some form of agreement with what Dean was saying. Grace sat quietly while the two men went back and forth about the difficulty of being a strong Christian man in a world where good, submissive Christian women were hard to find. As their discourse continued, Grace's stomach began to knot up and she started thinking that perhaps this counseling session was not such a good idea. She listened miserably as Dean hurled all sorts of accusations and insults at her: She was too attentive to the girls and put them before him; their sex life sucked; she spent too much of his money; she had put on a ton of weight and was making no attempts to lose it; yes, he had high standards for how he expected his house to look, but since she didn't work that's the least she could do. Humiliated, Grace wanted to interrupt but was afraid to. Instead, she completely checked out of the conversation. Grace had developed the keen ability to mentally place herself somewhere else in times of struggle. This was one of those times. She could see that Rev. Riley was building up to something negative against her.

Grace was absolutely right. "Grace, do you think you have a problem being submissive?" Rev. Riley asked her.

"Excuse me?"

Suddenly, the door swung open. Grace had never been so happy to see Brooke Anderson, Rev. Riley's personal secretary and one of his reputed mistresses. Brooke was surprised to see them all sitting there. Her face conveyed her embarrassment, and Rev. Riley looked put-upon as well. It was easy to infer that the Hardaways were infringing on the illicit lovers' alone time.

"Uh, I'll be with you in a little while, if you'd like to wait for me in your office, Brooke," Rev. Riley said to the young college student uncomfortably.

She nodded her head and exited quickly, closing the door behind her.

Rev. Riley had gotten a good enough glimpse of the shapely young woman's partially exposed breasts peeking out from the top of her tight blouse to be ready to wrap things up.

"Grace, what do you think it means to be submissive?" he asked.

Grace looked down at her lap. "It means that Dean is the head of the household. I don't have a problem with that."

"I think you do, but you might not be aware of it," Rev. Riley said. "I understand that perhaps your guard is up because of your troubled past. Dean came and spoke with me about that a few days ago."

Infuriated, Grace turned to Dean. She had never told Rev. Riley about her past and had no intention of doing so. Dean had betrayed her and stacked the deck against her. No wonder Rev. Riley was being so dismissive of her concern. He was probably thinking that a former addict and whore that had been lucky enough to find a military man willing to look beyond her past and marry her had no business complaining. Dean refused to meet her icy gaze.

"What does my past have to do with how I'm currently being treated?" Grace snapped.

"I think it goes without saying that our pasts shape our attitudes and behavior," Rev. Riley replied. "I think it's possible you are still holding on to some anger from your past. But more than that, I think both of you need to work on getting back to the place where you were when you first decided you loved each other. I understand that marriages can be strained when young children are involved. Sometimes you women get so caught up in taking care of the kids that you forget there is a husband there with needs too. Wilma and I have gone through the same thing; it's not rare at all. Grace, try to remember that before you were a mother you were a wife, and although your children are definitely important and require proper attention, as a Christian woman your marital duties and responsibilities to your husband are to come first. I'm assuming that in your vows you pledged to love, honor and obey Dean, correct? With him being the man, sometimes he has to make decisions that aren't popular with you, and maybe you don't understand them at the time because God reveals his desires for the family's direction to the husband, not the wife. If Dean is hard on the family, it's because he wants the best, and his leadership of the family is directed by God. You can't really argue with that."

Grace gave Rev. Riley a cold, blank look that he ignored.

"And Dean, try talking to Grace about what is bothering you instead of hitting. You can't hit your wife. Lighten up a little. You take things too seriously, even here at church. You are way too intense. And as for the cheating, it goes without saying that that is unacceptable." He stood up, signaling that the "counseling" session was over.

Dean stood, smiling. He was pleased. The bulk of the admonishing had gone toward Grace; of course he was happy. He shook Rev. Riley's hand. "I'll do better," he promised.

In the car, Dean turned on gospel music and sang along. As usual, Grace and the girls were silent. Once they got home, Grace fixed the family something to eat. When they were done eating Dean said, "I'll help clean up in here."

The girls stared at Dean, as did Grace.

"Um, you don't have to," Grace said uneasily. When Dean broke away from his routine or did something out of the ordinary, usually it meant something awful was on the horizon. She was not happy to have him offer to help.

"I know I don't have to. I want to. Girls, go play."

Feeling as uncomfortable as their mother, the girls left the dining room quickly. Hesitantly, and keeping her distance from her husband, Grace began to clear the table. He stood at the sink and turned on the faucet. As she handed him each empty plate, he rinsed it off and put it and the utensils into the dishwasher. They worked in silence for a few minutes before he spoke.

"I take it that didn't go the way you'd planned."

Grace wasn't sure how to respond to that statement. It was true, but the last thing she wanted was for Dean to probe her any further and back her into saying something that would make him angry. "It went okay."

"You're lying."

"Okay, fine," she said carefully. "I guess I thought the counseling would be more biblical, that's all. Rev. Riley didn't provide any Scriptures and what he said seemed to be based on his own understanding."

"Of course it was," Dean said. "What else would he base it off of?"

"He is supposed to be God's mouthpiece," Grace reminded him. "It didn't feel that way while we were in there."

"Probably because you were taking most of the heat."

"Yes, and you seemed perfectly content with that." It left her mouth before she realized it. Scared, she froze. Dean stared at her.

"I'm sorry."

Grace couldn't remember the last time he'd sincerely apologized for anything. Perhaps she had been wrong. "What?" she asked blankly.

"I'm sorry. I shouldn't have gone to Rev. Riley and talked about you. You know some things about me that I wouldn't want others to know, and while we were in there I hadn't given it much thought. It just hit me right now. Maybe it would have gone better if Rev. Riley hadn't fixated on that."

Tears filled her eyes. She hadn't spoke of her painful past in years. Grace had been active in church for almost a decade now, and even though she had heard dozens of sermons that talked about God's forgiveness, she still wasn't sure if her past sins were covered. She often wondered if her current life was punishment for having lived wrong in the first place. It just didn't seem right by her standards that God could ever look past who she used to be without judging her for it. A lot of the people who were members when Grace first joined, when she had confessed her past, were gone, replaced by a new crowd of superficial, judgmental pseudo-Christians. It terrified her to think of anyone at Christ First knowing her secrets, because despite how loved she was on the surface, Grace knew there would be plenty of people who were all too ready to find out some dirt on her.

"Why did you tell him?" she asked in a small voice.

"I was frustrated one day and wanted to vent to someone who I knew could keep a secret," Dean replied. "I don't even remember how it came out, I promise. But after I said one thing, he asked a couple questions and then I said something else."

"You had a secret meeting with our pastor just to talk about how horrible of a person I am?" Grace asked incredulously.

"No, no," Dean told her. "I was frustrated by a lot of things. I talked more about work than you."

"If you're having problems at work," Grace said, "why can't you talk to *me* about them? As you said, I know things about you that no one else does. So why do you feel like you have to hide yourself from me? The only emotion I see from you regularly is anger. I might not be perfect, but do I deserve that? Do these girls deserve to walk around their home on eggshells all day because they never know when you're going to explode, or why?"

Dean sat down at the table, looking dejected. "I don't want you to think I'm weak, Grace," he confessed. "When I was younger, people always treated me like I was weak and unimportant. That's one of the main reasons I joined the military. Not just because my dad was a Marine, but so I could prove to other people that they were wrong about me. Shoot, to prove to my own *family* that they were wrong about me."

He stood back up, walked over to Grace, and put his hands on her shoulders. "I've spent years bottling up problems," he admitted. "With the problems at my work and Dad dying, I'm starting to realize some things. I know I need to learn better ways to deal with my anger, Grace."

Grace felt a thousand pounds lighter.

Chapter Eight

"But godliness with contentment is great gain…" (1 Timothy 6:6)

Angelica was in a tizzy. Something had come over Dean, and whatever it was, it was throwing a monkey wrench in her plans.

All of a sudden Dean decided he loved Grace again. Angelica was furious when Dean texted her--he wasn't even man enough to come talk to her face to face--and told her he was going to try to work things out with Grace. When Angelica texted him back to ask why his response was just as flaky as he was: "God is not pleased with me and I want to be a better man."

Angelica laughed heartily when she read that text. What a joke he was! All of a sudden he cared what God thought? Out of all the disgusting men she had ever given the pleasure of her company, Dean was by far the biggest crybaby of all. He had no idea what it meant to be a "man", let alone a "better" one. She was convinced that he would be back at her doorstep within days.

When he wasn't, Angelica's worries began to compound. One Sunday when Dean and Grace shared a brief hug before they went into their separate Sunday school classrooms, she grew even more concerned that she was losing her grip on him. By the time the church service ended and Angelica realized that Dean had gone out of his way to avoid any contact with her, she knew she had to do something major to pull him away from his wife. Unfortunately for Dean, in his self-serving journey to gain sympathy from Angelica he had poured out to her all of his hopes, dreams and desires. Angelica knew that she had one thing Dean had always wanted and couldn't have: A son.

David was ripe for the picking as well. Angelica loved her son in her own way, but that didn't keep her from using him as a prop when necessary. He was struggling in school with math, and he had made the basketball team and often spent hours at the Ypsi Rec Center by himself honing his jump shot. Each time he went to the Rec to play he felt pangs of envy as he watched other boys shoot around with their fathers. Occasionally, they would invite him to play. He always accepted their invitation to do so and had a great time, but inevitably it would come to an end. Father and son would walk out together while he walked out alone.

Sometimes the desire for a father brought tears to David's eyes. The only thing Angelica had ever told David about his dad was that his name was Simon and that he was dead. Whenever David asked for more information about Simon Angelica either grew angry or changed the subject.

"All you need to know about him is that he didn't want you," she'd tell him. "Now drop it. I give you everything you need. You don't need a father."

But the thing is, *he did.* David was no different from any other child. Just because he had become accustomed to being raised by his mother didn't mean that he never considered how his life could have been positively impacted by a father. Who else could teach him how to fix things, talk to him about girls, take him to the barber shop? There was no one there to teach him how to change a tire, grill the perfect steak or tie a tie. There was no one there to help him with his jump shot.

Dean's desire for a son and David's desire for a father meant that Angelica had everything she needed to get her scheme back on track--despite this minor derailment.

November 22nd, Sarah and Rebekah's seventh birthday.

Typically, Dean didn't make any fuss over the girls' birthdays, but the new and improved Dean felt that he owed them a great birthday to make up for all of the subdued birthdays of the past. To the absolute shock of the entire family, Dean gave Sarah and Rebekah permission to have a birthday party outside of the house at the location of their choosing and invite a few of their friends. They picked skating.

The party was a ton of fun. That night as they readied for bed, Dean approached Grace sheepishly, rubbing his hands together. "Uh, Grace, I feel like things have been going well lately…"

"They have," Grace said with a smile, rubbing her aching ankles. She hadn't remembered skating being so painful. "You were a blast tonight, Dean. Did you see how happy the girl were?"

"Yeah," Dean said, smiling slowly. "I definitely saw that."

Grace patted the bed next to her. He sat. "I knew you had it in you. I don't think they'll ever forget this birthday."

"I did have fun," Dean admitted. "But uh, I need to run something by you."

Grace looked at him quizzically.

"Last month I invited a few of the guys from work over here for Thanksgiving. I forgot to mention it to you. I had forgotten myself until one of them brought it up."
Grace shrugged. "That's cool. I just need to know how many people so I can figure out how much food to make."

Hoping to win favor among some of his ITS colleagues, Dean had invited every member of Wes and Mike's team *except* Wes and Mike over for dinner. That Thursday was Thanksgiving, and in addition to making enough food for their family of seven, Grace had seventeen extra people to cook for. Not that she minded. Dean had been doing so well lately that she was willing to overlook the short notice.

Although Grace was exhausted by the time the night was over, it was a total success, and Dean couldn't have been happier. He ran his wife a hot bath, cleaned up the kitchen and dining room and returned upstairs to wash her up and help her to the bed, where he lotioned and tickled her body, making her laugh and blush.

Grace slept soundly that night, but Dean was startled awake when his cell phone began vibrating loudly on the night table next to the bed. Irritated, he reached for it, wondering who was texting him at this time of the night. To his surprise, it was Angelica.

"I understand you're back with Grace, but I have a favor to ask and I don't know anyone else I can trust. I'm having some problems with David. He seems to like and respect you. Was wondering if you could talk to him since you are his assigned deacon."

Dean blinked sleepily and reread the text. It was true that he was David's assigned deacon, so technically he *was* responsible for attending to the boy's spiritual needs unless there was a problem that needed to be escalated to the pastor's attention.

"Yes I am trying to work things out with my wife but I'd be happy to help with David. Will call later. Unless there is an emergency right now?"

At home, sitting in her bed, Angelica's lips curled into a satisfied smile. "He did leave home earlier but he came back. No emergency. Just starting to rebel and I can't handle him. Talk to you later. Thanks a million. Good night."

David looked down, making sure his feet were firmly planted on the three-point line. Inhaling deeply, he positioned the ball in his hands, and shot. The ball sank into the net. A satisfied smile on his face, David jogged to retrieve the ball, grabbed it and shot again. It went in.

"Nice shot."

The voice came from the gym's entrance. David turned. Up until then he had the pleasure of having the entire court to himself. It was Thanksgiving weekend, and apparently everyone else had holiday plans or fun things to do with their families that kept them away from the Rec. Not him. It was only open for a few hours that day, but David was there, waiting, when the building manager unlocked the doors that morning. Angelica had been unbearable the past few days, yelling at him about everything, things that weren't even his fault. A few times he had yelled back, only to get slapped in the mouth and forced to sleep in the car. He had been enjoying the solitude and wasn't interested in any company.

"Thanks," he mumbled listlessly as he watched the shadowy figure approach.

Once he finally made his way to the light, David was surprised to see that he recognized the man behind the voice. Holding a ball and a water bottle and dressed in an Adidas track suit, Dean Hardaway was headed right toward him. David didn't bother to hide his confusion. *What the heck is he doing here?* David had never seen him at the Rec before. Now all of a sudden he shows up?

"Mind if I play?" Dean asked.

Scowling, David shrugged. "Do what you want. It's not my court."

Dean took off his jacket and set it on the bleachers along with his water. Although David tried not to watch, he couldn't help but notice that Dean sank all of his warm-up shots. Dean went to the other half of the court and ran up several times, enticing David with his fancy handles. Within a few minutes David was no longer looking out of the corners of his eyes. He stood, holding his basketball, while Dean made three-pointer after three-pointer.

"Who's your favorite player?" Dean asked David as he sank another three.

"Steph Curry," David replied.

"Mine too. Imagine that. That last finals series was crazy, wasn't it?"

David had to smile. "Yeah, man."

For awhile, David forgot that he loathed Dean. It was nice to have an older guy to talk to. But when Dean challenged David to a game of one-on-one, David hesitated.

"I'll go easy on you," Dean teased.

David laughed. "I'm not worried about me, old man. I'm worried about how I'm going to pick you up off the floor after I break your ankles."

"Looks like it's on!" Dean announced, getting up from the bleachers where he had been comfortably taking a break. "First one to twenty?"

"Let's do it!"

At the end of a very close game, Dean came out on top. Although David definitely had far more energy, Dean had more experience and natural skill. During the game, Dean stopped multiple times to try to help David with his defense, his ball handling, and his shot. When it was over, they sat on the bleachers, huffing and puffing, drinking water and recounting the game.

"Whew!" said Dean, wiping sweat from his forehead. "That was my workout for the day. I enjoyed myself. Did you?"

"Yeah," David admitted. "I would have enjoyed myself more if I would've won, though."

"You keep at it, and you'll beat me before you know it," Dean said encouragingly. He checked his watch. "This place is about to close. Are you hungry? I'm gonna grab some lunch."

Again, David hesitated. He was hungry--no, correction, he was *starving*. Angelica had been too upset the last few days to bother to cook a decent meal for her son, so he had been surviving on cereal, sandwiches, hot dogs and microwaveable garbage that never completely satiated him. But what was behind all of Dean's kindness? They'd never spoken more than a few sentences to each other. Besides that, knowing that Dean was married but having an affair with Angelica made his character highly questionable. What was his motive?

"You don't trust me, do you."

Surprised, David looked at Dean and nodded slowly.

"I get it. I've made mistakes. I had no business being with your mom, ever. If you've noticed, I haven't been coming around because I put an end to it. I messed up and I'm trying to make it right. With God, with myself, with my wife."

David eyeballed him.

"I'm far from perfect," Dean said, "but I don't think it will do you any harm to eat some lunch. I'm sure you're hungry."

The thought of three deuce burgers and crispy French fries from Full House made his mouth water. Before he knew it, David was following Dean outside to his car.

As they ate, they had lively conversation about basketball, school, and more basketball. Dean never had to tell David that Angelica had mediated this encounter-- David gave him all the information he needed. It was obvious the boy was starved for personal, deep interaction and attention. In great detail he explained to Dean his difficulty with math, and was pleased to find out that Dean was good at the subject. Right there in Full House David pulled out his math textbook from his backpack and turned to the section that was causing him the most grief. Dean asked him for paper and a pencil and quickly solved all the problems, writing step-by-step instructions on how to do so in the margins for David to study. David was stunned by how easy it was once Dean explained it to him. Dean gave David a few practice problems. Using Dean's notes, he solved them correctly within minutes.

"My math teacher never taught us that method. He gets mad when we ask him questions. He makes me feel stupid."

"Obviously you're not stupid," Dean informed him. "If you need help or want to play some one-on-one in the future just call me. I had a great time today. I need to get home, though. Do you want a ride home?"

David shook his head emphatically. "Nah, I'm not trying to go back there."

Dean looked at him with his eyebrows raised. "So where are you going to go?"

"I guess I'll hang around here for awhile."

Dean sat back in his chair. "Why don't you want to go home, David?"

David grew uncomfortable. Sure, he was having an enjoyable afternoon with Dean--probably the most enjoyable morning and afternoon he'd had since he and Angelica moved to Ypsi. But as much as his mother and her mood swings and erratic behavior bothered him, he was not ready to betray her just yet. He shrugged. "Me and Moms are going through a little something," he mumbled, putting his hoodie on over his head.

"Anything you want to talk about? You want me to say anything to her?"

David shook his head emphatically. "Nah. I'll go home soon. Just not right now."

Dean took out his wallet and retrieved a twenty. "Here. Just in case you need it for bus fare or food," he told him.

"You've done enough, Deacon Hardaway."

"Enough with the formalities. Call me Dean. And I won't feel comfortable leaving you here with nothing. Take the twenty."

Reluctantly, David reached across the table, took the money, and shoved it into his pocket.

"If you need me, call," Dean said, rising to his feet. "But I understand needing your space. Sometimes women go through things, you know? And your mom is doing it all by herself. Try, if you can, to imagine how hard her life is. I'm not saying that's an excuse for treating you badly, but think about how stressful her life is. And if you need me to talk to her, let me know. I mean it. Okay?"

David smiled. "Okay."

In his car, Dean fished his cellphone out of his pocket and called Angelica. Her phone went to voice mail, so he left a message. "Hey," he said. "I just left David. He's okay. I bought him some lunch. He's at Full House. He said he doesn't want to come home just yet."

Sitting on her bed, Angelica smiled as she listened to the voice mail. This was going exactly as she had planned.

Over the next few days, Angelica purposely acted erratically in order to force David from the house. Each time David left, she called Dean in fabricated hysterics and asked him to go find him and bring him home. Dean, trying hard to live up to the role of a dutiful deacon, responded each time. Within two weeks Dean and David were together almost every day for as much time as Dean could offer after work. Grace and the girls saw him less and less, and Grace was not pleased with this new development. They had been getting along so well, and Dean had been making strides in his relationship with his daughters. Now Grace had to wonder what her husband was up to that was keeping him away so much. He hadn't mentioned another work project. One night as they were getting ready for bed, she asked him.

He was surprisingly forthright. "I've been meaning to tell you about that," he said as he stretched. "Maybe we can all do something this weekend. I owe y'all some time. The Billups boy has been keeping me busy."

"Billups?" Grace repeated. "You mean David? David from church?"

Dean nodded. "Yeah. He's kind of a troubled kid, if you hadn't noticed."

"I've definitely noticed," Grace agreed as she eased her way into bed next to him. "What's wrong?"

"He's acting out at home. His mother tends to think he needs a positive male influence in his life."

Grace wasn't particularly fond of Angelica Billups, but she did have a special place in her heart for David. "I'm sure she's right," she said.

"I've been taking him to play basketball and stuff. I try to talk to him about his behavior and help him where he's struggling in school. It seems like it's working."

"Good for you, Dean," Grace said approvingly. "That relationship would probably do the both of you some good."

"You think?" Dean asked sleepily.

"Yes. He needs a father figure and you've always wanted a son. Good-night."

As Grace settled into a restful sleep, her words echoed in Dean's head. She was right. He *had* always wanted a son. With Angelica, he had the chance to have the family he truly desired… Dean shook his head, trying to prevent the negative thought from developing further. Somehow, someway, he had to learn to be content with what he had been given.

CHAPTER NINE

"Behold, I am coming soon, bringing my recompense with me,
to repay each one for what he has done." (Rev. 22:12)

Grace was more than ready to get the tedious pastor's anniversary crap over with. As the date approached Dean began to regress to his former self. After having had no input whatsoever in getting the celebration together, he was fully dissatisfied with every decision Grace had made and voiced his displeasure--loudly. Several times he felt his temperature rising and knew he was about to lose control and slap her. Instead, he grabbed his jacket and car keys and stalked out of the house.

The party wasn't the only thing contributing to his anxiety. Since Dean had relaxed a little, Grace and the girls had gotten comfortable and began to relax too. A few times Dean had come home and the house looked sloppier than he would have allowed before. Most other men would have been perfectly fine coming home to a house where his wife and kids happily greeted him at the door but the towels weren't lined up perfectly or there was a crayon or two out of place, but not Dean.

Dean was on edge by the time the Monday night celebration kick-off service rolled around, and since he was on edge, so was Grace. She was glad that Dean was leaving instead of taking his anger out on her, but the fact that his anger had returned in the first place was very distressing. She was uneasy around him just like before and spent hours in prayer to God, asking that He help make the week go by as smoothly as possible so that Dean could just be *happy*.

Apparently Grace was highly favored by God. Each evening, Christ First was packed to capacity. The guest preachers were dynamic, and it seemed as though they had gotten together and coordinated a series of sermons that spoke directly to Rev. Riley--whether he noticed or not. They preached about the qualifications of a pastor, the judgment that was to come his way if he did not lead his flock according to God's Word, and the personal characteristics that a good pastor ought to have--including humility. The guest preachers brought their deacons, praise dancers, choirs, ushers and nurses. At the end of the night Grace made sure to talk to as many of the visitors as she could, enthusiastically thanking them for coming. She had had such a good time in the Lord she forgot the celebration was for someone she despised.

Saturday was the main event. Grace started preparing herself for the dinner on Thursday, going with several members of her assembled crew to Gordon Food

Service to purchase the food. From her old hospitality crew was Cecile, Paige Henderson, Trevor Findlay, and Dominic Santiago. In addition to her trusted comrades were five students from the EMU hospitality program that had been chosen to be team leaders.

Working with the crew Thursday and Friday was a dream come true. Grace's passion for food had never disappeared; if anything, it had grown stronger. The leadership qualities that had been suppressed for years, the same ones that had piloted two successful Veteran's Day dinners, poured forth unimpeded. In the kitchen at EMU, the students, Grace's colleagues, and her daughters watched, almost in awe, as Grace walked them through the preparation of the appetizers, the desserts, and finally the entrees.

Grace spent Friday evening submerged in prayer. She knew that she needed this event to go well in order to keep her husband's morale high. It didn't matter that the event was celebrating someone that Grace barely respected. Dean's happiness and their marriage was more important than her disdain for Rev. Riley.

Grace and her team arrived at the banquet hall at 3:00 p.m., rearing to go. If nothing else, her hours-long prayer the night before had definitely calmed any nerves she may have had. When she got to the banquet hall and saw the students there already, she was more excited than she had been in years. "Let the magic begin," she said to herself with a grin. "Come on, girls. You're going to be my apprentice chefs." They all squealed with delight, even Eve, as they tumbled out of the car.

The decorations committee had already been there. They had done a masterful job decorating the entire banquet hall with green and gold, Rev. Riley's favorite colors. The banquet hall employees had set up tables for the food. The cooking crew just had to bring it in and get it ready.

Everything went swimmingly. Grace and the girls headed home to get ready for the party. When they arrived, Dean met them at the door, frantic.

"How'd everything turn out?" he said, his tone of voice even slightly panicky.

Grace frowned as she hung up her coat. "Everything's fine, Dean."

"Was the decorations committee there?"

"No, they had gone in earlier and decorated. It looks really nice in there." She tried to head upstairs so she could hopefully have a few minutes alone, but Dean followed her.

"Did the techs come in and set up the projector and screen for the picture slide show?"

"Yes, Dean."

"Were the cakes there?"

"Yes, Dean."

"Were the chairs for Rev. and Sis. Riley decorated?"

"Dean." Exasperated, Grace turned. "Please calm down. Everything is fine. I promise you this is going to be the pastoral celebration to end all pastoral celebrations."

Dean inhaled and exhaled deeply. Nodding, he backed up and started back down the steps. "Okay. Okay. I'm sure you're right. I'm going to go get dressed."

They still had an hour and a half until the party started, but Dean bothered Grace so much that she thought it was best to head to the banquet hall, where Dean would hopefully calm down once he saw how perfect everything looked. It was a smart idea. As soon as they got there, Dean's anxiety visibly diminished. He walked into the banquet hall with a huge grin on his face.

Guests began to arrive as early as five thirty, which Grace had been expecting. Everyone knew the honorees would make a fashionably late entrance. Grace flitted about the room, making sure the girls were seated, that guests were aware of the appetizer table, and that everyone was seated where they were supposed to be seated. By the time Rev. Riley and Wilma descended the steps of the horse-drawn carriage that had brought them several feet from the parking lot to the door and waltzed into the full room to the sound of thunderous applause, Grace was already exhausted.

Her fatigue didn't stop her from being excited about the dinner that was to be served beginning at 6:30. As the time grew near, Curtis approached the DJ booth at the front of the room and picked up the microphone. He tapped it three times and cleared his voice. Everyone grew quiet and looked at him.

"Ladies and gentlemen," he said, a broad smile crossing his mustachioed face. "First, let me thank each and every one of you for attending tonight's celebration of our pastor, Reverend Benjamin 'Benny' Riley, and his wife, our first lady, Wilma. I will be tonight's emcee, and my first order of business is to get us ready to eat this good looking food!" He motioned to the tables that displayed the food and was rewarded with generous applause. Grace smiled to herself. Her former EMU colleagues and the hospitality students were lined up, ready to serve. She gave them the thumbs-up sign. They gave it back.

Curtis led the room in a word of prayer and gave the instructions for dinner. "Each table has a number in the middle. We will call you up to be served by table. Please wait your turn. The honorees and their family members will be served by the hospitality staff."

Grace watched as the first tables were dispatched and received their meals. Trying not to stare, she followed each person as they exited the banquet line and carried their plate back to their table. Grace observed the look of pure bliss and delight that crossed each person's face as they took their first few bites of her food.

Her daughters noticed as well. "Mom, they love your food!" Eve exclaimed.

"I think it's a hit," Grace agreed, smiling.

Dean came up from behind, startling her. "Grace, the food is getting rave reviews," he told her excitedly. "You outdid yourself!"

Grace sighed internally with relief. He was pleased. She had done it. Dean worked the room the entire night and sat down only to eat with his family before getting up and leaving again. Grace barely saw him for the rest of the evening.

The remainder of the program was a breeze--mainly because Grace tuned out of it. She was not interested in hearing Rev. Riley's embellished history, or in listening to various members of Christ First as they stood front and center and gushed about how great a pastor Rev. Riley was. Half the time they were lying. Rev. Riley sat at his table with his arms folded proudly across his chest, reveling in the praise. Next to him, Wilma, who had to know that some of the stories being told were just that--stories-- kept the same fake smile plastered across her face the entire time. Grace was happy each time one of her daughters asked her to accompany them to the bathroom because it meant she could get out of there and have a few moments alone to roll her eyes.

After the embarrassing brown nosing session was over the Christ First choir performed two songs. When they were finished, Rev. Riley joined them at the front of the room. He was supposed to give remarks and close out the program. He walked back and forth a few times with his head down and his lips pressed together tightly, pretending to be emotional.

"Take your time, pastor," someone called.

Grace groaned. It was now close to ten o'clock and she was ready to get out of that annoying black dress and rest her aching feet. The girls were getting tired too. Grace craned her neck, looking around the room for Dean. She found him sitting at the table with Angelica and David Billups. Instantly her heart dropped. It was inexplicable... Grace couldn't put a finger on it, but there was something about Angelica that always seemed disingenuous. The woman was nice to her face, but duplicitous vibes radiated from Angelica like a plume of smoke from a chimney.

Grace tried to fight the feeling in the pit of her stomach and focus on the garbage speech Rev. Riley was guaranteed to make.

"My brothers and sisters," he began melodramatically, "I am so full right now I can barely speak. This past week has been absolutely amazing. I can't tell you how good it feels to have the members of your church go to these lengths to show how much they love you. There are no words. Dean, get up here."

Dean almost toppled his chair over as he shot up like a rocket and headed up to the front of the room as the attendees applauded. Rev. Riley put an arm around Dean's shoulders.

"This guy here," Rev. Riley said, looking at Dean proudly, "this entire celebration was the brain child of this very hard-working deacon right here. I can't go any further without thanking him for his efforts. Judging by how everything came together, I'd gather to say that this thing took time to organize, and I really can't thank you enough for thinking so much of me as to go all out like this."

As the crowd applauded again, Grace couldn't help but wonder if she was going to get any credit at all for *her* hard work. In all honesty, Dean hadn't managed a single aspect of the entire celebration on his own. It was *Grace* who had done the work. Grace warred internally with herself. She knew that Christians weren't supposed to get bent on rewards and attention from people when it was the rewards and attention from God that she ought to be seeking, but Grace was human. Although she didn't need a standing ovation or anything, some type of acknowledgment would have been nice.

She didn't get it.

"I'd also like to thank each and every one of you who played an individual role in making this happen," Rev. Riley said. He gave Dean a bit of a nudge, which was his cue to go sit back down. As Dean headed off the dance floor, he was happy to hear more applause following him back to his seat with his family. Now that he knew all eyes were on him, he was back to playing the family man role. Grace fought the urge to become aggravated with him further.

Out of nowhere, Rev. Riley launched into a spirited rendition of "Every Praise" by Hezekiah Walker. It was obvious that he had planned beforehand to do the song-- the DJ had it ready when he hit his first note. That further proved that Rev. Riley's speech was rehearsed, just as Grace thought. Everything about the guy was insincere.

The Christ First choir was eager to back him up, and it didn't take long for the attendees to join in. The room turned into a mixture of a church service and a dance competition. While some of the people dancing were without a doubt doing so with a pure heart, others were doing way too much and it was obvious that they were more interested in being noticed for their footwork skills than their praise. Grace noticed that the people who were engaged in serious praise remained close to their chairs, while the attention-seekers shuffled their way to the dance floor where they could be seen better under the bright lights. The DJ, aptly prepared, responded by putting on a praise song with a much faster beat. At one point in time the dancers made a circle around Rev. Riley and hooped, hollered, clapped, and stomped their feet as he jitted across the floor. It got so good to him that he broke free from the circle and ran a lap around the entire room.

Grace watched, partially amused and partially annoyed, as people took turns getting in the middle of the circle and showing off their best moves. As soon as the song ended the dancers walked off the floor, fanning themselves with their hands and laughing and talking among themselves. Grace shook her head. The dancers were members of Christ First, many of them women much older than she. They should have known better.

Grace looked at the members of the other churches. While the vast majority of them had pulled out their best poker faces, others weren't bothering to hide their consternation. Grace was embarrassed.

Rev. Riley was not. Out of breath, he again picked up the microphone. "It's alright to have a little church, ain't it?" he said, grinning. He removed a handkerchief from his pocket and wiped his sweaty brow with a great flourish. "Now, let me finish what I came up here to do. It's getting a bit late in the evening, so again, I'd like to thank everyone for coming, and we're going to get you on your way here. Let's not leave this building until we have come together for a prayer of thanksgiving and for traveling grace and mercy."

Rev. Riley's party was slated to end at ten p.m., but as Grace expected, many members of Christ First, unsurprisingly led by Claudia, decided to turn the banquet hall into a dance club when they went to the DJ booth and asked him to turn off the smooth jazz he had been playing and put on some Jodeci. Ordinarily the music wouldn't bother Grace, but she knew as soon as she saw several bottles of alcohol that had appeared out of nowhere being passed around, she knew the party was going to take an ungodly turn. Horrified, she looked around to make sure the guest pastors had left. They had, but some of their members were there. A few of them were looking at the members of Christ First with wide eyes. Others obviously wanted to join in, but were hesitant.

Grace was not willing to have anything that she had organized turn out like this. Furious, she walked up to the members who she assumed had produced the bottles of alcohol, including Curtis. "Look, I can't tell you what to do in your own home," she hissed, "but this is a church-sponsored celebration for a *pastor*. Not to mention there are children here. Please put that away."

Curtis threw his hands up. "It wasn't me this time, Grace," he defended himself. "But I agree with the lady. Fellas, get rid of the booze. If y'all want, we can take the party back to my place."

Dean came up from behind Grace and put his hands on her shoulders. "Lighten up," he told her. "No one is forcing anyone to drink."

Grace whirled around, her eyes wide.

"But be a bit more inconspicuous with the drinks, okay?" Dean said to them. "No need to leave. We have the place until two a.m. Is the DJ taking requests?" He headed to the DJ booth, leaving Grace behind looking and feeling stupid. Her feet were aching. Her hands were aching. She was tired and sweaty, and he had the nerve to undermine her in front of everybody like that? Grace balled up her fists.

"Mommy?"

Naomi was tugging at her dress. Grace snapped out of her anger and back into loving Mommy mode. "Yes?"

"Are we leaving soon?"

Grace sighed. "Give us just a little time to get this place cleared out, okay? If you girls would like to rest, there are a few comfy-looking couches right outside the doors."

Naomi nodded. She turned and walked back to the round table where the rest of her sisters were sitting, looking exhausted. Shaking her head, Grace headed across the dance floor to the DJ booth where her husband was still talking to the DJ. Right before she reached Dean he turned around, a big smile on his face. From the speakers boomed "Stars" by Kindred Family Soul.

"I asked him to play this for you," he said with a lopsided smile that let her know that he had, at some point in time of which she was unaware, taken a nip or two from one of the bottles circulating the room. "Dance with me."

Of course she obliged. In a way, it felt good to be in her husband's arms. He was mostly sober, so it wasn't like dancing with him at the Toole's back to school barbecue. He was sweaty, but so was she. He held her tight and whirled her around the dance floor. Despite her annoyance at him undercutting her earlier, she found herself laughing as they made their way across the floor.

After the song was over, Grace attempted to tell him they needed to get their girls home. "Dean, the girls and I are awfully tired…"

"Just a couple more songs, okay?"

A couple more songs turned into an hour's worth. Dean was quite a dancer, and his moves earned him shouts of encouragement and laughter from the others who still remained. As usual, the attention bolstered his ego, and he would have danced all night if it wasn't for a banquet hall employee going to the DJ booth and saying into the microphone, "Sorry to interrupt folks, but it's time to close."

Grace gasped. That meant it was two o'clock! She broke away from Dean and went to the tables, wondering what her poor girls had been doing the entire time. They were nowhere to be found. Grace raced to the doors and threw them open. The girls were on the two couches Grace had pointed them to, fast asleep. Grace sighed.

Dean was still in the banquet hall running his mouth, much to the chagrin of the banquet hall employees who were tasked with cleaning it up after the party was over. "Dean," Grace said urgently. "We have to get out of here so the employees can close and go home."

Dean still talked for fifteen more minutes. As he did so, Grace made multiple trips to the car, carrying her younger daughters, one by one, to the SUV and putting them securely inside. Eve, who was almost Grace's height, was too awkward to carry. Just as Grace was considering what to do with her, Eve woke up. "Can we go now?" she asked crabbily.

When they finally got home, Dean told Grace, "I'll bring the girls in. Go on upstairs and get yourself a hot bath."

Grace sighed and smiled. "That sounds wonderful."

During the ride home, Grace had planned the rest of the night and calculated how much sleep she could get. The bath was first on her agenda, and the second item on her agenda was also her last... She couldn't wait to go to bed. She had been visualizing her bed the entire afternoon. Grace couldn't wait to lay down and go to sleep. She'd only be able to sleep five hours, but that was better than nothing.

Dean had other plans. Exhilarated from the success of the evening, he was waiting for Grace when she got out of her shower. Grace wrapped her hair and opened the bathroom door and was dismayed when she saw Dean laying on the bed, wearing only his boxers, with his hands behind his head.

"Tonight went well, don't you think?" Dean asked as Grace walked to the bed and pulled the covers back.

"I told you it would, didn't I?" she asked casually as she slipped into bed.

"Yes, you did. You sure did." He ran his hand up and down her leg.

With her back turned to him, she cringed. They'd been intimate more than usual within the last few weeks, and it had been decent, but tonight she was absolutely not in the mood. She was exhausted and just wanted to go to sweet sleep. But she already knew the consequences of saying no. In the past, when Grace was actually interested in sex with her husband, it was perfectly acceptable for Dean to turn Grace down if he were tired, and she wasn't allowed to get upset, but if the tables were turned, all hell would break loose. Not only would Dean pout and go down to the den and watch porn, he would also remind Grace that she was not doing her duty as a godly wife. "I'll be tempted to go get it elsewhere!" was his favorite go-to threat if ever Grace had the gall to be tired or just not in the mood.

So Grace gave in. Not only did she give in, she pretended to be an enthusiastic participant, trying to get it over with fast so she could go to sleep. When it was finally over, Dean was satisfied. Grace was too--satisfied that she could finally go to sleep.

It was rare for Grace to ever groan when the alarm clock woke her on a Sunday morning, but it was also rare for her to stay up past ten o'clock on a Saturday night. Grace was so tired after Rev. Riley's party that she hadn't wasted a single moment dreaming. Instead, she'd lapsed right into an almost coma-like sleep.

The girls were little crab apples too. The only person who was particularly pleased about the impending church service was Dean, and Grace knew why--because Rev. Riley would more than likely single him out for his good work on the celebration party again.

As her Sunday school charges filed into her classroom, Grace couldn't help but smile at how crotchety they all were. No one had gotten enough rest, and the way they slunk into the room was kind of endearing. Grace knew she had to do something to keep them engaged that day. She came up with a quick idea to get them moving.

Grace went to her desk and removed a roll of Scotch tape from the top drawer. She dragged a chair to a corner in the back of the room, stood on it, and placed a piece of tape up on the wall. When she got down, she put the chair back in her place and said, "Everybody line up."

They obliged.

"I want to see if anyone can reach that piece of tape."

Giggling, the kids all took multiple turns trying to jump as high as they could to reach the tape. The only one who got remotely close was David, who was the tallest person in the class, but even he came up short.

After instructing the kids to get back to their desks, Grace said, "None of us made the cut. Did you guys catch that? We all fell short, right?"

Looking around at each other, the kids nodded in agreement. They were wide awake now.

"That is the central idea of our lesson today," Grace said. "Based on the Scriptures in Romans 3:23, we will be discussing that we're all sinners, we've all fallen short of the glory of God, and with that being said, we want to recognize a few things: One, that salvation is a free gift from God that is not based on anything that we have done, and two, since we've all fallen short, we cannot act as though we are better than someone else simply because they may sin *differently* than we do. Has everyone found today's lesson in your workbooks?"

Grace waited until pages stopped turning to continue. "If you guys look at your first activity, it is asking you to number the sins listed--murder, stealing, lying, oppressing others, and idolatry--with number one being the sin you think is the worst, and number five being the sin that you think is the least. The idea here is that the sin you pick is the worst is the one that you think deserves the harshest punishment from God. I'll give you a few minutes." She went to her laptop and pulled up an snippet of the music from *Final Jeopardy*. The kids laughed and got to work. They looked up eagerly when the music went off, signaling that the activity had come to an end.

"Let's go around the room and see what everyone thinks."

A lively discussion ensued as the students discussed and debated their viewpoints. Grace noticed that David hadn't said a single word since the start of the activity. "David?" she asked gently. "Would you like to share your thoughts?"

He shrugged, looking slightly embarrassed. "I didn't put what anyone else put."

"That's okay. I'd still like to hear what you think."

"I gave them all a one," he replied. "I don't think that any sin is worse or better than any other. I think all sins are sins."

Grace stood up and applauded. "Well, that's the end of the lesson today!" she declared, throwing her hands up in the air. David grinned sheepishly. "Class, David is absolutely right. You know how in our court system, crimes are often graded? For example, there is first-degree manslaughter, second-degree manslaughter, etcetera? First-degree is always the worst, and that comes along with a harsher punishment. The same system does not exist with God and sin. In God's eyes, there are no degrees to sin. If something goes against what God would have one do, it is a sin, and according to our Bible, the wages of sin is death."

David perked up. "Is that true, though?" he asked. "Because I can admit to doing plenty of sinning and I'm still alive."

"Great question," Grace said with a smile. "The type of death being referred to here is spiritual death. Broken fellowship with God and all of the negative feelings that come along with sinning, if you are a Christian--guilt, shame, all of those things. And eventually, if a person who claims to be a Christian continues on in sin, God may bring him or her home earlier than originally planned."

David looked troubled.

"David?" Grace prodded. "Is all this talk about death bothering you?"

He put his head down and shrugged, his arms folded across his chest.

"Because you have nothing to worry about," Grace reminded him. "If you have accepted Jesus as your Lord and Savior, death is not the end of it all--it's just a new eternal journey. It's nothing to fear. If you think about it, it's nice to know that there's a much better place than this waiting for us."

David pondered this information and said, "Can another person's sin make you fall out with God?"

Grace cocked her head to the side in thought. "I'm not really sure," she said slowly. "Can you give me an example?"

"Let's just say that you know someone has done something bad and you don't tell anybody. Will God be mad with you? Does that make you a bad person?"

Grace was slightly concerned. She wondered if perhaps David was trying to tell her something without really telling her. Was he in trouble at school? Possibly hanging with the wrong crowd? "I don't believe it makes you a bad person at all," she finally said. "But do I think God approves? No. I can give you a personal reference." She sat in her chair and pulled it closer to the students. "When I was eighteen, I got tied up with a group of people who by society's standards were bad people. In my opinion, they were just people who had been dealt a bad hand in life and needed help. Either way it goes, this group was in the practice of stealing from other people. At first, I wasn't into it, but I was usually around when they did it. Now that I look back, I feel guilty because who knows if the wallet that was taken had someone's last ten dollars in it? Even worse, after awhile of being around that group, I started stealing myself."

"You?" David asked incredulously, his eyes wide. "I can't imagine you doing anything wrong, Miss Grace."

She laughed. "Oh, David. If only you knew. Yes, I do things wrong even now. We all do. It's called being human. God gave us this pesky thing called free will, and sometimes we abuse it. We're never going to achieve perfection on this earth, and neither are the people around us. And because we all have things we've done that we're ashamed of, and because we all have flaws, we have no business trying to look down upon someone who is just as human as we are. At the end of the day, even if we think a person is not worthy of Jesus because of their sin, God can take that person and use them to do marvelous things. If you look through your Bibles, you will find that every last one of those major Biblical figures that we learn about was a regular, flawed person."

"Were any of them murderers?" David asked, his curiosity piqued.

"Absolutely. Moses was a murderer, for starters."

"Really?" David squawked.

Grace was happy to yield to David's zeal about this information that was obviously new to him. She instructed the class to turn in their Bibles to Exodus chapter two so they could read the story.

The class was over too soon. The students stood up and gathered up their workbooks, exhilarated, and put their materials away. All of them raced upstairs to the sanctuary for the summary session. Except David.

Grace was straightening up her desk and hadn't noticed that David was still in the room. When she turned around to head upstairs herself, she gasped. "Oh, Lord Jesus," she said, placing her hand over her rapidly beating heart. "I thought the room was empty. You scared me!"
"Sorry," David said ruefully.

"I'm glad you stuck around," Grace said, leaning up against her desk. "Is everything okay? You're not in some kind of trouble, are you?"

David hesitated.

"I just want you to be safe and stay out of trouble," Grace said, putting her hand on his arm. "Is there anything you want to talk to me about?"

He shrugged. "Nah, it's not a huge deal," he lied. "I know a person who keeps up a bunch of trouble, and maybe I should do a better job at trying to convince that person that what she--I mean he--is doing is wrong."

Grace definitely noticed that David had said "she" first, so she knew that he was covering for a girl. "Is this person planning on hurting other people or herself... himself?"

"No," David lied again.

"Unfortunately, David, there will always be people out there trying to convince you to go along with the ways of the world, to think only of themselves, and to do awful, selfish things. In most cases I would encourage you to stay away from those types of people so they don't bring you down with their mess, but I would also admonish you to lead by example. Try to talk to that person and not only tell her that what she is doing is wrong, it can also get her in big trouble, and that you care about her and don't want to see that happen. Whether or not she listens is on her. In the meantime, you being a Christian, you always have to take the higher moral road, even if it's not popular or convenient."

David nodded slowly, his eyes downcast. "Thanks, Miss Grace."

"My pleasure." She watched as he jogged up the steps to the sanctuary.

Church service was eventful as well. Rev. Riley and the deacons usually prayed before service in his office. As they were doing so, five sharply-dressed burly young men who had been coming to Christ First and sitting in the pews with the rest of the congregation for the past few weeks walked in and went to the front of the room. Grace wondered who they were--they'd never joined the church. She was even more confused when they sat behind the pulpit, a place that was typically reserved for other ordained ministers. Grace knew it was wrong to judge a book by its cover, but none of them looked particularly minister-ly.

Before he began his sermon, Rev. Riley instructed for Dean and Grace to stand so that they could be applauded for the job they did coordinating the anniversary celebration. "I don't really see how that one can be topped," Rev. Riley quipped. "Did y'all see that horse that brought us in? And wasn't that PhotoBooth fun? I was in there taking pictures like I was Denzel Washington! And sweet Jesus, that *food*! Did we eat like kings, or what?" Dean beamed with pride as random smatterings of conversation erupted throughout the sanctuary.

It was good that Rev. Riley had pumped Dean's ego up before he got to his next order of business. He cleared his throat. That was his way of telling the congregation to be quiet.

"I'm sure you all have noticed these men around the church," Rev. Riley said, gesturing to the five men in question. "I think it's about time for me to formally introduce them to you. This is Byron Pipkins, Aaron Wolf, Daquan Madden, Montez Sawyer and Keith Sanders. I have been mentoring these young men of God, and they are going to be our associate ministers."

The congregation began to murmur among themselves. Rev. Riley held up a hand to silence them.

"It is my job as an aging pastor to give back," he said. "It is my duty to help and train these young brother preachers, and I expect that all of my members will welcome them with open arms in the name of Jesus. Every now and then one of them might bring the message. Other than that, their main job here will be to assist me and to learn how to appropriately tend to a flock."

They need to go somewhere else if they're trying to learn that, Grace thought witheringly.

On the front pew, the deacons were completely blindsided. In the past, when Rev. Buckley had considered bringing a new minister in, even if it was just for training purposes, he asked the deacons for their thoughts and prayers on the matter. And now here was Rev. Riley, bringing in not one, but *five*? And what pastoral duties would they be "assisting" with? It was the deacon's job to assist the pastor.

After church, Curtis gathered the deacons and said, "Did any of you know about this?"

All of them shook their heads.

"But you know what," Tyler said slowly, "Theo did ask me to sign off on a check for Byron last week."

All heads turned to him. "For what?" Allen demanded.

"I was told that Byron had done some work on the roof," Tyler said, his voice full of doubt.

As if on cue, Theo Branch, one of the trustees that handled the church's financial matters, approached the group with a check in his hand and a pen. "Can I get one of you to sign this, please?"

The group crowded around and peered at the check. It was made out to Keith Sanders in the amount of $300. "Why is he getting a check?" Allen thundered.

Theo, looking put-upon, realized that he had walked into a hostile situation. "Rev. Riley requested it," he said uncomfortably. "He said that Keith's been doing some work around the church."

"We need to talk to Riley," Allen said grimly.

"Do what you have to,'" Theo said, "but in the meantime, can one of you sign this, please? I don't want to deal with whatever it is you guys are into right now."

Dean took it from him and signed his name. "Thank you," Theo muttered as he raced back to the trustee's office.

Rev. Riley's door was closed. Patrick knocked. Byron opened it and stood in the way. "Yes?" he said curtly.

Patrick was taken aback by his tone. "We need to see Rev. Riley."

Rev. Riley came flying out the office. "Sorry deacons, it's going to have to wait. I have a dinner reservation and I can't be late," he called over his shoulders. The five associates trailed behind him. The deacons watched as Keith ducked into the trustee's office to collect his check.

"Have all of those guys been getting checks?" Dallas demanded.

Together, they walked to the trustee's office. Theo and Earlene Smith were preparing to lock the door. They did not look pleased when they saw the group of grim-faced men approaching.

Theo sighed.

"Have we been paying those guys?" Andre asked.

Theo looked miserable. "Look, guys. I know Rev. Riley is a lot different from Rev. Buckley, but he is still the pastor and I trust that he knows what he is doing."

"Have we been paying them?" Andre barked.

Earlene spoke up. "All five of 'em," she said airily. "Rev. Riley claims that they're all down on their luck so he has been letting them do odd jobs around the church so they can get paid a little money."

"Have they all been getting three hundred bucks?" Tyler asked.

"Every Sunday for the past four weeks now," Earlene replied. It was obvious that she had her reservations about Rev. Riley's motives. She was all too pleased to tell the deacons everything she knew.

"Guys, it's not like the church can't afford it," Theo defended. "Rev. Riley has done a great job at getting people in here. That's why I'm not too worried about this."

"You should be," Curtis snapped. "Sweet Jesus, Theo, why didn't you say anything? This doesn't strike you as odd? You were here when Rev. Buckley was. Do you ever remember him being involved with the church's finances?"

Theo dropped his head. "I just don't think it's my place to tell the man what to do with his church."

"It's not *his* church, it's *our* church!" Allen corrected him. "And we all have a right to decide where the money that we give to the church goes, and I for one don't want twelve hundred bucks of it going to some man's pocket every month!"

"Well, what do you want *me* to do about it?" Theo said hotly.

Allen and Theo argued back and forth for a few minutes before Curtis held up his hands. "Fellas, fellas," he said, "let's get back to a calm place, okay? Theo, if I came off strong, I apologize, my brother. My frustration is not with you."

Theo sighed. "Apology accepted, Curt."

"I'm sorry too," Allen said gruffly. "I just don't trust this pastor. Not one bit." He pulled out his cell phone and dialed a number. Someone answered. "Rev. Riley?" Allen said coldly. "This is Allen from the church. Now, you left out of here in a hurry, and we had something very important we needed to ask you about!"

The other deacons plus Theo and Earlene watched as Allen fell silent, listening to Rev. Riley's response. Allen held the phone out at arm's length and motioned for the group to come in closer. He then put it on speakerphone.

"What's so pressing that it couldn't wait?" Rev. Riley asked. The agitation in his voice was apparent. There was loud music--not the gospel kind either--and plenty of talking in the background.

"We wanted to ask you about these five guys that you done brought up in here and handing out money to. That's what couldn't wait," Allen snapped. "Does the congregation know that their money is paying for these people?"

"Deacon, don't you get out of line," Rev. Riley warned, his voice rising an octave. "I thought I made it perfectly clear why I brought these men in. It's *my* decision and I have every right to bring these young brothers in for training. As for the money, these fellows are down on their luck. Just between us, they have had legal problems in the past that make it problematic for them to get decent jobs and they're struggling a bit. Instead of just handing them some cash, I thought it'd be better to at least make them earn the money. Wouldn't you agree? Isn't it our job to help our fellow brothers? Would you rather they starve, Allen?"

"Of course not," Allen barked. "But why wasn't this brought to our attention beforehand?"

"Because I didn't need your help making the decision," Rev. Riley told him. "And maybe those guys don't want the entire church knowing they're having money problems. With all due respect, Allen, everything that I do for this congregation is not your business. Now I'm here at the restaurant, and I am about to go eat. Have a good day, Allen."

He hung up. Allen was furious.

After several seconds of collective stunned silence, Tyler spoke. Dean rolled his eyes."I don't have a good feeling about this," he said. "I mean, did you hear all that noise in the background? He's probably with those guys right now. They're enjoying Sunday dinner on the church's dime."

As soon as his nemesis finished talking Dean had a rebuttal. "Don't crucify me, but I see Rev. Riley's point. We can't have it both ways. Either we want to help people as a church or we don't. It's safe to say that it's better for the church financially to have these guys working for us as opposed to just taking a handout, right? And it was our fault that the Helping Hands fund that we used to have, the one that was specifically for congregants facing financial distress, is gone. We convinced Rev. Riley to roll that money into the general fund. Remember?"

Allen threw his hand up in Dean's face in disgust.

Curtis patted Allen's arm. "I think we should see how this plays out before we get our panties into a bunch," he joked. "Let's all just go home and enjoy the rest of our Sunday. Who's watching the game?"

The guys parted after friendly banter. On their way home, Grace asked, "'Did you know that Riley was going to do that?"

Dean shrugged her off. Just like the rest of the deacons, he didn't appreciate being left out of the loop, and despite his defense of Rev. Riley, he wasn't so sure that these five guys wouldn't infringe on his territory. It was natural for Dean to be bothered any time a new male came into the fray. Had he not been so vested in remaining in constant opposition to Tyler, he would have agreed that paying the five guys seemed suspicious. Regardless, Dean was getting a bit tired of Grace's prodding. She was questioning him more than she should have been. Dean also didn't appreciate that she was now so comfortable that she had all but abandoned the rules he used to govern their home. The common areas of the house remained pretty spotless, but numerous times he came home and found the basement in disarray, the towels not perfectly lined up and streaks on the appliances. Those things, those little things, drove him nuts. Each time he saw them his blood boiled and he had to step back and try to pray through it. It didn't help that the washing machine was now making a weird clunking noise, and Dean was pretty sure it was going to be something that wasn't easily or cheaply fixable.

The prayers didn't seem to be as effective as they first were, and Dean had had to remove himself from Grace's presence on several occasions to avoid hitting her.

Dean was also growing bored by his new clean life. Now that Grace was a bit more willing in the bedroom, their sex life wasn't as bad as it used to be, but she was no comparison to Angelica. Angelica, passionate, vivacious Angelica, who wasn't afraid to try much of anything if it came to pleasing her man--bringing toys, costumes and even other women into the bedroom.

Dean dreamed of her every night. Sometimes he even dreamed of her when he was intimate with Grace.

Dean was trying to be a more hands-on father, and that included him dropping the girls off at school and staying for their morning assembly several times over the past few weeks. The younger girls, who were a lot more forgiving than Eve, were happy to walk into the school holding his hand and couldn't wait to show him to their classmates--nobody had ever seen him. Eve, who had seen more and been the brunt of Dean's anger more than her sisters, was a harder nut to crack, and although she hung back from Dean during the first few days of his transition, within a week and a half she finally let herself go and allowed herself to enjoy having a Dad.

When he got off work, Dean was always physically and emotionally exhausted and wanted nothing more than a hot shower and to eat his dinner in the den with the television on ESPN. That's not what he got. As soon as he walked in the door, five little girls met him, talking all at once about what had happened during their day--who got kicked out of class, who moved their card, the grade they made on their test, who made what team, blah blah blah. Truth was, and Dean knew it was horrible, is that he simply wasn't interested. He was sure he looked as tired as he felt. But they didn't care.

By Christmas, Dean's temper was on its way to getting the best of him, and he tried to shut it down by disengaging a bit. It was hard. He was bored, he was sexually frustrated, and to top it off, Grace had spent way too much of his money on gifts for the girls. He had managed to scrape up enough money to get her Suburban back, but it had set him back a bit. On Christmas morning, Dean sat in his armchair and looked on, emotionless, as his daughters opened their gifts, squealing with happiness. Even when they came to him and threw their arms around him, he responded with annoyance. They made him spill his coffee.

After they finished opening their gifts, Dean retreated to the master bathroom to take a shower and think. Mentally, he was empty. He didn't feel anything at all. He wasn't necessarily sad, but he definitely wasn't happy either. He felt like a shell of himself, and he didn't like it. In the shower, he continued his brooding, growing angrier by the minute. Why was he the only one expected to sacrifice? Why was it his responsibility to change for the better but okay for Grace to get worse? Grace had blown almost an entire paycheck on gifts for Christmas and he hadn't gotten much in return. It was him going to work everyday, dealing with a bunch of jerks, and for what? To come home to an unkempt house, a frumpy wife, and self-absorbed daughters who couldn't even let him sit down for five seconds before deluging him with brainless anecdotes about their day? What about *his* day? *What about him?*

CHAPTER TEN

"And he walked in all the sins that his father did before him, and his heart was not wholly true to the Lord his God, as the heart of David his father." (1 Kings 15:3)

Grace knew that Dean's transition had been too swift and too good to be true.

His detached behavior on Christmas was very concerning. There was a faraway look in his eyes, and the only time he showed emotion was when the girls jumped on him after they opened their gifts and spilled two drops of his precious coffee. Other than that, Dean was acting very strangely, and Grace knew his deportment all too well.

She tried to adjust her own behavior to head off any type of relapse. The day after Christmas, Dean got up early to check out the after-Christmas day sales, something he did each year, alone. While he was gone, Grace ran about the house painstakingly checking the towels, the appliances, the floors, every nook and cranny that might have the one blemish that would send him over the edge.

Unfortunately, her meticulousness was not the tipping point.

When Dean returned that afternoon he was in an even worse mood, having been bumped in the back and the ankles by overzealous shoppers who hadn't even bothered to apologize as they carelessly navigated their way through the aisles of Target and Best Buy multiple times. He'd been hoping the shopping trip would calm his nerves, but it didn't. He went into the bedroom and lay across the bed, hoping Grace would leave him alone.

She didn't. Minutes after he'd gotten himself comfortable, she barged into the bedroom and started talking.

"I had an idea I wanted to run past you," she said lightly. "What do you think of possibly taking the girls to that new water park while they're on Christmas vacation? I mean, things have been going pretty well, and we've never had a proper family vacation…"

Dean sat up and cut her off. "And why do you think we've never had a 'proper family vacation'?" he asked.

Grace backed up. The familiar snarl had returned. She knew what that meant. "I…it was just a thought."

"It's easy to have 'thoughts' when you're not the one who has to pay for it," Dean snapped. "Were you thinking at all when you bought all those presents?"

Grace's eyebrows went up in surprise. "I did what you said. I only spent $100 on each of the girls."

"Bull," Dean barked. "You know how I know you're lying? You didn't show me any receipts. Where are the receipts?"

"Dean, I did offer to show you the receipts. If you want, I still have them."

"Go get them. Right now."

Her heart racing, Grace went to the file cabinet in their walk-in closet and found the receipts from the gifts. She handed them to Dean and started to leave the room.

"Stay here," he ordered her.

Grace's eyes filled with tears as she watched him go over each and every purchase, mentally adding everything up in his head as he went. Although she had stayed within the budget he'd given her, she knew that when Dean was in this bad a mood, he was going to find some reason to take his anger out on her. She uttered a quick prayer to God, asking that He would give Dean the strength to walk away before his behavior got out of control.

For whatever reason, the prayer went unanswered. Dean got up, flew across the room and slapped her in the mouth with all his might. She stumbled and fell to the floor.

"No, no, no no!" Grace wailed. "Why? Why?"

"Every last one of these receipts shows that you went over $100!"

"I did not!" Grace protested. "What are you talking about?"

One by one, Dean read the totals off the receipts and threw them down on her. "One hundred three dollars and twenty-two cents… A hundred and one dollars and fifteen cents here…"

"But Dean, that was the tax that put the stuff over one hundred dollars! I stayed under!"

"I didn't ask for you to get smart!" he shouted. "I *told* you to keep it under one hundred for each of them. Do you know how hard I work to pay for all this stuff? Do you even care what I go through for you to just spend money like water? And then you had the *audacity* to come in here and suggest I take y'all on a vacation?"

"You promised," Grace said tearfully. "You said you wouldn't hit me anymore."

"I said I'd *try*," Dean barked. "I did try. I tried to do better, but as soon as I did, you started doing worse. I'm not going to change who I am so you'll have an excuse to be a lazy, fat, self-centered pig. I'm not happy with the way things have been around here. I don't know what to tell you. I can't live like this. And I won't. Not in *my* house."

He stalked out of the room and went downstairs to the den. He slammed the French doors hard enough that the entire house shook.

Humiliated, Grace sat on the floor with her head in her hands. She remained there, in that position for hours, barely flinching when she heard the kitchen door open and slam shut. Dean had left. Only then did she snap back into reality. Undoubtedly the girls had heard the argument, and she hadn't fed them. Grace scrambled to her feet and checked their bedrooms. They weren't there.

Sighing, Grace went to the basement and found them tucked into their hiding places of old. Seeing them back in their safe zones grieved her greatly. One by one she coaxed them out. Abby was the last to come out. When she did, Grace held all five of her daughters in her arms and fought the urge to cry as she did her best to comfort them.

"I'm sorry you had to hear that," she said soothingly, wiping away tears and smoothing mussed hair. "Daddy's been under a lot of stress, and sometimes grownups don't always handle stress appropriately. We have to pray for him and his strength…"

"He hit you, didn't he?" Eve interrupted.

Grace closed her eyes, inhaling deeply.

"That's all the answer I need," Eve told her sharply. "We're not interested in hearing any excuses for his behavior. It won't mean anything, because everything is going to go right back to the way it was, and you know why? Because at the end of the day he doesn't care if we're happy. At all." She turned around and raced up the stairs.

The other girls stared at Grace dejectedly.

"Are things really going to go back to the way they used to be?" Naomi asked in a small voice.

Grace forced herself to smile a little. "I think this was just a minor setback," she told Naomi, trying to convince herself of the same. "Your father has gotten really used to dealing with bad feelings in a certain way, and you know the saying…old habits die hard. It's going to take some time for him to get into a good habit."

"But does that mean he is going to hit you and be mean to us until he learns the good habits?" Sarah wondered.

Grace found this last question hard to answer. She didn't want the girls to be worried, but she didn't want to lie to them either. In her heavy heart, she knew that the peace that had permeated their home for the last month and a half had met its abrupt and tragic end. Dean had been simmering for the last few days. The condition of the house wasn't the major problem. Grace knew even if the house had been in pristine condition Dean still would have found a reason to explode. He had a problem, plain and simple. And Grace was confident that Dean would resist any further interventions.

That fast, with one encounter between husband and wife, the Hardaway home returned to its former acrimonious atmosphere.

While the other girls responded with disappointment, Eve was exceedingly angry. She was angry at Dean for getting their hopes up that they just might have a normal family for once and reverting back to his old self; angry with Grace for being so stupid as to think Dean was capable of making such a change and weak enough to allow the abuse to happen; and even angrier with herself for letting her guard down and trusting the dirtbag in the first place. Dean had made a total fool of her, and she didn't appreciate it. Eve was suspicious when Dean had first made his apparent turnaround--it came out of nowhere, and it was way too fast of a transformation. She doubted his authenticity from the beginning, but deep down inside, she was like any other girl. She wanted attention and approval from her father. And when she finally started getting it for the first time in her life, it felt good.

Eve was dealing with quite a bit of pressure. She was a late bloomer--most of the girls in her grade had had breasts and hips for years and were quite comfortable with them. Eve was just now beginning to develop a shape, and it made her self-conscious--especially when she found out that the boys were paying attention as well. Eve wasn't about to tell either of her parents that some of her peers were already sexually active and she had been teased because she wasn't. The last part wasn't a problem. Eve also wasn't about to tell her parents that she had slapped and punched a couple girls as well as a couple of guys for running their mouth about what she would and would not do. Because she never backed down from a physical altercation, Eve had developed a reputation for being tough, and after her first handful of skirmishes no one else really had much to say about her.

When Dean first expressed what she thought was a sincere interest in getting to know her, he'd taken her to Tim Horton's for breakfast. Both of them were nervous at first, but Dean knew it was his responsibility to engage his oldest daughter in conversation. After all, their detachment was his fault. As he stared at her across the table, Dean noticed how much alike they looked. Out of all five girls, Eve resembled him the most. He almost smiled as he stared into the cold, hard face that mirrored his own.

"I played myself, Eve," he told her softly. "I was just looking at you and I realized how much you look like me. And I know there's a lot about us that is alike. And I haven't taken time to get to know it."

Eve didn't say anything. She took a sip of her orange juice.

"I know rebuilding what I've destroyed will take time," he continued. "But I thought this would be a nice start."

Still nothing.

"You didn't want anything except that orange juice?" Dean pressed. "No coffee, no breakfast sandwich, no doughnut, nothing?"

Eve hesitated. "Am I allowed to have coffee?"

"I don't see why not," Dean said, flustered. "Here. Take my card up there and order whatever you want."

He held the card out to her. She stood up and looked at it.

"Go on," Dean urged.

Slowly, she took the card and went to the register. Dean watched as she mumbled her order to the cashier and waited. While she did so, an older guy in a faded blue hoodie and an unshaven, sunken in face, that was standing behind Eve said something to her. Eve turned around and frowned at him. Before he knew it, Dean was out of his seat, rushing over to her. He placed himself between Eve and the man and said coldly, "May I help you?"

"No…no… everything is cool," the man stammered, backing up.

"What did you say to my daughter?"

"I was just joking with her, man," the guy insisted. "I asked her if she could spot me a doughnut, that's all."

"She doesn't look twelve to you?" Dean snarled.

"Look man, I'm sorry," the man replied, backing away toward the door. "I didn't mean any harm. I think I'll just go."

Eve looked at Dean with a newfound respect, although she was still suspicious. He had cleared the entire room in less than two seconds. Dean waited for Eve to get her order and they returned to their table together.

"So maybe you do like me," Eve said listlessly.

"You're my kid. I love you."

"You don't act like it."

"I just don't know how to relate to little girls, Eve," Dean said helplessly. "I know that's not a decent excuse, but it's the truth. And I really don't know what role I can play in your life as you grow into a young lady."

"Stop worrying about defining a role and just be my dad. How about that? I'm sure if you just chilled out with us more often, you'd find something about all of us that you actually liked. We're not boring little girly-girls all the time, you know."

It was an extremely impactful statement for a pre-teen to make. Dean watched as she sipped her coffee, her eyes on him the entire time. She was absolutely right. He spent so much time fretting over how to interact with his daughters, finding reasons not to engage with them, over-thinking everything. And for what? His attention, positive attention, was sufficient.

Now, as she reflected back on their breakfast date, Eve's agitation amplified. She had finally allowed herself to get comfortable with Dean, and he had betrayed her. Never again would she allow him to toy with her emotions.

The washing machine finally gave up the ghost.

A repairman came to the house and pronounced it dead when Dean got off work. Grace watched, her eyes wide, as the repairman provided Dean with an estimate of how much it would take to fix the machine. Dean's eyes grew wide as well as he examined the obviously high number. On his way out the door, the repairman told Dean, "You're better off getting a new one, sir."

Dean stomped back into the house, swearing under his breath, and as soon as he found Grace, he advanced upon her with a series of slaps. It didn't matter that the repairman had informed Dean that the machine was old and that it had lasted longer than similar machines. All Dean cared about was the fact that Grace had caused yet another expense and he was going to have to come up with money that he didn't have, *again.*

It also didn't matter that it wasn't Grace's fault that Dean didn't have the money. After paying off the remaining debts incurred from Rev. Riley's lavish anniversary celebration with his Christmas bonus, Dean had used the rest to book a Presidential Suite for himself and Angelica at the Belamere Suites Hotel in Perrysburg, Ohio, an hour away. It was there he spent New Year's. He told Grace that he was getting a room in Ann Arbor by himself because he needed to think. She knew better, but said nothing. She and the girls spent the evening having a wonderful party by themselves, cooking appetizers and mini-cheesecakes, decorating wine glasses with paint and glitter, and blending fruit daiquiris to pour into the glasses. They toasted in the New Year with their freshly-painted masterpieces and blended concoctions, then blew their noisemakers and danced around the house. Grace was actually glad Dean was gone.

The girls had a couple of weeks off school for winter break. All of them had been dreading it, as it meant more time stuck in the house with their feuding parents. And church. On one hand, church was one of the few ways they were guaranteed to get out of the house, but the girls, especially Eve, were getting increasingly fed up with the roles they were expected to play. They were tired of the superficiality of the church. Eve and the older twins were becoming more aware of the dysfunction within the church and they were not impressed. Each time Eve watched one of the adults smile in the face of another church member and then turn around and talk about him (or her), she grew angry. She was tired of fake people. The only bright spot of winter vacation was January 6th when Eve turned thirteen. Dean actually let her get a mani-pedi and Grace cooked her favorite dinner and a delicious ooey-gooey birthday cake.

David was on winter break as well, and Dean spent the vast majority of his time with him...well, actually, Angelica. For the first couple of days Dean came over right after work and ate dinner with them. During dinner the evening of his first day of winter vacation, Dean asked David about his problems, but David wasn't necessarily interested in involving his mother in the conversation so he kept quiet, hoping that he could speak with Dean privately after dinner. Unfortunately, Dean and Angelica took their dessert and went upstairs to her room for the remainder of the night. David was upset, but shrugged it off. When it happened the next three consecutive days, he realized he'd been played like a fiddle. Dean wasn't coming around to be with him. He was lucky to get a ten-minute conversation with Dean as he stood in the doorway to David's room before disappearing into Angelica's room. The time Dean spent with David grew shorter in duration and frequency and after Dean's and Angelica's trip to Belamere, nonexistent. David's hatred for Dean and his mother magnified. He knew his mother well enough to deduce that she had effectively used him as bait to lure Dean back in and away from Miss Grace, and of course Dean was stupid enough to fall for it. To think he knew everything, he had to be one of the dumbest dudes David had ever met. David was looking forward to Angelica dealing with Dean. He deserved whatever he had coming to him.

David didn't know, but his rage toward Dean was matched by Eve. While Dean was away, she was able to ease into a small sense of happiness and security, only to have it dashed away by the sound of his footsteps. She hated him. Absolutely, absolutely hated him.

It had been a hectic Monday so far. The girls moved like molasses throughout their morning routine, causing their typically even-keeled mother to snap at them several times. Additionally, several inches of snow had accumulated overnight, making for a fairly treacherous journey to Cornerstone Christian Academy. Grace passed three accidents on the way and narrowly avoided one of her own. For some reason, although it was easy to surmise that most of the drivers on the road were native Michiganders who should have been accustomed to navigating snowy roads, everyone seemingly had forgotten how to drive defensively during the warmer months. A man attempted to speed past her in his Ford F250, momentarily lost control of the huge truck when he hit an ice slick and almost swerved into their SUV. The girls screamed as Grace reflexively turned the wheel to avoid the potential accident. A word escaped Grace's lips that she thought she had banished from her vocabulary years ago. The girls looked at her in shock and amusement, but said nothing about the expletive. By the time they reached Cornerstone and had to rush inside before they were deemed late by the morning bell, Grace was not in a very sociable mood.

Luckily, with it being Monday her required interaction with students, teachers and other parents would be relatively minimal. Mondays tended to be heavy-laden with paperwork. Permission slips, homework packets and fliers for school events had to be copied and stuffed into the kids' take-home folders. Grace hurried the younger girls to their classrooms and raced down the hall with Eve to her homeroom. Mrs. Ledbetter, Eve's homeroom teacher, placed a crate near the classroom door each Monday with the materials that she needed copied. When they got to the classroom, Mrs. Ledbetter was standing next to the crate, apparently waiting on Grace.

"Good morning, Eve," Mrs. Ledbetter said, shaking Eve's hand. "Go on in. I left your morning task on your desk."

"Have a good day, sweetie," Grace said as she prepared to retrieve the crate. "How are you today, Mrs. Ledbetter?"

"I'm good, thanks for asking. May we have a word before you head off?"

"Of course," Grace said, straightening back up. "Is everything okay?"

"I'm afraid not," Mrs. Ledbetter said uneasily. "I didn't want to wait until conferences because this needs to be addressed right now before it escalates. Eve has been very aggressive with her classmates--the boys in particular. I've spoken to all of her former teachers here and they were very surprised. They all informed me that aggressive behavior is not typical of her character, although they did say that Eve is a high-performing student and tends to place a lot of unhealthy pressure on herself. She is very competitive. Up until very recently Eve had the highest grade point average of anyone in her entire class, but it dropped a bit because she's been having some difficulties in math. Very briefly a male student overtook her as having the top GPA, and Eve did not take it too well. He mentioned it in class one day and from what I understand, after class, she pushed him into the lockers. Hard."

Grace swallowed hard. "Anything else?" she asked lightly.

"Eve is also very argumentative with her male classmates. In the event that we have a debate or a question in class and one of her male counterparts provides a point of view that differs from her own, Eve gets angry, and fast. She is just really lashing out at the boys. Now, Mrs. Hardaway, don't get offended, but I must ask. Is it possible that Eve is going through a sexual identity crisis?"

Grace scrunched her face in confusion. "Excuse me?" she asked blankly.

Mrs. Ledbetter looked extremely uncomfortable. "Again, I am not trying to offend you; I want to help Eve any way that I can. I know that these years of a child's life can be very confusing, and these kids are trying to figure out who they are sexually… Considering Eve's overly aggressive behavior, might it be possible that she is trying to work her way through homosexual feelings?"

Grace laughed out loud, causing Mrs. Ledbetter's face to go pale.

"Mrs. Ledbetter," Grace said tersely, "forgive my laughter. It wasn't necessarily at you. I guess I just wasn't prepared for you to say that."

"Mrs. Hardaway, please understand that this entire exchange is just as unpleasant for me as it is for you," Mrs. Ledbetter said, just as tersely. "I am trying to help Eve before her behavior escalates and results in disciplinary action. So far I haven't seen any of her physical aggression; I've only heard of it, and none of the boys she has pushed are willing to rat her out. But if this pattern of behavior continues, we are going to have to treat Eve just like we would any other student in this school. We have high standards for behavior. Whatever Eve is going through, she must learn to control herself, and if she needs help, she needs to ask."

Ashamed of the giggle that had burst through her lips, the severity of the situation finally sank in. A knot began to form in Grace's stomach. She knew the reason why Eve was treating the boys so terribly. She was trying to assert herself; to let them know she wouldn't be walked on—unlike her doormat of a mother at home.

It was all her fault.

Grace felt herself beginning to crumble and knew she had to get away from Mrs. Ledbetter before the tears started flowing.

"As far as I know, Eve likes boys," she said quietly. "We've had many conversations about sex and sexuality. If she was having homosexual desires I'm sure she'd be comfortable enough to come and tell me."

"Would she be accepted if she were?" Mrs. Ledbetter queried.

"I would never turn my back on any of my children, Mrs. Ledbetter."

Mrs. Ledbetter gave Grace a hard stare. "Do you have any idea what the problem may be?"

"No," Grace lied, "but I will find out."

Mrs. Ledbetter gave her a quick nod. "I have to get back to my class. Thanks for your time."

Without another word, Grace picked up her crate and fled the scene. As she dashed down the hall, she prayed that the parent office would be empty, and it was. She set her crate down and raced into the bathroom, locking the door behind her before she slipped to the floor, crying quietly, her head in her hands. Her spinelessness was ruining her baby. All this time, she hadn't given much thought to how their home life was impacting her daughters because they were rarely the recipients of the physical violence. Of course, in her heart of hearts, Grace knew that it wasn't healthy for the girls to see and hear their father beat their mother, but up until the very moment that Mrs. Ledbetter looked her very coldly in the face and asked her if she knew what the problem was, Grace had grown oddly comfortable with making excuses to justify staying with Dean.

As she sat sobbing on the cold floor, Grace berated herself for having been so selfish. Her poor babies. She remembered how she felt when she saw them for the first time, on the ultrasound screen, how happy and hopeful she was. She remembered how joyful she was when Eve was born, her first baby, and how she couldn't stop thanking God for blessing her despite her many faults and failures. As she'd kissed Eve's little nose and brown head, Grace had promised Eve she would be a great mother to her and love her with all the strength in her body.

The tears fell harder and faster as Grace realized that she had broken that promise. Part of being a great mother meant making sure that her children lived in an environment that allowed them to thrive. It wasn't enough that she took the girls to church multiple days throughout the week. How effective were Bible lessons when they weren't being lived out before the girls' eyes? Why would they be interested in hearing sermons about the goodness of God when they were miserable in the one place that should be the embodiment of love, peace and solitude—their home?

Freshly determined, Grace stood to her feet, washed her face in the sink and dabbed it dry with rough brown paper towels. In the parent room, she hurriedly completed her morning copying, found several pieces of paper and a pen, and went to the corner of the room where several telephones were parked.

With trembling hands, Grace picked up the phone and dialed a number that she had memorized years ago but never thought of using—that of the local domestic violence shelter helpline.

A woman with a plucky voice answered. "Safe Haven help line, how may I assist you?"

Her throat was suddenly as dry as the Sahara. Grace swallowed a few times and cleared her throat. "I…uh… I need help. I need to figure out a way to leave my husband."

"Are you in danger right now?"

"No."

"Good, good. Would you like to give me your name, or some way I can refer to you? It doesn't have to be your real name, and let me assure you, everything we discuss today is confidential. No one will know you've called."

"I'm Grace."

"Grace, I'm Jolene. Nice to meet you. I'd be happy to help you today. You're looking to leave your husband. Can you tell me why?"

"He beats me," Grace whispered, looking over her shoulder.

"I'm so sorry. I commend you for realizing you deserve better. I'm sure this was not an easy decision for you to make."

"No, it wasn't," Grace said tearfully. "I've got five daughters. I can't just… pick up and go anywhere."

"Okay, so there are children involved… gotcha." Grace could hear Jolene typing in the background. "It will be no problem for us to accommodate you and your daughters, so don't worry about that, okay? Once you get here, you'll be fine. This place is under tight security day and night, and it cannot be seen from the street. Can you and the girls get here now?"

"I don't think I can come right now."

"Do you need transportation? We can get you picked up."

"No, I have a car… I just…I don't know if I'm ready to leave right this moment…"

"Okay. That's perfectly fine. Let's do some planning so we can get you all here safely when you are ready to leave, okay?"

"'Safely'?" Grace repeated blankly. "Why wouldn't I be safe?"

"I'm sure you know your husband better than I do, and of course I don't want to say anything to scare you from leaving, but I have to provide the information you need to be safe. Leaving can be very dangerous. That is why I want to walk you through some things that will get you here if you commit to it. If you decide not to come here, I still want to help you."

Grace's spirits were momentarily bolstered…and dissipated steadily throughout the conversation despite Jolene's calm and easy demeanor. Jolene asked if Dean had guns. Grace knew he had some, but he had never been truly forthcoming about how many weapons he actually owned. So no, it wouldn't be possible for Grace to make sure the guns weren't loaded, because she didn't know how many there were, and she didn't have access to them.

The conversation was surreal; Grace couldn't even believe she was talking about her husband, her marriage: "Has he ever threatened to kill you or the girls?" "What does he say he will do if you ever left him?" The questions about their finances left her feeling completely powerless: "Is there any way that you could squirrel a little money away to help when you leave?" *No.*

Grace realized she had rugswept many of Dean's previous gaslighting behaviors that were precursors to the impending physical abuse. When Jolene detailed the characteristics of an abusive relationship, it became painfully clear to Grace that her entire relationship with Dean had been abusive. She wasn't aware that emotional abuse was still *abuse*. Grace remembered when they first started dating how Dean used to make her feel guilty for wanting to spend time with her friends from the cooking department. Even if they had nothing more planned than an innocent night of going to Meijer, buying a bunch of random ingredients and trying out recipes for the restaurants, food trucks and catering companies they all planned to own upon graduation, Dean had a problem with it. Usually he would wait until Grace announced her intentions to hang out and angrily inform her that he had planned a romantic date for them, forcing her to choose. In all actuality Dean really didn't have anything planned. He just didn't want her to go out without him.

When they did go out together, he was overprotective and rude to other men who spoke to her. Grace remembered the only night she convinced Dean to come to a party on campus with her. She'd run into many of her male friends from class, and whenever she introduced one of them to Dean, he glowered at them and gave them a handshake with a grip too firm to be considered friendly. When she attempted to make conversation with other women, Dean listened in. Not to contribute to the exchange; to see if he could fish any information out of the women that painted Grace in a bad light to be used as ammunition against her. Embarrassed by Dean's behavior, Grace had ended the night early,

With each scenario Jolene described and each question she asked, Grace's illumination grew. Dean always had excuses for his jealousy and degrading comments. "I just love you so much and the thought of you with someone else bothers me." "I'm just looking out for you because you're a bit naive." "You've been through so much already; I'm just trying to protect you." "It's obvious no one ever taught you this, that's why I have to." "If you leave me I don't know what I'd do. I wouldn't want to live."

When the physical abuse started, it was often followed with gifts, tears, and guilt trips, at least at first. After Dean was comfortable that his control over Grace was firmly established—particularly after all of the girls were born-- the make-up gifts and tears had stopped, although the guilt trips continued. Now it was rare for Dean to apologize. As Jolene pointed out, Grace had internalized that everything wrong in their marriage was her fault, so it was up to *her* to apologize.

It was too much. Grace hadn't thought of the possible danger she might be putting herself and the girls in if she left. There could be the emotional damage associated with making an abrupt exit from the only home they'd ever known only to go to what Grace imagined was an overcrowded shelter with little to no privacy— kind of like the group home she lived in as a teenager. There was the threat of physical violence. Even though Dean didn't care about Grace or the girls, without a doubt he would not be pleased if Grace took the girls and fled. The very thought of what he might do terrified her. He *did* have a cache of weapons and a military background. And when she left, what would she do? She had no money. Not a dime that wasn't somehow attached to Dean. Grace was embarrassed. She had been so willing to be a dutiful Christian wife that she had set herself up for this. Reflecting back, she realized she should have fought harder to keep her cooking career. Dean had her exactly where he wanted her—penniless and powerless.

Other parents were beginning to enter the room. "I can't do this," Grace whispered hoarsely. "I'm sorry."

"You don't have to apologize, Grace," said Jolene soothingly. "I know this is a lot to consider. If you're not ready to leave, that's okay. But can we spend a few minutes hashing out some protective measures in case your husband attacks you again?"

Grace lowered her voice. "Yes, but I won't be able to respond as much. There are other people in the room with me now."

"That's fine. Thanks for letting me know. I'll try to formulate my questions so that all you'll need to say is 'yes' or 'no', okay?"

"Okay."

"Have you ever called the police on Dean?"

"No."

"I know it seems embarrassing and scary, but it would be helpful for when you do decide to leave if there is a paper trail to follow you. If you are not comfortable calling the police, can you possibly document the abuse in other ways? Can you keep a journal with dates and detailed accounts of what happened?"

"Yes."

"Do you have a camera that you might be able to use to take pictures of any bruises or injuries?"

"No."

"If you can get your hands on one, that would be a huge help."

"Okay."

They moved on to ways that Grace could try to be safe if she again came under attack. Some of the measures Jolene described were things she already tried to do. Over the years Grace had become familiar with Dean's actions and behavior before he was about to strike. She would always try to defuse the situation. Jolene encouraged her to leave once she knew that an attack was oncoming. Grace was not about to leave the house without the girls, so that meant getting away from Dean fast enough to go and round up the girls, get her keys and hurry to the garage. It wasn't bound to happen.

Jolene advised Grace to try to get to a safe spot in the home when an attack was impending. Grace tried to avoid arguments in the bathroom and kitchen, since those were the places where she was most likely to bang her head on a counter when she fell. Up until her conversation with Jolene Grace thought the bedroom was the safest room in the house because of the lack of hard surfaces. Jolene encouraged her to try to be in a room or area in the house where she might be able to run and get outside. It was profound. Grace was used to the slaps, punches and kicks. She had never considered that the beatings could get worse.

When Grace mentioned this to Jolene, she replied, "Unfortunately, batterers don't just stop battering. The abuse is likely to escalate. Is there any neighbor that you might be able to involve in your safety plan?"

Grace thought. In her heart she knew she could very well ask Tim to help her. But her humiliation wouldn't let her go there just yet. "I don't know," she said miserably.

"I know asking for help is humiliating. But being momentarily embarrassed is worth the possibility of a safe life for you and your daughters. Remember that, okay?"

"I will."

"You deserve better. Do you believe that?"

It was a question that Grace was unprepared to answer honestly. Over the years she had allowed Dean to convince her that, in light of her past, he was the best she could do. She wasn't confident in her own ability to make even minor decisions, as Dean had convinced her she was stupid and worthless. As she'd gained more and more weight and the abuse and stress took a toll on her physical appearance he'd doubled down on his opinion that she was incapable of finding another man that would be willing to marry her.

Grace wasn't sure that she deserved better.

Jolene sensed her hesitation. "You deserve better," she repeated emphatically. "And so do your children."

A bell rang, startling Grace so much that she almost dropped the receiver. "Oh my goodness, I have to go," she said, flustered. "I have to go help with lunch."

"Call back any time, Grace."

Grace tried unsuccessfully to turn on theatrical auto-pilot mode. Her stratospheric anxiety impeded her ability to concentrate on even the smallest of tasks, and she found herself having to double- and triple-check her work after she found herself stuffing the wrong materials into the wrong folders. She was glad when the day was over until she realized that meant she would have to have an uncomfortable discussion with Eve.

When they got home, Grace made sure the house was presentable and got to work on dinner. "Eve!" she called as she retrieved her potato masher from the drawer. "Come down here, please."

Eve flounced down the stairs and poked her head into the kitchen. "Do you need help?"

"No, baby, I need to talk to you about something."

Eve slid into a kitchen chair, looking uncomfortable. "What?" she said, her voice full of trepidation.

"I was told you haven't been getting along so well with the boys in your grade."

Eve's eyes narrowed. "Who told you that?"

"It doesn't matter. How about we talk about it though?"

Eve shrugged. "Fine."

"You go first."

Eve sighed. "There's not much to talk about. I am not the one to get jerked around by some guy. A couple of them have come at me on some disrespectful mess and got handled. Simple as that."

"No, it's not 'simple as that'. What do you mean, they 'came at you on some disrespectful mess and got handled'?"

"Are you making shepherd's pie?"

"Yes."

"Can you make cornbread too?"

"Yes, Eve. Now, back to what we're talking about. I need to understand what is going on with you and these boys. Do we need to set up some meetings between you and these boys and me and their parents?"

Eve smacked her lips. "That will only make it worse. I don't need your help, Mom. Really. It's not that big a deal."

Grace went to the stove and started browning the lamb. "Are you trying to make sure they know better than to treat you how your father treats me?"

Eve's eyes widened.

"Because if that's what you're trying to do—and I think that's what's happening, whether you're truly aware of it or not—I get it, Eve. I've set a terrible example for you and I know why you don't want to be like me. But you can't take your anger over what goes on here on those guys at school."

"Mom, they are obnoxious."

"Teenage boys tend to be obnoxious." Grace tried to smile reassuringly, but she felt a twinge of disappointment when Eve didn't bother to rebut Grace's deduction that she had set a poor example for her. "Look, Eve…you and those boys are at a weird time in your lives. You're not children, but you're not adults either. Everyone is trying to figure out who they want to be right now, and they're taking cues from other people around them, their parents, television, you name it. Boys are trying to wrap their minds around what being a boy really means. Same goes for the girls."

"I get what you mean," Eve said thoughtfully. "It just seems like they're always doing so much. It's annoying. Even when we're doing something that is not meant to be a boys-versus-girls thing, they turn it into a competition. And I'm not the one for that."

Grace chuckled. "I know you're not, Eve. But listen. I've always taught you not to worry about what other people say or think. You have to measure your behavior up against the standards of God. That's how you keep yourself in check. You can't keep other people from annoying you, but you can choose to respond with dignity. You have to keep yourself under control or else you're going to get in trouble. And you know I don't have much tolerance for you pushing or hitting people unless you are defending yourself."

Eve sighed. "I know."

"So let's wrap this up… Boys are obnoxious, but you have to deal with them better, because the pushing and hitting is not okay. And I know you're a tough little cookie, but if those boys fight you back you might get hurt. Keep your hands to yourself, Eve."

"I will."

"What do you think you'll do the next time a boy annoys you?"

"I'm going to ignore him or laugh in his face, probably." She sighed.

"Okay. Since you're in here, would you mind cutting up some carrots?"

Nodding enthusiastically, Eve reached across the kitchen island for the carrots. As she did so, the sleeves of her medium-length shirt came up a little. When they did, Grace noticed what looked like healed cuts on the lower part of her arms, just beneath her elbows. Her heart sank.

"What happened to your arms?"

Eve straightened up quickly and pulled her sleeves down. "It's nothing."

"Let me see."

Eve dropped her eyes.

"Let me see your arms, Eve."

Miserably, Eve rolled up her sleeves. None of the cuts looked particularly fresh or deep, but it was obvious they had been done deliberately, possibly by a razor. Like her mother, Eve didn't grow much body hair, but early on in the school year she had requested her own package of razors and shaving cream after making the volleyball team and complaining about the microscopic hairs on her legs. Grace had bought her the supplies and taught her how to use them. She could have never expected Eve would use those razors to cut herself.

After watching the color drain from her mother's face, tears filled Eve's eyes. "I didn't want you to see this," she said tearfully.

"I guess I don't need to ask you why," Grace told her despondently. "I'm sorry that I haven't given you the life you deserve, Eve. I know you're unhappy. But please don't hurt yourself. Please."

"I kind of stopped."

"'Kind of'?" Grace repeated. "That's not good enough. Honey, it's so dangerous to cut yourself. You know that. The cuts can get infected, or you can cut a vein, and then you might die, Eve. You understand that?"

A heavy and sudden sob escaped Eve's lips. Grace grabbed her and held her. They cried together.

"I'm going to get us out of here," Grace whispered in her ear. "But can you please not hurt yourself until I figure this out? Please? I want to get us out of here, but I want to do it safely. I talked to someone today and…" She stopped. "I want to do it safely," she repeated.

Eve looked into her mother's eyes and saw a surprising determination that she hadn't seen before. "You talked to somebody?" she asked in a small voice.

"Yes, I did. It was a hard conversation but necessary. I have to get some things together so that when we leave, we will be gone for good. I've gotten myself into a situation where I am completely dependent upon your father and it was a huge mistake. Promise me that when you grow up and fall in love, don't let that quench your sense of independence. Always make sure you have your own. Okay?"

"I'm not going to fall in love, but okay."

Grace smiled a little. "You know I'm taking those razors away, right?"

Eve sniffed and nodded. "Yeah."

"And I'm going to find someone for you to talk to."

Eve sighed. "I don't need counseling, Mom. I need to be free from this house."

Me too, Grace thought as she defiantly chopped up the carrots for dinner. *I have to get my babies out of here. No matter what it takes.*

CHAPTER ELEVEN

"A friend loves at all times, and a brother is born for a time of adversity." (Proverbs 17:17)

Out of nowhere, the dryer died shortly after the washer. Dean was livid. As Grace expected, Dean slapped her a few times and ranted and raved that it was somehow her fault that the fifteen-year-old appliance was no longer working.

"This is your problem," he sneered as she cowered in a ball in a corner in their bedroom. "You get to deal with it. Have fun at the laundromat. I have other things to pay for. I'm not in any rush to go out and get a new washer and dryer because you're too stupid to take care of them. You'll have to convince me that you even deserve a new set!"

It ended up being a dream come true. It was another opportunity for Grace to leave the house for several hours. She pretended that it was a huge inconvenience for her, knowing that if Dean thought it made her life harder for her to go to the laundromat he would drag his feet about replacing the washer and dryer out of spite. Actually, Grace loved going to the laundromat. Grace made a good--and very important--friend during her first trip there.

Being the control freak that he was, even though he had no interest in going to the laundromat or doing anything laundry-related, Dean had to be involved in planning the initial trip to the laundromat. While they were eating breakfast Saturday morning, Dean asked coldly, "When were you planning on getting these clothes washed?"

"Whenever you gave me the okay," she replied quietly.

"I found a place on Whittaker that you can go to. I called there and got the prices for the washers and dryers. This should be enough money for you to do several loads of clothes." Dean pushed some money across the table. "There are machines there for you to get quarters and there is a pizza place close by for you and the girls to get lunch. It shouldn't take you longer than two hours depending on how busy the place is."

The girls looked excited to leave, but contained themselves. After breakfast Grace cleared the table and washed the breakfast dishes. She completed the rest of her Saturday tasks from her checklist and called the girls into her bedroom.

"This is new, I know," she told them with a smile. "I've got a little project for my little helpers. I have laundry bags for each of you to use. Go into your bedrooms and put your dirty white clothes in one of these white bags and your colored clothes in one of these purple bags."

Eve took her bags and ran to her room. The twins took their bags and did the same. In record time they had their clothes sorted and were dragging the bags downstairs.

"Bye, Daddy," they chorused insincerely as they raced into the garage.

He was in the den and hadn't heard them or didn't care to respond. It didn't matter--the girls were only saying bye because they knew they would have hell to pay if they didn't.

Although she knew most people weren't excited by the prospect of using a laundromat, Grace was. It was refreshing to be around other people, even if those people were strangers who weren't paying her a lick of attention. She liked the atmosphere and the bustle around her. The laundromat was a very clean and well-maintained place that even had a play area for children, complete with a flat-screen television that was showing the Nickelodeon channel. There was a corner with refreshments--a popcorn machine, a Keurig with a variety of K-cups, vending machines with chips and candy and another with pop. The owners of this laundromat had thought of everything.

The younger girls made their way to the play area. Eve pulled a book out of her backpack and sat in a chair close by to supervise them while Grace set to work. After she got their clothes into washers, she made her way to the play area to check on her daughters. Eve was engrossed in her book and the younger girls had made friends with a cute blond-haired girl who appeared to be Abby's and Naomi's age. Smiling, Grace sat down and waited for the clothes to finish their wash cycle, taking the time to flip through the magazines that were on the table beside her. *People, Essence, InTouch.* Dean did not allow for such rubbish to be in his home. The only materials Grace could bring in the house to read other than newspapers were books with a Christian focus. She found *Essence* to be pretty engaging. The other magazines, showing photo after photo of some insanely rich celebrity in a huge home or on a beautiful beach of white sand did nothing other than make her jealous.

An hour later all of the clothes were dry. Grace pulled the clothes out of the first dryer, put them in a cart, and wheeled them to a table to fold. As she began her task she caught the gaze of a beautiful blond woman with sparkly blue eyes at the table across from her. Grace smiled politely. The woman grinned.

"I think our daughters have become instant BFFs," she remarked.

Grace looked to the play area, where her daughters and the little blond girl were jabbering away. It was as if they had known each other for years. Grace smiled back. "Looks like they're having quite the conversation," she said.

"It must be pretty good!"

The two continued to fold their clothes uneventfully until a well-dressed woman--dressed too well for an afternoon at the laundromat, complete with pretentiously ornate diamond jewelry and a Michael Kors bag--came into the laundromat, complaining loudly. An iPhone rested in the crick of her neck as she clumsily tried to maneuver one of the laundry carts into the building with one hand. Trailing behind her were three teenagers, two boys and a girl. They were completely engrossed in their iPhones and weren't paying their mother a lick of attention.

"This is absolutely ridiculous," the woman fumed into her phone. "I tell you, Ted might be sleeping on the couch when he gets back. I am in a laundromat right now. Can you believe it? Me, in a *laundromat*! It's the biggest inconvenience of my life!"

Grace looked across her table at the blond woman. They both shook their heads.

As the woman made several trips out to her SUV to collect her laundry, she talked loudly into the phone. It was obvious that she was above coming to the laundromat. Her children had taken seats at the back of the laundromat, apparently trying to distance themselves from their mother as much as possible. Not a single one of them attempted to help her with their clothes.

"I told Ted to get the repairman out to the house before he left, but does he listen?" she shouted into the phone. "That's what happens when you get cheap. How do you have a half-million dollar house and a $1000 washer? If he would have gotten the LG model, but no! And now look. I have these kids' uniforms to wash and all this other stuff and he is in France on business. Luckily for him if he closes this deal he'll get a huge bonus. For this inconvenience I better get half of it!"

The other customers watched as the woman, with her phone glued to her ear the entire time, moaned and groaned about her difficult entitled life as she loaded several washers with clothes. After a very short time it was obvious that the woman was annoying the other customers with her attitude and her children grew embarrassed. They got up and walked past her, heading for the front door.

"Where do you think you're going?" she asked them, almost dropping her phone.

"You need to get a grip, Mom," said the daughter, rolling her eyes. "You're annoying. And you're embarrassing us. We're going to the pizza place."

The woman started to protest. "So none of you are going to stay and wash *your* uniforms?"

The teens exited the laundromat without a word. That burned the woman up even more, and she began to complain about her ungrateful children to whomever the long-suffering individual was on the other end of the line. Grace was hoping it was a therapist. This woman was definitely histrionic.

When Grace was finished folding the final washcloth, she checked her watch. She still had some time before she had to be home. Across from her, the blond woman was finishing up as well. Grace packed the clothes into two carts and loaded them in the SUV. She went back into the laundromat to retrieve her daughters. Naomi met her with a pleading look on her face. "Can we go to the pizza place and get a pizza with Madison?"

Grace's face wrinkled with confusion.

Abby gestured to her new little friend. "Her and her mom are going to get pizza at Jet's. Can we go too? She's our new friend."

Madison's mother walked up and stuck her hand out. "Seems as though our girls made arrangements," she said with an apologetic laugh. "I'm Karen."

"Grace," Grace replied, shaking her hand with a smile. "I guess that's okay. We do need some lunch."

As they headed toward Jet's, Karen asked, "So how did you like the show?"

Again confused, Grace looked at her. "What show?"

"The show Miss Hoity-Toity put on in there," Karen said with a snicker. "She wanted to make sure the rest of us lowly peasants knew that she didn't belong there, didn't she?"

"Oh, gosh yes!" Grace said, laughing. "I really wanted her to shut up."

Karen graciously held the door to Jet's Pizza open as the girls and Grace walked inside. "Thank you," they said politely.

Madison led the way to the front counter. The girls waited while their mothers placed their pizza orders. As they did so, Eve looked around the restaurant and spotted a familiar face. Seated by himself toward the back of the store with an entire pizza in front of him was David Billups.

Eve tapped Grace's shoulder. "Isn't that David?" she whispered.

Grace turned and looked. Surprised, she nodded. "Yes, that sure is David. I wonder if he is here by himself?"

"It certainly looks like it," Eve replied.

"Why don't you be nice and go say hi? See if he would like to sit with us, okay?"

"I'm sure he wants to sit with two old ladies and a bunch of little girls," Eve said witheringly. "I was actually thinking of asking him if I can sit in his booth with him. I'll bet it's a lot quieter."

Grace laughed. "Really? You don't want to sit with us?"

"No," Eve admitted. "They're getting on my nerves." She motioned to her little sisters, who were again chatting loudly with Madison about which Disney princess was their favorite and why.

Grace smiled, shaking her head. "Wait until your order is up. But if David doesn't mind the company…" She shrugged.

Carefully balancing the tray that held her pepperoni pizza and Coke, Eve couldn't get away fast enough. But as she got closer to David's table she started to hesitate. Really, she didn't know him well enough to invite herself to sit at his table. They had seen each other for almost every Sunday for the past five and a half months now, and they often talked to each other in Sunday school and church, but that didn't make them friends—or did it? Eve wanted to stop walking, but when she heard one of her sisters let out a high-pitched giggle, she cringed and kept moving. David was consumed by whatever was on his phone and didn't see her approaching. When she reached his table, Eve said bluntly, "My sisters are annoying and I don't want to sit with them. Mind if I sit here?"

Startled by her presence and candor, David shook his head. "No, go ahead."

Eve set her tray down on the table and slid into the seat across from David. There was awkward silence as they both tried to figure out what to say to each other. Irritated by her own reasonable discomfort, Eve picked up a slice of pizza and started eating.

David felt stupid just sitting there in silence. "So… are y'all just hanging out for your Saturday afternoon?"

Happy that he had gotten the conversational ball rolling, Eve breathed an internal sigh of relief. "We were at the laundromat. What about you? Do you live around here?"

"Yeah, I'm just a short bike ride away. I usually spend Saturdays out this way."

"By yourself?" Eve asked.

David nodded. "Yep. That's kind of how I like it though."

"Must be nice," Eve mumbled witheringly, glancing again at her little sisters, who were still as loud as they had been when they first came in.

"They can't be that bad," David said, chuckling.

Eve shrugged. "Nah, they're okay most of the time. But they depend on me for a lot and sometimes I get tired of it."

"Better than being all by yourself though." David put his head down.

Eve hadn't thought of it that way. He had a point. Her life did suck, and even though they got on her nerves sometimes, Eve knew that her sisters were crazy about her. Sometimes it was endearing how they clung to her. As far as she knew, David didn't have anybody but his mom.

"Do you have any family here or anywhere else?"

David shook his head, still looking down at the pizza in front of him. "Nope. It's just me and Moms. That's how it's been all of my life."

"Where's your dad?"

"He died a long time ago."

"You don't have any aunts or uncles or grandparents or anything?"

"Nope. My mom was an only child, and her mother died years ago."

"Wow." He hadn't been exaggerating. David really didn't have anyone. "I guess I'm luckier than I thought."

David just nodded quietly.

Eve suddenly felt compassion for him. "I heard you say you made the basketball team at Sunday school," she said, changing the subject. "Have you had any games yet?"

"Nope, not yet," David said, brightening. "Not for another week. Your dad kind of helped me get my game up, so I invited him to come. You should come too."

Eve frowned. "My dad did what?" she asked blankly.

David took a sip of his Coke. "Your dad was helping me practice at the Rec Center for awhile before tryouts."

"My dad is Dean Hardaway," Eve informed him. "Do you have the right person?"

David looked at Eve evenly. He was curious as to how Dean operated as an adulterous father, but was unsure if Eve was trustworthy or not. While he wanted to come right out and ask Eve if she knew her dad was unfaithful, he also knew that she probably loved her dad and wasn't interested in hearing anything negative about him.

"Yeah," he said, "I have the right person."

Eve threw herself up against the back of the booth with her arms folded, fuming. "But our extracurricular activities bore him though," she mused aloud. "I like basketball too, and that's technically not 'girl stuff', but do you think he offered to help me practice when I went out for the team?"

David's eyes widened. "Umm…" he said uneasily. "I'm sorry I mentioned it."

"You don't need to apologize. It's not your fault my dad is a jerk."

David swallowed. "Is he really that bad?"

Eve took a rather vicious bite of her pizza and chewed vigorously before responding. Whereas David was being careful in his approach about Dean, Eve had been waiting on the opportunity to unload her feelings about her dad on anyone who asked, and that person just happened to be David. "No, he's not that bad--he's worse," she spat. "He doesn't do anything with me or my sisters but he can go play basketball with *you*?"

"I think my mom asked him to," David said.

"So what? And who exactly is your mom to him? My mom is his wife and he doesn't show her any respect. None. You probably think he's a decent guy because he shot a couple hoops with you, don't you? Well, he's not. Decent guys don't hit their wives, now do they?"

David's mouth dropped open. "Your dad hits Miss Grace?" he said in a low voice.

Cringing, Eve realized that she had gone too far. Aside from their small conversations in Sunday school, she really hadn't had enough interaction with David to gauge his trustworthiness, and now she had let him in on the biggest secret in her-- and her mother's--life.

Sensing her apprehension, David took a deep breath. In a way, her admission provided him with a sense of relief. Obviously Eve's family was putting on a big show, and he often felt the same about him and his mother--everything about them was a big show. Angelica played the doting single mother and David the mild-mannered, adoring son, but behind the scenes, their life was a mess and their mother-son relationship was a quagmire of codependency.

"My mom isn't what everyone thinks she is, either," David revealed.

Eyes big, Eve looked up from her plate across the table. "Really?"

"Yeah, really."

"How so?"

"She looks more put-together than she actually is," David informed her. "Everybody looks at her and thinks she has it going on but the truth is that she's a mess. That's why I'm usually not at home. I go anywhere I can so that we're not in the house together for too long."

Eve was surprised. David's mom was one of the most stunning women she'd ever seen in person. Every Sunday, Angelica came to church wearing an expensive suit with a matching hat, handbag and shoes. Her makeup looked professionally done. Her nails were always manicured. She was well-spoken and gave the appearance of being relatively well-educated. "Does she hit you?"

"Sometimes."

"Why?"

David shrugged. "Because I'm there. That's why I try not to be. I can't stand to be around her for too long. She's crazy."

Eve sat back in her seat and chuckled. David looked at her, confused. As far as he concerned, there was nothing said during this exchange of highly personal and painful information that was worth laughing at. Seeing his face, Eve explained herself quickly. "I'm sorry your life is what it is, David, but honestly… it was nice to hear that someone else hates their home life as much as I hate mine."

David's face melted in a smile. "I know, right?"

When Eve smiled back, her eyes sparkling behind her glasses, something happened. Their conversation hadn't been long, but it was highly meaningful. Kindred spirits had connected; a spark had ignited. All in a matter of fifteen minutes in the middle of a noisy pizza kitchen.

Across the restaurant a strong friendship was in the making for Grace and Karen. Initially the two had sat together so that their daughters could talk, but Grace soon fell prey to Karen's engaging personality and sardonic, dry wit. Grace was in tears as Karen regaled her with numerous parental anecdotes.

Karen was also very observant. As they conversed, Karen noticed that Grace seemed very nervous. If a man even looked in her direction, she quickly dropped her head, and she checked her phone repeatedly. After she had done so for the millionth time, Karen asked politely, "Do you need to go? Don't let me and Maddy hold you up."

"Oh…oh no. No, I'm fine. It's okay," Grace stammered, flustered, as she shoved the phone back in her purse. "I just wanted to make sure my husband wasn't trying to call me."

Karen tried to hide her frown. The restaurant was noisy, but not so much that Grace wouldn't have been able to hear her phone ring or even buzz if a text message came through. "Is he at home?"

"Yeah."

Silence.

It was obvious Grace wasn't interested in talking about her husband. In Karen's past experience, that was yet another red flag. "What does he do for a living?"

"He works at ITS in Ann Arbor as a project manager."

"Some of the guys and gals my husband served with work there! Do you know Irene Quintanilla, Karl Strickland, Rick Hightower or Antonio Ayala?"

Grace shook her head. "No, I'm afraid I don't."

"I guess that was a stupid question. There's hundreds of workers there."

"It wasn't a stupid question at all. I just don't really know much about the people that Dean works with. Your husband is military?"

"He's a Marine," Karen said proudly.

"Dean is too," Grace informed her.

Karen gasped with delight. "Imagine that! We have something in common. So you know what it's like to be a military wife!"

"Well, not really," Grace said, a bit embarrassed. "Dean was pretty much done by the time we got married."

"Oh," Karen said, softening a bit. "Did he retire? Was he injured or something?"

Grace cocked her head to the side in thought. "He's never really told me why he isn't a Marine anymore. I just assumed that after coming back from Afghanistan he wanted out."

Karen fought to keep her mouth from dropping open. Her husband, Jake, affectionately referred to by his friends as "Alf" because of his hairy body, had been in the Marines since he was eighteen. She knew that once one enlisted with the Marines and signed a contract, he or she could not simply quit because they "wanted out". Coupled with the fact that Grace didn't even know how her husband exited the service, Karen was highly suspicious. Something didn't sound right here. Unfortunately, getting information out of Grace about her husband wasn't easy.

Suddenly Grace jumped up. "Oh wow, look at the time," she said, her eyes glued to her phone screen. "Girls, we need to get going."

The four girls recognized the sound of slight panic in their mother's voice and rose obediently. Across the restaurant, Eve did as well, looking at David. "That's our cue to get home before the king throws a hissy fit," she said witheringly.

David looked at her sympathetically. "Sorry," he said. "Do you have a phone? I mean, just in case you guys come this way again and I am not here? I'd rather not eat alone all the time if I don't have to."

Eve was embarrassed. A cute, decent boy--an older one at that--was asking for her phone number and she didn't even have a phone. "Dean won't let me have a phone," she mumbled.

David's brow furrowed. "Are you serious? Why not?"

Eve scowled. "He doesn't think I'm old enough for a phone. He thinks that if I have a phone, I'll use it to talk to boys, and that once I start talking to boys I'll start having sex in the school bathroom with them and get pregnant, and disgrace my entire family."

David laughed. "You can't be for real," he said disbelievingly.

"I wish I wasn't," Eve said, shaking her head. She couldn't help but to chuckle at her own misfortune. "Mom tried to convince him to get me one, and that is what he told her. He doesn't want his daughters to be fast."

"That's a new one Eve." David shook his head too. "I can't believe your dad is that big a control freak."

"He's just a freak altogether," Eve said acerbically. "See you tomorrow?"

"Yeah. We'll be there. See you tomorrow."

David and Karen were troubled for the rest of the day after their interactions with the Hardaway ladies. After having made such a sensitive connection with Eve, David's heart was filled with tenderness toward her, and after he left Jet's he wasted no time pedaling his bike to Wal-Mart where he used the rest of the money he had gotten from Angelica--who had probably gotten the money from Dean--to buy a Verizon LG Optimus Zone prepaid Smartphone that he planned to give her discreetly during church tomorrow.

At home, Karen relayed her afternoon to Alf over dinner. "She reminds me a lot of Kelsey," she told her husband quietly. "A lot."

Alf looked at her with his eyebrows raised.

Kelsey was Karen's twin sister who had been killed by her abusive husband fifteen years ago. Karen experienced great difficulty dealing with the loss of her twin. The guilt over not pushing Kelsey harder to leave her husband drove Karen to two years' worth of therapy. Since then Karen had been active in various organizations, causes and programs associated with ending domestic violence, and part of her training including education on how to identify warning signs. Grace exhibited several: Her attachment to her phone, the way she took great care to avoid contact with men, and her initial inability to say much about her husband.

Alf could tell his wife was deeply troubled. "Do you need my help with anything?" he asked gently.

Karen took a sip of her wine and pursed her lips in thought. "Maybe," she said slowly. "There were a few things Grace said about her husband that I thought was kind of strange. She had no idea how or why her husband was no longer a Marine. She made it sound like he just quit."

Alf pondered this. "You don't just quit the Marines. You have to abide by the terms in your enlistment contract. But there are conditions that can result in a Marine being ejected for being unfit for service. You said the guy works at ITS?"

Karen nodded. "And you know what else was weird? Their family doesn't take advantage of any of the benefits offered to military families. She didn't even know what TRICARE was."

"Depending on how he removed from the Marines, participation in TRICARE is not a requirement," Alf informed his wife. "So he could still be eligible to buy into TRICARE, but if he found that his employer-sponsored insurance is better, he could use that instead. But if he was dishonorably discharged, he would have none of the rights and privileges afforded to Marines in good standing, retired or otherwise."

"Is it possible for you to find out his discharge status?" Karen asked. "I know it sounds like I am prying, but…I got a bad feeling about this Dean character."

"I'll have to get some basic info on the guy in order to do that, but I can do it," Alf told her. "You know I'll do whatever I can to help your friend. I don't want you to worry too much in the meantime. You hear me?"

She smiled at him. "Yes, I do. I sure do."

"If she has to come here, five kids and all… the more the merrier, I always say."

Karen sighed deeply to herself, wondering how she could have gotten so lucky in the husband department. It was love at first sight when they first met two decades ago, and he had been nothing but supportive as she struggled to conceive children, miscarried twice, and struggled through a nerve-wracking pregnancy with Maddy. He knew his strong-willed wife had dreams and ambitions and he stood behind her. In return, she held down the fort with pride whenever her husband had to leave the family to tend to his military duties. It made Karen sad to think that Grace wasn't receiving the love of which she was so deserving from her own husband.

The next morning Eve woke up with her stomach all aflutter. She rarely got excited to do much of anything anymore, but she was actually happy to go to church today and see David. Eve took a little extra time getting ready, wondering if she was being silly, feeling a bit shy and embarrassed by her thoughts. As she styled her hair, she tried to convince herself to be cool. "We only talked once," she reminded herself. "He could still be a jerk."

Once she got to church and found David waiting at the door for her, her consternation diminished. David knew she had to act cool while Dean was around so he didn't even let on that he had been waiting for her, instead pretending that he was getting a drink from the nearby water fountain. Without saying a word and trying their hardest to avoid making eye contact lest they slip up and smile at each other, they headed down to the classroom behind Grace for Sunday school.

After Sunday school, David caught Eve before she headed upstairs for refreshments. Grace was still tidying up the classroom, so now was the time to slip Eve the phone. "You got a purse or something?" David asked her.

"Yeah, why?" Eve asked, confused.

"How big is it?"

Perplexed, Eve showed him her black purse. It was small, but big enough to hide the phone. Looking around, David reached into his pocket. "Open it up."

Eve had no idea what David was up to, but not only was she intrigued, she trusted him for some reason. She obliged. She was shocked to see him slip a little black Smartphone into her purse.

"Close your purse. Let's head upstairs."

As they raced up the steps, Eve whispered, "What am I supposed to do with that? I mean, are you giving it to me?"

"Yeah. You might need it one day."

"This is crazy! Are you serious?"

"Yes, I'm serious. Shoot. I almost forgot. Take this charger."

Eve took the charger he pressed in her hand and hurriedly stuffed it in the purse. "Did you buy this?"

"Yes."

"I don't feel right taking this from you."

"It didn't cost much," David told her. "Take it. You might need it. For real. If you get low on minutes you have to let me know."

They were at the entrance doors to the fellowship hall. It was crowded and people were waiting impatiently to get in. The two only had a couple of minutes to talk before prying eyes noticed.

Eve swallowed. "Is it only for emergencies or can I text you sometime?"

"I put my number in there for you."

At that moment Dean appeared out of nowhere. The two teens pretended like they hadn't been talking to one another. It was for naught, because Dean was looking over their heads anyway. They smiled at each other and parted.

Much of Dean's money was going toward keeping Angelica appeased so he was unable to get the washer and dryer replaced quickly, which was perfectly okay with Grace. She didn't mind when she had to spend the next four consecutive Saturdays at the laundromat, and neither did the girls.

Although Karen had replaced her broken washer shortly after she and Grace first met, she continued to come to the laundromat on Saturdays to spend time with her troubled new friend. Slowly and steadily Grace opened up to Karen bit by bit and confirmed to her Karen's worst suspicions: That Dean Hardaway was an abusive monster using cherry-picked Christian principles to justify his supremacy. Karen vowed not to let what happened to Kelsey happen to Grace.

Eve also looked forward to Saturdays and what had now become a standing lunch date with David. She was very careful with her new phone. There was a series of shoe boxes under her bed that served as a perfect hiding place for a phone. At nighttime she and David would text back and forth for hours before one of them would simply fall asleep. She made sure to never have the volume up on the phone, because although David promised he wouldn't call, he reminded her that someone might dial a wrong number--her number--and cause it to ring. It was best to keep it on silent or vibrate and in her bedroom.

Both Grace and Eve were flourishing as a result of their newfound connections. Months had passed since the pastoral anniversary dinner, and that had been the last time Grace was able to speak freely to other adults in a setting outside the church. Each conversation with Karen served as a sad reminder of the person Grace used to be before marriage: Driven, ambitious, confident despite her past, content. Karen truly brought out the best in Grace.

The same could be said for David. Now that Eve had David to focus on and was allowing herself to bask in his positive attention and support, her happiness and improved self-confidence was reflected in how she treated her male classmates at school. Somehow, word got out that Eve had a boyfriend who was in high school, a rumor that elevated her status. When asked by her friends if David was indeed her boyfriend, Eve demurred. Undoubtedly she was very taken with David, but she wasn't sure if he qualified as her boyfriend or not, or how she even went about establishing whether or not they were in an actual relationship. It was all very foreign to her.

David helped her figure it out. On their fourth Saturday afternoon at Jet's, two of his teammates from basketball sauntered into the restaurant with their parents. They looked embarrassed to be seen with their mother and father and gave David a sheepish grin and a wave. He smiled and waved back. After they ordered their pizza, the two guys approached the table and the three boys exchanged exuberant greetings. They made small talk for a minute before one of them fixed his eyes on Eve.

"You didn't tell us you had a girlfriend," he said rather teasingly.

Eve shifted in her seat, visibly uncomfortable.

David was not. "Yeah, this is Eve. Eve, this is Kendrick and Cedrick. We play ball together."

Her heart beating out of her chest, Eve tried to contain her excitement so that she could render David's friends a proper greeting. She couldn't wait to tell her friends. They had seen pictures of David on Eve's phone, and they were majorly impressed. And green with envy.

Grace's friendship with Karen and David's relationship with Eve took a turn several weeks after their first laundromat trip. David had been agonizing as to whether not he should tell Eve about Dean's relationship with his mother. Indeed, David was tired of Dean being at his house, and he was tired of being party to Dean's and his mother's treachery against Grace--and against God. As Eve sat across the table from him eating her pizza, he became downtrodden, thinking that she would be upset with him for not telling her sooner.

"I've been keeping something from you about your dad."

Eve looked up, her curiosity aroused. "If that fool isn't about to die or something I don't really care what it is." It sounded harsh, but it was how she was feeling. Dean had been hitting Grace regularly and had also grabbed her by her arm and yanked her a few times over the past week.

"I just kind of feel like I should tell you. I hope you won't be mad at me for not saying something. I think I should have told you awhile ago, honestly."

"Okay, what is it?"

"Your dad has been messing around with my mom."

Eve recoiled in shock. "What the heck does your mom want with *him?*"

David was unprepared for her indignant response. He couldn't help but chuckle. "Honestly...money. That's all."

Eve put her slice of pizza down on her plate and stared at David, her mouth agape. "So... let me get this straight. This guy totally disrespects my mom, tells her she ain't nothing, tells her she can't be trusted, all this and all that... and *he's* the one out doing dirt?"

"That's usually how it works, Eve."

"For Christ's sake!" Eve said angrily. "The *nerve* of that guy! After all he puts my mom through, he goes out and cheats on *her?*"

"I know."

"And wait a second," Eve said, fully fired up, "your mom knows my mom is Dean's wife, so what in the heck is she doing with him?"

Embarrassed, David said quietly, "She's after his money, Eve."

"What money?" Eve said, her voice rising an octave. "I always hear him complaining about money. Mom spends too much on groceries. Mom spends too much on gas. Oh, and you should have *heard* him when the washer and dryer broke down. He acted like it was the worst thing in life that a couple crusty machines didn't last forever!" Grunting, she picked up her pizza and took a vicious bite.

"Well," David told her uncomfortably, "I think he is having money problems because he is helping my mom with her bills."

Eve dropped her pizza and stared at him.

"No flipping way."

"It's what my mom does, Eve. Always has," David said miserably. "I'm not crazy about it. I'm just now really getting to a point where I actually understand her entire scheme. She finds these dumb desperate dudes to give her money. Your dad just happens to be her current dumb desperate dude."

Eve was gobsmacked and her appetite quickly left her body. She sat back and folded her arms across her chest, fuming.

David watched her in silence. He could tell by her flashing eyes that she needed a minute. He knew there was a lot more he could tell Eve about his mom--that she was responsible for the deaths of multiple men--but that was a terrible secret he was not yet ready to reveal to anybody. David wanted the guilt of harboring the secret off his chest, but he knew there was a good chance both he and his mother might end up in prison if he divulged information about his mother's transgressions. Although he despised his mother, David wasn't so sure he was ready to see her go to prison. After all, he had no one else.

"I'm not mad at you," Eve finally told him. "I know it's hard to keep your parents' secrets and even harder to tell them."

"You don't know the half of it," David muttered, returning his attention to his own plate of uneaten barbecue chicken pizza.

On the other side of the restaurant, Karen was nervous. She had no idea how she was going to approach Grace with the facts Alf had recovered about Dean. All Karen knew was that Grace had to know who Dean was and what he was capable of. She had come prepared with ten dollars worth of quarters so that Maddy and the twins could play the arcade games at the back of the restaurant.

As soon as the girls were no longer within earshot, Karen fixed a serious gaze upon her face and said in a low voice, "Grace, I need you to listen to me. I hope you trust me by now. I hope you think of me as a friend. I want you to know that us being friends is not limited to this pizza place only. I want you to know that if you need help, I am here for you. Okay?"

Alarmed by Karen's tone and her departure from her normally sunny demeanor, Grace put her salad fork down and nodded. "Karen, what's wrong?"

Karen reached into the satchel beside her and pulled out some papers. "I'll let you look through these if you want," she said, "but the gist of it is, Dean, your husband, was discharged from the Marines after being tried for murder."

Grace gasped. "What? What do you mean? How do you get discharged for murder if you are killing enemy threats?"

"Because in his case it did not appear that he killed *actual* threats," Karen said, turning the pages of the document. "People said that Dean was power-hungry and trigger-happy when he was over in Afghanistan. He was not well-liked by any of his fellow Marines. He bragged about killing several civilians for sport and was turned in. Dean was court martialed, but he said at the time he thought the civilians were a threat, that his bragging was just insincere bluster, and since he was inexplicably alone at the time that he encountered those 'threats', no one was able to conclusively prove that he was or was not under duress when he killed those people. But it looks like his record was unsatisfactory overall, and he was dishonorably discharged after being found not guilty after serving some time in the brig for Conduct Unbecoming an Officer."

Karen pushed the report toward the middle of the table slowly. Grace wasn't sure if she wanted to read it or not. "Are there details as to how those civilians were killed?" she asked quietly.

"They were shot to death at close range, Grace."

"This…this can't be Dean." Feeling nauseous, Grace pulled the report all the way across the table and started thumbing through the pages. Underneath the top page, which was a cover sheet, was all of the identifying information about Dean that one could possibly collect. There was also a black-and-white photocopy of his enlistment photo. It was definitely Dean's record.

Dumbfounded, Grace skimmed the entire report, paying special attention to the passages that appeared to be character statements from other Marines or perhaps Dean's superiors. The words and phrases they used to describe Dean served as further confirmation: "He is a loose cannon; reckless, impetuous, and in my opinion, not fit for this honorable service." "His arrogance and overestimation of his mental and physical abilities has afforded him no small amount of ire from his peers. Dean's refusal to accept correction and his inability to compromise is detrimental to this service." Dean was referred to as "condescending", "thirsty for power and prestige", and "lacking empathy". There wasn't a single positive thing said about Dean in the entire document. It was obvious that even if he hadn't been charged with the civilian murders Dean had no future in the Marines.

"I saw that Dean's dad was a Marine," Karen remarked quietly. "I kind of wondered how someone with those personality traits was even able to get in, but I'm sure you know that those types of people tend to be good actors, and they're usually pretty intelligent. And maybe the recruiting Marines looked at his dad's record and thought Dean would live up to that."

Grace sighed and laid her head back, closing her eyes. Now the conflict among Dean, his parents, and his sisters made perfect sense. Dean had completely dishonored the family with his actions and indirectly sullied his father's spotless Marine record in the process. It also made sense that Dean kept his family from Grace so that she would not find out the truth. Dean wasn't a distinguished Marine at all. The longer Grace thought about it, the more she was inclined to believe that Dean had definitely killed those civilians and bragged about it.

She looked at Karen with renewed alarm. "I have to leave him. But I don't think I should tell him what I know."

"No, you shouldn't," Karen agreed. "Please don't. I'm sorry I had to do this, Grace. But regardless of whether you truly believe Dean is capable of harming you to the point of death or not, you have to admit this is pretty scary stuff. I of course have no idea whether Dean would kill you. But, I also didn't think my twin's husband would kill her, either."

Grace gasped. It was the first she'd heard of this. "What?"

With tears in her eyes, Karen relayed the story about Kelsey's tragic, short marriage and violent death. "There was so much about Lance that reminds me of Dean," she said, dabbing the corners of her eyes with a rough restaurant napkin. "When you talk about the things he says to you and how he runs your household... I can't think of anyone else other than Kelsey. Grace, you don't do that to people you love. Controlling someone, by fear, manipulation, finances or whatever--is not what you do to someone you love. You just don't."

The two put their heads together and brainstormed a plan and a timeline for Grace to safely leave Dean. After they'd talked for almost an hour, Grace swallowed and asked Karen, "May I use your phone?"

"Of course," Karen said, pulling it out of her satchel and handing it to Grace. "You're not calling him, are you? I don't want him to have my number."

"No... I was actually thinking of calling his sister, Denise. She's a lawyer, and I met her for the first time when Dean's father passed. She gave me her card and told me to call her if I needed help."

Karen nodded.

With trembling fingers, unsure as to what she would say and how Denise would respond, Grace retrieved Denise's card from the innermost pouch in her purse and punched the numbers into Karen's phone. Denise answered on the third ring.

"Grace?"

Shocked, Grace sputtered, "How did you know it was me?"

"I don't even really know," Denise replied, sounding surprised herself. "I just saw the area code and a part of me has been expecting your call for awhile. I'm glad you trusted me enough to call."

Grace put her head in her hand, tears streaming down her face. "I found out why you guys hate Dean so much. I found out that he killed people while he was in the Marines. Why didn't you guys tell me?"

"Honestly, I didn't know how you'd take that," Denise said sympathetically. "I didn't know if you would believe it, and then I didn't want to tell you and have you go back and ask Dean about it and get hurt. I assume now that you know you're looking to get out. Am I right?"

"Yeah. I can't be with him anymore. The hitting is getting worse, and he's targeting Eve more. I can't have that."

Denise went into lawyer mode and gave Grace valuable ideas as to how to make a smooth exit, one where Grace would be basically guaranteed full custody of the girls and enough alimony to help her get on her feet. Denise asked to speak to Karen and the three women developed an escape plan for Grace to enact immediately.

When they hung up with Denise, Grace and Karen put their first part of the plan into action. Grace went to the table where Eve was sitting with David. "Eve," she said quietly, "I'm going to go right across the street to the Huntington Bank. I'll be right back. Can you keep your eye on your sisters and Maddy for a few minutes?"

Confused but hopeful, Eve nodded. "Take your time…"

At the bank, Karen opened a checking account with Grace's name on it for Grace to use without Dean's knowledge. As soon as the account had been established, Grace called Denise back to let her know it had been done. What Denise said stunned her again.

"There will be three grand in there by the end of the week."

Grace gasped. "How so?"

"A grand from me, one from Mom, one from Diana. And no, we don't need you to pay it back, we know you're thankful. We need to get you and our nieces to safety."

Grace was overcome with emotion and couldn't finish the call. She had not been expecting such overwhelming support. Karen hadn't thought twice about putting her name on the account, showing that she trusted Grace and truly wanted to help. And for Denise, Pamela and Diana to give her thousands of dollars when they'd only spoken to her a handful of times was absolutely remarkable.

Karen and Grace's next item of business was getting Grace a prepaid phone. In case of an emergency, if Dean decided to cut off the house phone, and so that she might be able to take pictures of her bruises, she needed a phone. They ran up the street to Wal-Mart and purchased a Verizon LG Optimus Zone prepaid Smartphone--incidentally, the exact same phone that David had given Eve.

When the girls got home, Dean wasn't there, much to Grace's pleasure. His absence gave her time to regroup and relax. Dean didn't return for the entire evening. Grace and the girls prepared dinner and ate together. While the girls played in the basement, Grace submitted herself to a night of prayer. *If this is my way out--please be with me.*

CHAPTER TWELVE

"For there is nothing hidden that will not be made manifest, nor is anything secret that will not be known and come to light." (Luke 8:17)

Dean and Grace were both actively preparing to leave the marriage and both of them were acting strangely around the other.

Having been together for so long, the Hardaways knew when the other was up to something. Grace seemed a bit jumpier than usual, but she was also in a much better mood lately. Dean didn't know what conclusions to draw from her behavior and thought Grace might be cheating. He watched her closely during church to see if she so much as smiled at any of the other men there for too long--she didn't. For a week, he crept into Cornerstone Christian Academy on the days when Grace was supposed to be there and walked around the building to make sure she was really there. She was. Each time he saw her, she was standing at the copier. There were no men in the room. She never saw him.

Baffled, Dean finally asked Grace about her behavior.

"You seem awful chipper lately," he remarked one evening after dinner as she stood at the sink, washing dishes.

Grace tried not to panic. She thought she'd been doing a good job being unassuming. "What do you mean?" she asked lightly.

"I don't even know how to describe it, but you seem... Happier, I guess."

"Is that a bad thing?"

"Well, no, but... I haven't seen much of that lately."

A light bulb went off in Grace's head. Giving Dean the biggest, fakest smile she could muster, she said, "I guess I was hoping that if I changed my attitude and showed a bit more gratitude, it would reflect positively on the atmosphere here." She knew she had to say something that fed into his narcissism, and by implying her attitude was a problem Dean was more likely to buy into it.

Flustered, Dean replied awkwardly, "It does make a difference, actually."

Grace knew exactly what the impetus was behind Dean's behavior. He was involved with another woman. He could have just come out and told her for all she cared. Truthfully, Grace was glad, because this meant Dean had somewhere else to go and someone else to fulfill his sexual desires. Grace had no interest in Dean's company or intimacy.

Dean was too arrogant to believe anyone capable of pulling the wool over his eyes. He was in for a major shock. His wife was planning to leave him; his mistress was planning to kill him. He was in a precarious position at work and the grumblings within Christ First were growing. People were increasingly disillusioned with the direction the church was taking under Rev. Riley. He had relinquished the responsibility of teaching Bible study to his associate ministers, and while the church members were initially accepting of this, they quickly found out that the "ministers" had little understanding of what was considered basic Bible doctrine. The members felt that the deacons were abusing their position and making decisions among themselves that the congregation should have been voting on, and many of them knew this usurpation was mainly due to Dean's influence. While Dean thought he was sitting on top of the world, the makings of his demise on all fronts was underway.

Dean was giddy with anticipation as he walked through Christ First's double doors. One of the deacons had called an emergency meeting. Dean had no idea what the meeting was about, but whatever it was, it was bound to be juicy.

One by one all of the deacons arrived and exchanged greetings. Once everyone had settled down, Tyler stood at the front of the room and held up his hands to get everyone's attention. Dean fought the urge to groan.

"Guys," Tyler said in a low voice, "we have an urgent matter to discuss here. I thank you all for coming out on this short of a notice on a Saturday, but what I've discovered is just that important."

Everyone quieted down.

"Look," Tyler went on, looking embarrassed. "I have direct proof that Rev. Riley is involved with several women in the congregation, some of them married."

The deacons erupted into scattered conversation, but none of them appeared to be surprised.

"Now, how do you know this?" Curtis asked.

Tyler gave him a long look that could not be decoded. "Samantha told me. Two women she was working with in the kitchen on Tuesday almost got into an altercation because they found out they were both involved with Riley. Samantha has been on the phone asking around and found out that there are at least six other women that the pastor has slept with, or is still sleeping with, and more that he has made advances on."

"Do you have names?" Patrick asked.

Tyler nodded. "I have names of some, but Samantha forbade me from putting their names out there unless I absolutely had to. Again, some of them are married and have reconciled the affair with their husband privately. Others may not have told their husband, some are single. Either way it goes, this all is a mess, and yes these women shoulder some of the fault, but I think what we really ought to be talking about today is whether or not we should fire Rev. Riley."

More scattered chatter erupted before Andre got the deacons back in order. "Guys, guys!" he said loudly in his booming voice, "we can't all talk at once." He looked at Tyler. "Man, you just laid some heavy stuff on us, bruh."

Tyler shrugged helplessly. "I know," he replied. "And I know none of us would be comfortable asking Rev. Riley to resign and then having to inform the congregation, but this is why I came to you guys with this after I'd confirmed everything. We cannot expect for this house of God to be fruitful when the angel of the house can't keep it in his pants. And come on guys… are any of you really satisfied with the job he is doing?"

Dean was quiet, but underneath the surface his mind was spinning thoughts at a mile a minute. He didn't care whether or not Tyler's claims had any merit. All he knew was that he was tired of Tyler and would rather have him leave than Rev. Riley. If he could spin this thing, he might have an opportunity to be rid of that self-righteous, annoying little jerk for once and for all.

He stood to his feet.

"I, for one, *am* satisfied with our pastor," he said sternly, looking Tyler in the eye, "and I think meeting here behind his back and discussing unverified claims made by a bunch of cackling broads in the kitchen is low down."

Understandably, Tyler was shocked. "Are you for real?" he asked Dean incredulously. "You're more concerned about the fact that I came to you guys with these claims than you are the claims themselves? Guys, come on," he said, appealing to the other deacons. "Riley already had a reputation that came along with him from his previous church. That was the main reason I opposed his installation as our pastor from the start. The majority of you supported him, so I went along with it, but I regret my decision to do so."

"What exactly do you think he is supposed to be doing that he's not?" Dean countered. "None of us are perfect. I don't doubt the man has flaws. But look at how this church has been growing in the last few months. It's not because of anyone but him."

Allen found his voice. This was the conversation that he had been waiting for. "I'm with Tyler," he said. "Yes, the numbers are up. The church is taking in more money than ever. Fine. But that's not the only way we measure our success. Riley is not teaching sound doctrine anymore."

"Allen, you're still mad about what went down with Rev. Buckley," Dean said exasperatedly. "You've never even given Riley a chance, so I'm not surprised you're on the opposing side here."

Tyler was easily intimidated by Dean, but Allen was not. He stood up, walked over to Dean, and stared him squarely in the eyes. "Last I checked, my opinion here was as valid as that of anyone else," he said gravely, "and I will not apologize for having high expectations of the pastor of this church. The fact that you are content to ride Riley's coattails to whatever position or status you're hoping for means nothing to me. The man hasn't mentioned the Gospel message in his sermons in a month of Sundays. You tell me how a preacher who doesn't preach the Gospel is doing his job?"

"You think people need or want to hear the same thing every Sunday?" Dean said. "Rev. Riley is simply preaching what he knows his congregation needs to hear. Our members have problems. They're sick--they want to hear that they can be healed. They're broke--they want to hear that they can have prosperity…"

"That is only *half* of it," Tyler, now emboldened by having an ally in Allen, interrupted. "How is it that believers can be healed or brought through financial droughts? Only because we have aligned ourselves with Jesus. The central component of our faith, the very thing that *defines* our faith, is the death, burial and resurrection of Jesus. If you guys can honestly stand here and tell me that you're okay with the pastor of this church not even mentioning that regularly because he puts on a good enough show to get people in the doors, then maybe *I'm* at the wrong church!"

"Wow," Dean said in feigned disbelief, "who are *you* to decide what the shepherd feeds his flock? How do you know God isn't giving Riley exactly what he wants him to say? Don't you think that if Riley weren't following God's instructions, this church wouldn't be growing as much as it is?"

Dean walked around Allen and got closer to Tyler. "What is this really all about?" he asked in a low voice. "You have been against Riley from the start. Did you just cook all of this up to get rid of him?"

Tyler momentarily looked put-upon, then angry. "You calling me a liar?" he snarled.

The other deacons, seeing that the situation was about to escalate to dangerous levels, finally stepped in. Patrick got between Dean and Tyler and pushed Dean into one corner of the room while Allen and Curtis pulled Tyler to another. The other deacons talked among themselves in the middle of the room until Andre again called them all to attention.

"I personally am not one to discount what Tyler has brought before us," Andre said solemnly. "Given Riley's track record, I wouldn't be shocked to find truth to these allegations. But until these women identify themselves and tell us directly that these things happened, I think it is unfair to dismiss the pastor of the church and disgrace him based on allegations alone."

"I don't know what to think *or* do," Patrick confessed. "I'm confused right now. I don't know if this church could stand losing another pastor. We lost a ton of members after Rev. Buckley died."

"It wasn't *because* he died," Allen corrected him, "it was because of how *this* deacon board treated him, and because we put Riley in the pulpit!"

Dean shook his head and sighed, his arms folded across his chest. "Can I put forth a motion to quiet Deacon Chandler?"

The other deacons looked at him in shock. Per their charter, the deacons did have the option to silence another deacon during a meeting if they felt his comments or behavior were not conducive to the business of the meeting, but no one had ever invoked that right.

150

"How dare you," Allen growled.

As uncomfortable as it was, the motion had to be dealt with. "Deacon Hardaway, why are you asking to silence your brother?" Marlon asked.

"Because his opinion will continue to be as it always has been in matters concerning Rev. Riley--*biased*," Dean spat. "His dislike for Rev. Riley overshadows any ability to think reasonably. Anytime we have had to discuss an issue involving Rev. Riley, Allen has always been on the opposing side. While some of his complaints may have had some merit, I think it is safe to say that there were some matters where, had we been discussing Rev. Buckley, he would have been a bit more flexible."

"Deacon Chandler, what is your response to Deacon Hardaway's charge?" Marlon queried.

Allen walked slowly to a nearby chair and sank down into it. "This isn't for me anymore," he said quietly. "I am over eighty. I love serving the Lord with all my heart and soul. But I don't have the fight in me anymore that I used to. I have been at this church longer than any of you. Heck, I was one of the carpenters that laid the foundation for this building. Rev. Buckley had a vision for this church, a vision he shared with me, and I won't apologize for trying to do whatever I can to see that vision come to fruition. With that being said, I do not think Rev. Riley is doing a good enough job teaching the Word, and I have no doubt in my mind that he is fooling around with other women. None." Shaking his head, Allen subtly rubbed away the tears that had formed in his eyes. His love for Christ First was genuine. Unfortunately for him Dean's disdain for Tyler and desire for more power and prestige was more important.

Now calm, Tyler spoke next. "'Well, gentlemen," he said, "I think we have to take a vote here." He walked to the front of the room. "I would hope that after all of these years of service together, you would know me better than to believe that I would make up these accusations. I am sincerely concerned for the future of this church. I vote that we remove Rev. Riley from the office of pastor."

"Dean?" Simon, who had been silent the entire time, approached Dean tentatively. "You got anything else?"

Nodding, Dean went to the front of the room and stood an arm's length away from Tyler. Sensing that Tyler had reached his breaking point, he knew his final word had to be exceptionally persuasive. Dean wanted Tyler to know, without a doubt, that he was *not* running things. He could possibly kill two birds with one stone and be done with Allen, too. If he said the right things, appealed to both sides, certainly he could get most of the guys on board with him.

"We have to understand that whatever decision we make here is going to impact a lot of people," he said seriously. "I know it might seem like my opinion is simply based on my respect for Rev. Riley--it's not. I just think we ought to tread lightly in terms of how we treat another man of God. In some ways, I agree with you, Deacon Chandler--Rev. Buckley *was* handled inappropriately."

Allen looked up, surprised by the acknowledgement. The expression on his face let Dean know that he was not convinced of Dean's sincerity. Allen was wise. Dean didn't care about what had happened with Rev. Buckley at all. He was just trying to appeal to the rest of the deacon board by appearing to be sympathetic.

"And who knows if some of the strife we have dealt with in this church, and in our personal lives, dare I say, is *because* of how we treated him?" Dean continued. "I am not comfortable, like Andre said, displacing a pastor and possibly destroying his reputation and marriage with unfounded allegations. Tyler, is there any chance any of these women would be willing to actually identify themselves and discuss these matters with us?"

Looking stone-faced, Tyler shrugged. "I was under the impression that these women did not want their affairs with the reverend to become church fodder," he replied. "I will talk with Samantha and see if she can convince any of them to come forward."

Dean shrugged. "Fair enough," he said nonchalantly. "Until we get something we can actually investigate for ourselves, I do not see how we can come to any sort of fair and reasonable conclusion. I personally do not want the wrath of God to come down on me because I judged a pastor based on a bunch of gossiping women. I also don't want to put this church through another pastoral change if necessary, especially since, as it's been pointed out, we are growing again. I do not think Christ First can survive another change in leadership."

"Fine," Tyler said tersely. "I suggest we all put this issue to prayer until I can get some of the women to come forward. Maybe we should tentatively plan on meeting again next Saturday, same time."

The meeting ended informally when Tyler gathered up his coat and prepared to walk out. At the exit, he stopped suddenly, turned around and gave Curtis another odd look. It appeared he wanted to say something and second-guessed himself. Shaking his head, Tyler left the church.

Curtis had seen the look Tyler gave him. Dean jogged over to him, hoping to instigate some bad feelings between the two that he could use to his advantage. "What was that all about?" he asked.

"You saw that look too?" Curtis asked as he slipped into his jacket. "Man, I wish I knew. He been acting funny around me for a couple weeks now."

"Do you believe what he was saying?" Dean inquired.

Curtis shrugged. "I don't put anything past anybody," he replied. "And come on Dean… we all know that Riley has a sketchy past."

"We all have sketchy pasts," Dean countered.

"We're not pastors, Dean," Curtis said. "I know I have my faults, but at the end of the day, I think I'm a pretty decent guy, you know? Yeah, I like to have a good time. I drink a little. I smoke a little. But I love my wife and take care of my family and would give anyone in need the shirt off my back. I gotta admit, I've been questioning Riley's effectiveness for a bit of time myself."

"You agree with Tyler??"

Curtis looked annoyed. "For Christ's sake, Dean," he said gruffly, "this is not a Dean versus Tyler issue. I know that's what you're trying to make it out to be. It's not. Grow up, man."

He walked out, leaving Dean with his mouth hanging agape. Curtis had never spoken to him so roughly. Something about this meeting had apparently touched a nerve. The other deacons filed out without saying so much as a word to Dean. This angered and worried him. Now he wasn't so confident that any of his fellow deacons were on his side. It looked like Tyler might come out on top again.

After a sleepless night in bed, Dean awoke to the makings of a decent Sunday morning. He could smell the breakfast cooking and heard light chatter between Grace and the girls in the kitchen. Dean sat up, yawned and stretched, and swung his legs out to get out of bed. As soon as his feet touched the floor, the talking downstairs stopped. The girls had heard him and knew he would be making his way down soon.

At church, the atmosphere among the deacons was dark and brooding. Strangely enough, Curtis and Tyler were absent from Sunday school. It was unusual for either one of them to miss, and both of them had never been absent on the same Sunday. Dean's anxiety levels shot up as he considered that the two of them might be together.

As usual, the deacons headed toward Rev. Riley's office to pray with him before church began. However, Byron, the biggest and burliest of the associate ministers, barred them from coming in.

"New rule, fellas," he said, "Rev. Riley only wants us in there while he's getting ready in the morning. Y'all can still pray as a group, but there's not enough room in here for all of us anymore."

It was a complete lie. Rev. Riley's office and the adjoining room had more than enough space for the deacons and associates to be involved in the prayer. But before anyone had the chance to say something, Byron closed the door in their faces. There were already people seated in the pews, and they definitely noticed the shunning that had just taken place. The deacons knew they had to play it off lest the congregation become aware of the dysfunction among their church's leadership. They pretended to check the pulpit to make sure the sound system was functioning properly and that the pastor's water pitcher was full. Grumbling, they then took their places on the front pew.

Tyler came in with Samantha shortly before church began. Instead of joining his fellow deacons, he stayed with his wife and children, something he had never done before. The other deacons exchanged glances. It wasn't against the rules for a deacon to choose to sit with his family every now and then, especially for the deacons who had children, but it was definitely a rare occurrence. Their job was to stay close to the pastor in case he needed something. Tyler's refusal to sit with the deacons was highly symbolic. He was, in a way, separating himself from the deacon board and from Rev. Riley.

Another associate minister, Aaron, approached the pulpit and tapped the mic to make sure it was on. "It is eleven a.m., and we'd like to get things started," he said in his raspy voice. "Please join me and the other associate ministers in devotion."

The deacons, who had been preparing to go to the front and perform the devotional part of the service as usual, exchanged shocked glances. What the heck was Aaron doing? They watched, aghast, as the associate ministers gathered in front of the pulpit, which is where *they* typically stood during devotion. They signaled the organist and began to sing a hymn. Allen pulled the shirt sleeve of the associate nearest to him, Keith. Keith whispered something in his ear. Allen apparently didn't like what he heard, because he threw up his hands, picked up his worn Bible from his seat, and started to leave the sanctuary. Confused, Marlon hurried behind him.

Marlon came back minutes later and motioned for the other deacons to follow him out into the hallway. Allen was standing there, but he was wearing his hat and coat and had his car keys in hand.

"Rev. Riley *forgot* to mention to us that he wants his associate ministers to do the devotion from now on," Marlon informed the group.

"*What?*" Dallas said. "That's our job. It's always been our job!"

"He claims he wants his associates to get experience running the entire service," Allen told them. "Y'all can call it what you want, but I'mma go ahead and call it BS. Y'alls reverend has been taking responsibilities away from us and handing them over to his band of crooks for months now, just so he can justify them getting paid. I'm through."

"What do you mean, you're *through?*" Patrick asked.

"I mean, I'm done with this place. I have to go. God knows I hate to say this, but Christ First ain't for me anymore, and it won't be as long as that man is here." With that, he tipped his hat at them and walked out of the church's front doors without looking back.

Dean was pleased, but the others stood there in stunned silence. However, their silence was short lived. Minutes after Allen had left the building, Curtis burst in.

He was a sight to be seen. Typically well-groomed and the epitome of cool, calm and collected, Curtis was disheveled, with wild uncombed hair and blood-shot eyes. It was obvious by his unsteady gait and the strong smell of vodka that emanated from his body that he had been drinking heavily. He wore a plaid shirt that was only buttoned halfway. His black slacks were wrinkled and his fly was down.

"Holy crap," Andre muttered. "Curtis, what the heck, man?"

"Mind your business," Curtis snapped as he pushed past them and tried to enter the sanctuary.

Dean and Dallas blocked his way. "Curt, bro, are you sick? What is wrong with you right now?" Dean asked.

"I will be just fine," Curtis replied, trying to sound calm, "but right now, I really need y'all to get out of my way. If you let me be, no one will get hurt."

Dean and Dallas exchanged glances. They eased up on their grip on Curtis's shoulders and waist only a little, but that little bit was enough for him to struggle with them and finally break free. He burst into the sanctuary and proceeded right down the middle aisle.

"Heeeeeeeeey, everybody!" Curtis shouted. Everyone turned to look at him, confused. "How's everybody today?" He stopped to shake the hands of a few bewildered congregants. "Sorry to interrupt," he continued as he made his way to the front, "but I have a big, big announcement to make to everybody here today. Yep, I want all of y'all to hear this. It's big, really big! As a matter of fact…" He had reached the front of the pulpit. Curtis turned left and walked to where Reggie, the drummer, sat perched behind his set of drums. Curtis reached over Reggie and plucked his drumsticks from his hands. "…I need a drumroll for this!" Curtis pounded on the drums and then banged on the cymbal so hard it fell off its holder. He then held his arm out straight to the side and dropped the drumsticks like they were a microphone. "Pick that up for me, would you?" he asked Reggie casually as he walked toward the pulpit.

"And now, the moment you all have been waiting for," he said dramatically. "The big announcement. Y'all ready for it?"

He pointed at Rev. Riley. "Pastor, can you join me, please?"

Rev. Riley, just as confused as everyone else, looked hesitant. When he descended the pulpit, a couple of his associates tried to join him as well. "Are you the pastor?" Curtis snapped. "If you ain't no pastor, go on back up there where you don't even belong. Go on." They took one step back, but did not go back up the steps.

"Stay there if you want, but you better not touch me," Curtis warned them. With a big grin on his face, he slung an arm around Rev. Riley, who patted his chest awkwardly and said, "Deacon Toole, do you need help? Are you sick?"

Curtis shook his head. "No, but I'll tell you what…I just found out," Curtis said breathlessly, "that our beloved pastor has been banging my wife!"

Right after the declaration escaped his lips, Curtis turned and decked Rev. Riley right in the face. The associates hurriedly attempted to break up the fracas but they were no match for Curtis's anger. By the time the associates were able to put Curtis into a chokehold he had already lumped Rev. Riley up to the point where his nose was bleeding. Rev. Riley pulled a handkerchief from the pocket of his robe and held it to his face as he sat on the ground, dazed. Two of the associates helped him to his feet, put their arms under his shoulders for support, and carried him to his office. The remaining associates roughly picked Curtis up off the floor and prepared to throw him out of the church. The church members in attendance stood and watched the entire debacle in shock and awe.

Unfortunately, the show wasn't over yet. Claudia had apparently found out that her husband was planning to confront Rev. Riley and drove to the church hoping to head off the confrontation. She arrived just as Curtis was being pushed out the front doors. The deacons and some of the other members of the church gathered to watch. As Curtis was being thrown out, Claudia tried to push her way in. Already hysterical, she grew even more furious as she watched her husband be pushed to the ground. Claudia fell to her knees beside him and tried to pull him up. Curtis put up a finger, letting her know that he needed a minute to catch his breath. Claudia stood up. Her hazel eyes looked wild, and for once in her life, her hair was not perfectly coiffed. Her shoes were mismatched and she wore a wrinkled pair of mom jeans that were not two sizes too small, as the rest of her clothes were. Apparently both Tooles had had a rough night.

"Where is Samantha?" she shrieked. "Where is she? You tell her to come out here right now!" By her tone of voice and how vigorously she was fighting to get into the building, it was obvious what Claudia's plans were if she were given the opportunity to reach Samantha.

When she realized no one was going to let her in, she backed off, her chest heaving up and down. "It's cool," she yelled hysterically. "It's cool. She's safe while she's in there. Fine. But she's going to have to come out. She's going to have to go home. She's going to have to come out of her house. And you know what, Samantha? I'll find you. I *promise* I'll find you." She went back to her husband and yanked him up off the ground. "Go get in the car!"

Curtis slowly rose from the ground, stumbled toward the car and got in. Claudia burned rubber as she peeled out of the parking lot.

Back inside the church, Keith and Aaron were in the pulpit attempting to move forward with the service, but serious damage had been done. Several members of the congregation were gathering their things so that they could leave. One of the oldest members was on her feet, demanding to know if what Deacon Toole had said was accurate. True to their form, Keith and Aaron, who knew good and well that Rev. Riley had in fact been sleeping with Claudia, stood in the pulpit and lied through their teeth, claiming that Deacon Toole was just drunk.

Tyler and Samantha emerged from the coatroom with their children and their belongings. Samantha was in tears, shaken up by what had just transpired. "I didn't mean for this to happen," she told her husband tearfully. "I shouldn't have said anything. But I thought you guys should know."

He rubbed her shoulders lovingly. "It's not your fault."

As they walked toward the front doors of Christ First, some of the women had come out of the sanctuary to give Samantha angry looks and whisper to each other behind cupped hands. Tyler walked past the deacons and held the door open for his wife and children. On his way out, Tyler paused, looked over his shoulder, and said, "I wish you all the best."

The deacons watched as Tyler and his family got into their SUV and sped out of the parking lot. It had only taken minutes for their deacon board to crumble. Not only had Rev. Riley been systematically diminishing their roles within the church, they knew that Allen, Curtis and Tyler were not going to come back. Dean was strangely titillated by all of the uproar, but the other deacons were downtrodden. They knew that all of this upheaval was not good for the church, and they actually loved their fellow deacons.

Rev. Riley emerged from his office, still holding the bloody handkerchief to his face. As if he were a wounded celebrity, his entourage hustled him out to his Escalade and helped him into the passenger seat. Wilma Riley followed by herself. Humiliated, she had her head down and didn't look at anyone or speak. One of the associates held the back door open for her to climb inside. The Escalade left the parking lot minutes later, speeding off as though Rev. Riley's injury was life-threatening.

The sanctuary was almost empty. Grace and the girls were still there, only because Dean had not told her what to do. The girls were riveted to their seats. Eve, being the oldest, completely understood what had just happened and why. She knew Rev. Riley was a slimeball. She had caught him on several occasions patting and pinching behinds in church before, and hadn't even had the fortitude to care when she saw him. He just winked and laughed. The younger girls, however, were confused and kept asking questions. Grace was not in the mood.

"I need you to be quiet!" she snapped.

Dean appeared in the doorway and signaled for them all to come out. Grace and the girls grabbed their things and headed out to the parking lot. "I'll be out in a minute," he told them, handing Grace the keys to the car.

Nestled comfortably into the passenger seat of the SUV, Grace sighed heavily. She knew the day would come when Christ First would implode, but she hated what had just happened. Although she had little respect for Rev. Riley, she was concerned about how everything would impact the new members, the babes in Christ. Several college students had just joined the church within the last few weeks. A few of them had never been to church in their entire lives. Grace could only imagine how confusing all of this drama had to be for them.

She was also disappointed knowing that she had just seen Samantha Ware for the last time, and felt sorry that Samantha had been put in such a situation. Grace also felt guilty because she had known a long time ago that Rev. Riley was sleeping with several members of the congregation, yet she had said nothing. She was now ashamed of her silence. Grace felt convicted enough to offer a quick apology to God for her complicity.

Dean hopped into the car, startling her. He quickly turned over the engine and headed out of the parking lot.

"Everyone is leaving?" Grace asked.

"Yep. Church is done for today. No one is really trying to hear the Word after the commotion Curtis just caused."

Grace squinted her eyes in confusion. "Don't you think Rev. Riley is partially responsible for the commotion, though?"

"Rev. Riley didn't just assault someone in mid-service, Grace."

Grace dropped her head. She was hoping that perhaps this mess would be the straw that would break her husband's back and force him to re-evaluate their membership at Christ First. She was wrong. Apparently he intended to maintain his ridiculous loyalty to Rev. Riley. Just another reason to leave him. The goings-on at the church were giving her daughters mixed messages.

Grace didn't understand that Dean wasn't necessarily loyal to Rev. Riley. He was loyal to his position there at Christ First. Underneath the facade of having everything together, Dean wasn't really a people person. Dean liked his status at Christ First and wasn't ready to give it up just yet. He didn't want to have to start over somewhere and have to prove himself to anyone.

That night Dean fielded multiple phone calls from numerous church members who were calling to either gossip or share their concerns about what had gone on in church that day. To Grace's disgust and dismay, Dean sounded almost giddy as he talked to the more gossipy members. He was enjoying this. Dean was too excited to sleep by himself in the den that night. Much to Grace's chagrin he came barging into the bedroom while she was in the bathroom wrapping her hair and turned on the television. Grace sighed and hoped he wasn't in the mood as she headed out into the bedroom. Luckily, Dean wasn't in the mood to do anything other than ramble on excitedly about the day's events. In doing so, he inadvertently let on why he was so happy despite the turmoil.

"I tell you, I wasn't disappointed to see Tyler go," he said as he pulled the covers up over his legs. "I know you thought Samantha was the greatest thing since sliced bread, but you see now why I wanted you to keep your distance?"

"I'm sure she did what she thought was best for the church."

"You would say that," Dean said witheringly. "You always want to see something good in people. People aren't good all the time, Grace. A whole church might come apart because she couldn't keep her mouth shut and you say 'she did what she thought was best for the church'." He shook his head. "Anyway, I'm not upset that Tyler and Allen left. I am kind of disappointed that Curtis left, but then again with all of them gone, now I'll probably be able to get to be the president of the deacon board."

Grace, who had been laying on her side with her back to Dean, perked up. "What?" she asked blankly.

Dean shrugged. "The other guys are more likely to listen to me without those three there," he replied nonchalantly. "I'm sure I'll get the presidency. And who knows what else?" He turned off his lamp, laid down, and was sound asleep within minutes.

Grace exhaled deeply. She should have known. Dean and his selfish ambitions were at it again. Deplorable, but not surprising.

The Rev. Riley show was not yet over.

The following Sunday Christ First was packed to capacity. Word about the fight had spread rapidly throughout the small town, and people came to see if there would be a round two. Rev. Riley skipped Sunday school and stayed in his office, sheltered from the massive crowd, refusing to allow anyone except his associates to enter, until it was time for him to come to the pulpit to preach his sermon.

Still bruised from the beating, Rev. Riley adjusted his tie several times before he spoke. What he said shocked everyone in the church, including the remaining deacons.

"My brothers and sisters in Christ," he intoned gravely, "I have to sincerely apologize to you all about what you witnessed here last weekend. It was a travesty and should not have happened in the house of God. I do hope you will pray for Deacon Toole and his wife Claudia. I have no ill will toward either of them, and I hope none of you do, either."

Grace was riveted to her seat. Was Rev. Riley going to admit wrongdoing for once in his pastoral tenure? Had Curtis beat some humility into him?

Nope.

"The good thing is that what happened last week helped me to put my position here at Christ First into perspective," Rev. Riley continued. "I cannot say that I have the same zeal for this church as I did when I was first installed. While some of that may be attributed to my own personal shortcomings, a lot of it has been due to the stresses brought on by several of the auxiliaries here who do not seem to support my vision for this church." He fixed his gaze on the deacons. They exchanged glances with each other.

Rev. Riley continued. "Some of you have also been unkind to my beautiful wife Wilma, who has done nothing but be the best first lady and wife she could be."

Wilma dropped her head. It was a gesture the church was accustomed to seeing from her. She always looked sad. Grace felt terribly for her.

"With that being said," Rev. Riley went on, "I have decided that it is in my best interest to resign as the pastor of this church effective immediately. I pray that you find someone who can lead you in the ways of the Lord."

As the church burst into conversation, Rev. Riley descended the pulpit, walked to the third row where Wilma sat, and extended his hand. Wearing an expression no one could comprehend, Wilma rose, but refused to take her husband's hand. Instead, she walked out of the church, making eye contact with no one. Rev. Riley followed behind her, nodding grimly at a few confused members as he made his way to the exit. The associate ministers followed behind him.

No one knew what to do. Multiple people in the congregation jumped to their feet and rushed to the door, along with the deacons. "Are they really leaving?" they asked in disbelief.

They were. Dean watched as Rev. Riley and his crew packed themselves into two SUVs and sped out of the church parking lot at top speed.

"Everyone, everyone!" Dallas yelled, gesturing for everyone to quiet down. "Please, go back in the sanctuary. The service must continue."

The other deacons turned to him. "How is the service going to continue without any ministers?" Andre asked in a hushed voice, eyeballing the church members as they hesitantly went back into the sanctuary.

Dallas folded his arms. "In the absence of the pastor, whose job is it to bring the message?"

Marlon and Patrick adopted a stance similar to Patrick's and turned to face Dean. "The deacons," they chorused.

Dean looked back and forth at his peers, his eyes wide. "Why are you all looking at me?" he squawked.

"Because this is what you've always wanted," Dallas told him coldly. "Now's your time to shine, Dean. You've got the spotlight that you've been after. You weren't happy having decent guys like Allen and Tyler on the board, and you know what… had either of them been here right now, I'm sure they'd have no problem putting together a sermon."

Andre shrugged uncomfortably. "He's right, Dean. Allen and Tyler were trying to get us to the see the light on Riley and they were right. I don't know why I sided with you sometimes. I really thought I was doing the right thing then, but now…" He shook his head and walked off.

Patrick put his head in his hands. "Look… One of us needs to go up there and get control of the congregation. Let them know that service will move forth in about ten minutes. Have the choir sing a couple songs until Dean gets himself together."

Dean's head was swirling. Yes, he wanted to be the president of the deacon board, but at no point in time had he ever wanted to be the *pastor.* And how was he supposed to preach a sermon? Truth be told, he never picked up a Bible when he was outside of church. Never.

His heart pounding, Dean made his way to Rev. Riley's former office. He needed a quiet place to figure things out. When he got to the office and flung the door open, what he saw made his blood run cold.

"Fellas!" he yelled hoarsely.

The other deacons ran to him. "What?" asked Marlon, annoyed.

Dean pointed into the office.

It was obvious that Rev. Riley had planned his departure well. He had taken some parting gifts--the desk and its matching bookcase and chair, the microwave, the DVD and CD player, the little refrigerator, the flat-screen television--all items that had been bought using the church's money. Dallas got so angry he let several curse words escape his lips.

"That little low-down piece of garbage!" Patrick shouted. "How could he take that stuff? Should we call the police? That's *not* his stuff!"

"Oh my God. Oh, my God," Dean repeated weakly, pacing back and forth. "I don't know what to do!"

Dallas again turned on him, looking incredulous. "You don't know what to do?" he repeated mockingly. "Well, color me surprised! Maybe now you see that you don't have everything under control like you always thought you did!"

He turned to Andre and barked, "Marlon, go out there and tell the congregation that Dean will be out there to give the message. Then we will have the benediction and head home. We will do Communion next Sunday. You're going to have a long week, Mr. Diva. You're going to have to call the pastors at the local churches and see if they can line up some preachers until we get a new one elected."

"But…but…" Dean sputtered.

"No buts," Dallas said angrily. "You wanted the presidency, you got it. Congratulations and good luck."

He walked out of the office, bumping into Dean's shoulder as he did so. One by one, the others followed. The only one who looked at him at all was Andre, and it was only to shake his head.

Alone in the office, Dean's stomach bubbled as he continued to pace back and forth, trying to figure out what he could possibly say to the congregation. He rummaged through the remaining items in the office and found nothing. Then, a light bulb went off in Dean's head. He grabbed his phone and quickly typed "www.findasermon.com" into the search box. He scrolled through the list of sermon topics, picked one, and headed out into the sanctuary, where the grumbling congregation was growing impatient and angry.

Dean gripped the pulpit desk with both hands, nervous. He leaned forward to speak into the microphone. When he did so, his voice was more amplified than he expected, and a few members in the congregation recoiled at the sound. "Good afternoon, and thanks for bearing with us," he said, trying to sound confident. "As they say, the show must go on."

Mother Bonita Shoemaker, one of the oldest members of the church and one who had been very critical of Dean since the moment he was installed as a deacon, wobbled to her feet. "So you really about to preach?" she said doubtfully.

Stankin' old bag better sit down, Dean thought. He fixed a smile on his face and said, "Yes, Mother Shoemaker, in the absence of the pastor, the deacons have to bring the Word."

"We'll see how this goes," Mother Shoemaker said witheringly as she sat back down.

Dean was incensed but kept himself under control. He looked down at his phone screen, which was now blank. He pressed the button on the side of the phone and it came alive. He tried to open the tab that displayed the sermon he had found online. All of a sudden, the link was not working. It was most certainly due to the spotty Internet connection in the church--there were multiple areas in Christ First where the Wi-Fi connection was questionable at best. Unfortunately for Dean at the moment, the pulpit was one of those blind areas.

"Deacon, don't tell me you don't even have a Bible," Mother Shoemaker shouted.

When Dean looked up from his phone, his face no longer masked the anger and irritation he was feeling. Although he hurriedly tried to fix his face, the congregation had seen his expression. A few of them gasped. Others talked among themselves in whispers. To Dean's dismay, some people stood up to walk out, shaking their heads.

"Just bear with me. I have a Bible right here on my phone…"

Fully panicked, Dean picked up the phone and tapped the screen furiously. In their seats, Grace and Eve were having a hard time keeping their composure. It was a struggle to keep from laughing out loud at Dean's mishap. Just as Dean was about to throw the phone in frustration, Mother Shoemaker again rose to her feet, this time asking for her fellow mothers to clear out so she could leave.

"Deacon, this is ridiculous," she barked as she slowly exited the pew. "You better hope we come back next Sunday. I'll pray for y'all in the meantime, because it's obvious you have no idea what you're doing." She threw a dismissive hand up at Dean as she walked out of the church. The other mothers whispered among themselves before standing and following her. As other members watched the backbone of the church leave, they grew disheartened, and soon, the others began to file out too.

Dejected and furious, Dean pitched his phone across the church. It hit a wall and shattered. Unmoved by his frustration, the other deacons waited until he descended the pulpit to pounce on him.

"Just as I thought," Dallas spat. "You ain't *nothin'*."

Before he could fully gain control of himself, Dean's fury overtook him and he lunged at Dallas. Andre restrained him. Dallas laughed in Dean's face before walking away, shaking his head. One by one, the other deacons walked away as well, shaking their heads too. Dean was left alone at the front of the church dazed, confused and humiliated. His reign at Christ First was over.

CHAPTER THIRTEEN

"As I have observed, those who plow evil and those who sow trouble reap it." (Job 4:8)

Grace was confident that she had enough together to move forward. She'd been diligently recording Dean's abuse in a secret notebook and taking photos of her bruises. She had found the key to the safe that he kept their important papers in, including her birth certificate and those of their daughters, took them to school, copied them, and stuck the originals back in the safe. Grace also went on a scavenger hunt throughout the house to itemize Dean's weapons. She was stunned when she found eight guns stored in various areas throughout the house. Some of them were not secured. Grace took pictures of this as well.

Karen, Pamela, Diana and Denise deposited money into the Huntington bank account weekly, making sure that Grace had more than enough money to pay for several months' rent while she looked for a job and applied for temporary assistance. Denise advised Grace to call the police when Dean hit her, have him arrested, and then take her proof of abuse to the court in order to obtain a Personal Protection Order and set the grounds for the divorce proceedings. This was Grace's final objective. All he had to do was hit her once, and it was on.

But then something happened. One day Dean came home from work at nine a.m., surprising Grace as she cleaned the kitchen. He flung open the door and staggered inside, face blanched. Grace frowned in irritation. It was obvious that Dean was sick, which was very rare for him. As he lurched forward into the house, carelessly dropping his briefcase in the middle of the hall, Grace noticed him clutching his stomach.

"What's wrong?" she asked, trying to sound more concerned than she felt.

Dean swallowed past a wave of nausea. "I must have caught a stomach bug from somebody. I felt kind of sick when I left earlier and threw up at work."

Sighing, she said, "How about a relaxing bath? And then you can lay down in the bed for the rest of the day. If it's a stomach bug, it should be out of your system before you know it."

Nodding helplessly, Dean headed toward the stairs. Something told Grace to accompany him. It was lucky for Dean that his wife was behind him, because as he got to the top of the stairs he grew woozy and almost fell backward. Grace caught him, almost stumbling back herself, pushed him back into a standing position, and gasped, "Dean!"

Dean had to sit down, catch his breath, and regain his balance before he was able to make it to the bedroom. As he lay on the bed, Grace ran him a warm bath with salts. Dean staggered into the bathroom, disrobed, and almost fell into the tub. His lack of coordination was baffling. Last Grace checked, a stomach bug didn't cause clumsiness.

Dean was confined to the bed for two days, throwing up every single piece of food that touched his lips for the first twenty-four hours of his sickness. On the second day he was finally able to keep down a bit of soup. He was weak and lethargic, but Grace assumed it was because he hadn't eaten. By the fourth day, he was well enough to return to work--and back to his routine of splitting his time between his home and Angelica's.

Within days of getting well Dean was sick again. This round was much worse than the first. Dean had diarrhea and vomiting, could barely stand up and walk straight, was peeing left and right, and complained of headaches. When he appeared to be confused and started slurring his speech, Grace knew there was something more to this sickness than just the stomach bug. She and the girls rushed Dean to the emergency room where he was admitted immediately. Grace was shocked when, hours after their arrival, the emergency room physician informed her that Dean's kidneys were failing. Dean spent three days in the hospital before stabilizing and being sent home. He was dismayed when he was referred to the local hemodialysis center.

Dean was suspicious. After having a clean bill of health his entire life, he wasn't so sure this entire kidney problem hadn't been brought on by something external. He wondered if Grace was poisoning him. That would explain her mood as of late--kind, overly helpful, attentive--she knew he would be on his way out soon. He went into the den, shut the doors tightly, and turned on his laptop. His Google search led him to believe he might have ingested antifreeze, but he wasn't sure. It seemed as though as if he had been fed antifreeze, he should already be dead.

As he read about the symptoms of ethylene glycol poisoning, Dean grew angrier and angrier. His illness definitely fit the bill. Dean found and ordered an antifreeze detection kit that was relatively simple to use. He wanted as much proof as possible that Grace was trying to kill him. It would make for an even cleaner break from Grace that he ever could have dreamed of--she would go to prison, so he wouldn't have to worry about alimony or child support, and he could figure out what to do with the girls and make the life with Angelica they'd been discussing. The kits arrived on a Thursday. Dean hid them behind several books on the bookcase in his den and waited for Grace to bring him dinner so he could catch her in the act and finally have the proof he needed to end himself of this terrible life, no strings attached.

David felt sick to his stomach, too.

Feebly, he rose to his feet, clutching his stomach, and attempted to get his algebra teacher's attention. "Mrs. Langley?" he said.

From the whiteboard, Mrs. Langley turned. When she saw David's pallid face and labored breathing, she instantly grew alarmed. She rushed to his desk and eased him back down into his seat. "My goodness, David," she said worriedly. "What is wrong?"

"My stomach feels weird," David croaked. "I think I need to go home."

"Let's get you to the office," Mrs. Langley said. "Brady, help me get David to the office, please." Brady, one of David's good friends, dutifully rose to his feet and looped David's arm over his shoulders while Mrs. Langley took the other. Once they were at the main office, David lay down on a cot in the principal's office while Irina, the school secretary, placed a call to Angelica, who, as David expected, did not answer.

David vomited several times into a nearby trashcan. After her fifth time dumping its contents, Irina stood in the doorway of the office with her arms folded. "David, I can't seem to get your mother. Is there someone else I can call for you?"

Sighing himself, David tried to pull his aching body into a sitting position. "I can just walk."

"Absolutely not," Irina declared firmly. "Who else can I call?"

David thought. The only people he knew were from Christ First, and he didn't really care for many of them--except Miss Grace and Deacon Tyler Ware. Those were the only two adults who had shown him genuine concern. David knew that Miss Grace probably wouldn't answer her phone, so he only had one option. Praying to himself, he scrolled through his cell phone contacts until he came upon Tyler's cell phone and work numbers. David handed the phone to Irina. She took it back to her desk and punched in a number. Tyler Ware answered on the second ring.

"Good afternoon, is this Tyler Ware?" David heard Irina say. "I'm calling from Ypsilanti High School. I have a sick student here--David Billups. He needs to go home, but I can't seem to reach his mother. He gave me your phone number..." She trailed off. "You're close by? Perfect. Thank you so much."

She came back into the office with a disposable thermometer and stuck it in David's mouth. "You're usually pretty healthy, kiddo," she told him. "Did you eat something that didn't agree with you?"

"Must have," David mumbled.

Irina pulled the thermometer from his mouth. "You have a slight temperature, but it's not too alarming," she told him. "Do you have anything at home you can take? Do you think your mom will be home soon to take care of you?"

David shrugged.

Irina's warm brown eyes showed her concern. "Maybe you need to stay here and rest if there's no one there to look after you," she said hesitantly. Although it was David's first year at the school, his teachers and the school administration had already picked up cues that his home life was questionable. None of them had ever seen Angelica, and David often came to school haggard in appearance and exhausted.

Without David informing them, they had no idea that he sometimes slept outside in Angelica's car to stay away from her, but they knew something was amiss.

David shook his head. He was used to caring for himself when he was sick, and right now he wanted nothing more than his own bed, regardless of whether his tyrant of a mother was at home or not. "It's probably just something I ate. I'm sure once I get rid of it I'll feel better."

Tyler arrived ten minutes later, his eyes showing concern as well. Having emptied out most of the contents of his stomach, David already felt a bit better, well enough to walk to Tyler's car, which was parked right at the curb. Once inside the car, David heaved a big sigh of relief and leaned his head back, eyes closed.

"Do I need to stop by the pharmacy and get anything for you?" Tyler asked.

David shrugged.

"Come on, son. If you need Vernor's, fever meds, let me know. I can grab that for you. That secretary said you were running a temp."

David nodded miserably. "I doubt we have anything at the house."

"Alright. I'll run in this CVS right here. Be right back out."

Tyler came back out with two bags full of supplies. As they drove to David's house, Tyler watched worriedly as the boy drifted in and out of sleep. "Are you just ill or is something else happening?"

David tried to pull himself into full consciousness. "I don't ever get sick to my stomach," he informed him. "I haven't been eating right, so maybe that's the problem."

"Why haven't you been eating right?"

David shrugged. "I have been busy with baseball. Usually by the time I get home, it's late, so I've been only eating chips and salsa or something so I can get to bed."

"Your mom doesn't make sure that you get a decent meal?"

David snickered ruefully.

Tyler took that as a "no". He wasn't surprised. Angelica didn't seem to be the most attentive mother, and Tyler wasn't fond of her at all. When she and David first began attending the church, Angelica openly flirted with him even after finding out he was married. He firmly struck her down. Despite his reservations about Angelica's character, he and David had struck up a friendship when they were put together to set up displays for the church's Christmas program several months back. It was obvious that David craved attention.

"You're a growing, active boy," Tyler told him. "You gotta make sure you're eating, and eating good stuff, David. Does Angelica cook or no?"

David shook his head.
"So what do you eat on a daily basis?"

David ran down his typical meal plan. A bowl of cereal or oatmeal for breakfast, lunch from school, and for dinner, usually chips and salsa, a couple of hot dogs with wheat bread substituted for buns and potato chips, or pizza rolls.

They had pulled up to David's house. Tyler sat with his head in his hands, thinking. "Not only are you not eating enough for your level of activity, you're eating crap food, David."

"I know."

Tyler tried to hide his anger, but nothing offended him more than negligent parents. As polished as she always was, it was disgusting that Angelica wasn't taking steps to make sure her only child was healthy. He knew he had to do something. As thin as David was, he definitely didn't need to be missing too many meals.

David looked at Tyler like he was crazy when he handed him a Discover credit card.
"What is this? I'm not about to take that."

"I barely use it. It only has a couple hundred dollar limit on it. My work hours are too crazy for me to know whether or not I'll always be available when you need food, but I'm not okay with the idea of you not eating."

"But it's a credit card."

"I'm aware of that. Your phone has Internet, right?"

David nodded.

"Good. Then you can use that card and order food when you get hungry, or take it to the grocery store and use it at the self-checkout to buy something. A lot of places that actually make decent food have delivery now. I trust that you won't abuse it."

David looked at him. "You do?"

"Yes, I do."

David was overwhelmed with emotion. He wasn't sure what to say; he knew if he opened his mouth he might cry. People who were strangers to him before--Miss Grace and now Tyler--were taking better care of him, talking with him, trying to guide him better than his own mother. As David took the card and the supplies and headed into the house, his emotions spilled over. The house was empty. Once inside, he headed right up to his room, stretched himself out on his bed and cried. Why couldn't he have a mom like Miss Grace or a dad like Tyler?

David fell asleep. When he woke up it was visibly darker outside. Angelica was still not home, and his stomach was bothering him again. As he suspected, he was going to have to take care of himself. Sighing angrily, he opened his bedroom door, preparing to head to the kitchen to get a cup of ginger ale, when something he saw out of the corner of his eye made him stop dead in his tracks.

Over the past couple of weeks Angelica had become especially secretive and uncharacteristically paranoid. David knew from prior experience that when Angelica was in the last stages of planning before she executed her evil scheme, she became more anxious and erratic. He knew that she had received multiple notices about late bills, and that also fed into her unpredictable temperament, but he suspected she might be up to more than just her typical treachery. The paranoia was new and alarming, so bad that she kept her bedroom door locked, even when she was in the house. Apparently Angelica had left home in a hurry. Her bedroom door was ajar. Curious, David crept toward the bedroom door and pushed it open.

It looked as though a tornado had ripped through the room. David was stunned. Despite her many conflicting flaws and quirks, Angelica was a very tidy person. The condition of the room was indicative of her current state of mind. David flipped on the light switch to examine the mess disorder more carefully.

The entire expanse of the room was littered with notebooks and papers. His eyebrows furrowed with confusion, David picked up the notebook that was closest within his reach and opened it. It was filled from the first page to the last with Angelica's handwriting, which ran the gamut from being neat and legible with every "i" dotted with a heart and every "t" crossed with an elaborate slanted slash on some days to being indecipherable on others. As David read several of the entries, he discovered that these notebooks were his mother's journals, and that she had been keeping them for years, recording her deepest, darkest thoughts and actions, and to his disgust, personal, intimate details about her male conquests. The entries that discussed the latter subject were typically the ones that were well-written, except for when Angelica was growing tired of her pursuit and getting ready to be done with him. The scribbled entries, which also looked like Angelica had been pushing down very hard as she wrote, also suggesting anger, were usually about one subject in particular--- David.

In entry after entry Angelica bemoaned her soft, spoiled son. On more than one occasion she mused about ways to get rid of him. David was completely unaware that she had contemplated leaving him at various rest stops as she made her way from one state to another. In each of those entries, she talked herself out of doing so by reminding herself that David was the only person she could blame for her crimes if she got caught.

David found Angelica's most recent journal. Ironically it was one that had been given to her when she first joined Christ First, one with a tree that bore brightly-colored fruit and the Scripture from Galatians 5:22-23--ironically, the Scriptures that referred to the fruit of the Spirit. What David read made his blood first run cold, then boil.

Angelica was planning to kill him too.

"Truth be told, I'm getting older and tired of going through the motions with these annoying men," she wrote. *"And I am tired of the U.S. I can't wait to finish with these two so I can retire comfortably to Costa Rica. If I handle both of these situations right, I'll end up with enough money to last me for a long time."*

In another entry full of furious writing, Angelica wrote, *"NOTHING I do can ever satisfy this kid. It doesn't matter what I give him, he still finds something to complain about. He keeps bringing home schedules for his games and telling me about them. I'm waiting on him to get the hint that I am not interested in NONE of that stuff that he is interested in, and I'm tired of pretending! Every day there is SOME reminder as to why I wanted a DAUGHTER! I just know I wouldn't be this miserable with a daughter."*

And the most alarming entry, which also happened to be the most recent: *"I have the papers stashed away; half a million on both of them.. I messed up not giving them enough of the stuff. It only made them sick, and I'm surprised David hasn't figured it out yet. I don't know why, but the dumb kid obviously still trusts me for some reason. I almost had Dean, though. Now I know exactly what I need to do for both of them."*

David's stomach issues weren't caused by poor eating habits at all. His mother, his own mother, had been poisoning him. David had no idea how, as Angelica hardly ever cooked any food. Then an alarm went off in his head. Although he didn't eat food cooked by his mother often, he always had his favorite beverage in the house, one that Angelica never drank--orange juice. Each morning with breakfast and sometimes in the evening, David drank several glasses of orange juice. Undoubtedly that was how she was administering the poison to her child.

David knew he had little time to panic, but thoughts whirled through his head at a mile a minute. Part of him didn't want to believe his mother was capable of such duplicity against her own flesh and blood, but the proof was right there in front of him in black and white--or in the case of Angelica's preferred gel pen, pink and white. He had no idea what to do. Call someone? Who? And tell them what? Call the police? He knew better than to do that. He'd seen his mother talk her way out of situations in which she was obviously criminally liable before. No one wanted to believe such a beautiful, polished and poised woman could be such a demon. All Angelica had to do was put the blame on David and no doubt he'd be locked up at least until adulthood, if not further.

David went back to his room, heartbeat thumping, and sat on the edge of his bed with his head in his hands. It could happen at any time. He could easily stop drinking the juice and refuse her food if she made any, but that only meant his mother would find a different way to kill him. He couldn't run away; he'd done so before and once apprehended been returned right back to his mother's custody with no questions asked. All Angelica had to do was tell the authorities her son was acting out against his poor, beleaguered single mother, and the grown-ups fell for it each time, hook, line and sinker. He knew if he told Miss Grace or Tyler, they would take him to the police immediately--*if* they even believed him.

As tears of rejection and anger fell from his eyes, David's pocket vibrated. It was his phone, and most likely Eve calling.

"David?" It was Eve, and she had obviously been crying. "Are you at the park? Or can you come to the park later on?"

"I can come now, if you need me to… what's going on?"

"It just got bad here, man," Eve said between sobs. "I don't know what happened between Mom and Dean, but he really went off."

"On your mom?"

"Yeah."

"Is she okay?"

"She's awake now, but he had knocked her out, and I went and tried to defend her, and he…" She stopped.

David stood to his feet, the anticipation as to what he knew she was about to say intensifying. "He what?" he coaxed in a low tone, trying to mask his fury.

"He punched me and kicked me. I was knocked out for a few seconds. Mom said she'll probably take me to the hospital but the cops are here and she is talking to them right now. But you know what, David? Even if Mom does leave, he'll never just let us go. He's too controlling. He's always told her if she leaves he will destroy her. We'll never live a normal life. And I'm sick of it! I hate living like this. I hate it." He listened as she cried for more than ten minutes.

That was it; David was done. Mentally, he snapped. Dean was never going to stop. He was going to continue being a tyrant for as long as he was allowed. Angelica, too. Someone had to stop them. His own pain was now inconsequential. Listening helplessly as she sobbed, David felt pity, and then anger. Right then, he knew there was definitely something he could do, something that would help Eve and Grace... let his mother get rid of Dean. Until that very moment David had been wrestling with his increased understanding of good and evil. Grace was a very effective Sunday school teacher who was passionate about building the Christian character of her charges, and the lessons she taught about doing what was right in the eyes of God as opposed to living by the world's wicked standards had been indelibly implanted in his mind. Each time David attended Sunday school he felt convicted; convicted and compelled to try to convince his mother that what she was doing was not the way to go.

That was before this. With each of Eve's sniffles, David's anger grew exponentially.

"Okay, Eve. It's okay. It's going to be fine. Do you want to meet at the park now?"

"Can you meet me later?" she asked, still sniffling. "I'm not sure how long the cops are going to be here. I don't think I need to go to the hospital but Mom might make me go anyway."

"Where is Dean?"

"I don't know. He ran out before the police got here. He said he wasn't coming back tonight though."

David sighed. "I'm willing to bet he is with my mother."

"Really?" Eve said incredulously. "They're sneaking around again?"

"Yeah. He always comes to my house when things aren't going well there, so I'd put money on it. Wherever my mom is, that's where he is. And he's not necessarily safe with her, so don't worry about him." It slipped out before he could stop himself.

"What do you mean, 'he's not safe'?" Eve repeated.

"Meaning that my mom has guns all around the house, and if he tries anything stupid with her, he might get shot," David said, thinking quickly.

"I hope she does," Eve huffed. "She'd be doing us all a big favor."

David changed the subject. "I think you guys are safe. I'm sure the cops showing up spooked him and he is going to try to lay low. Are your sisters there?" he asked.

"Yeah. They're all in my room. They're afraid of Dean coming back."

"Okay," David said slowly. "Alright, Eve. What time do you want to meet at the park?"

"Around eight-thirty."

"I'll see you at eight-thirty," David repeated. "If you need me before then, let me know."

"Okay."

David jumped into action. If Dean and Angelica weren't together already, David was sure Dean would make his way to their house sooner or later. He also knew that Angelica would be ready to be done with Dean--his violence toward his family was making him more of a liability. Just then he had a thought. He had informed Eve that his mother had guns all over the house... indeed, she did. Always afraid of the day karmic reparations came upon her, Angelica had amassed an impressive cache of weapons over the years. He needed to unload them just in case.

David put on a pair of black leather gloves. In his mother's room, David found Angelica's Glock and checked its chamber. It was fully loaded, as he suspected. He got down on his hands and knees and reached under Angelica's bed, patting the ground until he felt the two boxes of ammunition that he knew were hidden there. David went into Angelica's master bathroom, took the lid off the toilet, and picked up the handgun that she had duct-taped inside. He carefully removed the bullets and placed the gun back in its duct-tape holster and put the lid back on the toilet. Next, David went to the main floor, where he located the handguns that Angelica kept in the living room and kitchen, removed their bullets, and placed them back in their homes.

His next step was to go to the kitchen, where he opened the refrigerator and surveyed its contents in deep thought. There were a couple of opened bottles of wine, a Sprite, and a diet Cola. Two huge steaks were also marinating in a pan covered with foil. David eyeballed them curiously...

Fifteen minutes later he proceeded downstairs to the basement storage area, where he went to a shelf and pulled down all of Angelica's shoe boxes until he found the .357 magnum she had stolen two years ago from another of her conquests. It too was fully loaded. David removed the bullets from the .357, then, on second thought, put two back into the chamber, tucked the Glock into his waistband, went upstairs to his bedroom, and sat, waiting, thinking.

His thoughts were enough to drive him momentarily insane. If Angelica was in fact trying to kill him, was he prepared to defend himself against his own mother, a move that might possibly cause him to take her life? Nah... it couldn't be. What was he thinking??? Was he crazy? David punched at his head with his fists. He couldn't believe the thoughts that were coming into his head. He was seriously considering having to fight or even kill his own mom? It couldn't be, it just couldn't. David's stomach felt queasy. Maybe he should just leave and go to the police...

The front door downstairs opened, signaling Angelica's return. As David suspected, she was accompanied by Dean, and from the sound of his mother's voice, she was not happy with what he had done to his family. They argued as they made their way into the kitchen. Davud crept down the stairs to watch the scene unfold.

"You are *such* a moron," she raged. "What kind of life do you think we'll have while you're paying child support for five kids *and* alimony? Now that the cops are involved, that's what's going to happen! You won't get custody of the girls, so we won't be able to send them away, and now Grace will control everything! We could have been done with this whole situation in less than a month, but you couldn't control yourself and now you've probably ruined everything! Thanks to you a clean break from your stupid family is impossible!"

"I--I just lost control," Dean stammered. "What was I supposed to do, stay calm knowing that my wife is trying to kill me? And Eve stuck her nose in our business and I just exploded. I don't even know what came over me. I couldn't help myself."

"Funny how you can help yourself when it comes to me though," Angelica countered. "You've never so much as raised your voice at me. Is it because you know I'd kill you on the spot if you did?"

David watched as Angelica stomped around the kitchen, opening the refrigerator and various cabinets as she prepared to cook Dean what would be his last meal. He stared at her miserably as she continued to rampage against him. Dean was no match for this side of Angelica. She was out of her mind, and it was starting to make him look at her in another light. "Have you been drinking? Did you shove some more of that stuff up your nose again?"

Angelica turned toward him suddenly, brandishing the knife. Instinctively, Dean moved back.

"I'm. Sober."

She stared at Dean icily for a few minutes before turning back to the meat.

"You're acting crazy," Dean said quietly.

She put her hand up at him. "Just go away and let me do this. Go downstairs or something."

Shaking his head, Dean opened the basement door and descended the steps, muttering to himself. Lips pursed, Angelica returned her attention to the steaks that she had searing in a pan on the stove.

"I hear you on those stairs, David."

David gasped.

"Get in here."

Slowly, David descended the steps and made his way into the kitchen. Angelica removed the steaks from the pan and added them to plates alongside several spears of asparagus and baked potatoes.

Angelica stared at him. "You ready for this?"

David shrugged. "You've never cared before what I thought, so…"

"I need to know that you're not going to go run and tell that little girl that you're sneaking around with."

David was stunned. "What do you mean?" he asked timidly.

The knife was still within Angelica's reach. "You think I'm stupid?" she asked coldly. "I know you've been seeing Eve. So now I have to wonder how much you've told her. You been messing around with her?"

"Are you serious? She's thirteen."

Angelica laughed. "Do you know the kinds of things I was doing when I was thirteen? That means nothing!" she retorted. "Have you been messing around with her?"

"No!"

Angelica's face hardened again. She advanced upon her son. "What have you told her about me, David?"

He backed up.

"Have you told her about me, David?" she asked, her voice barely above a whisper.

"No," he said, whispering himself.

She had the knife in her hand; David hadn't even seen her pick it up. They were now standing face to face, with Angelica glaring up at her son. "Good," she spat, "because if you did, it wouldn't be good for either of you."

David's eyes widened. "You would hurt me?" he asked tenuously.

Inexplicably, Angelica retreated. She picked up one of the plates and a glass of wine. "Do you remember all those times I asked you to take Dean his food?"

"Yeah," David said uneasily.

"That food was poisoned. There was a reason I asked you to deliver it to him--so you can never think that what's about to happen to Dean isn't as much your fault as it is mine. Whether or not you knew the food was poisoned at that time was of no consequence... you still gave it to him. That makes you an accomplice. Don't think for one minute I'm going to go down by myself. You're responsible for what's happening with Dean too, and don't think if you try to sell me out to the police I won't tell them that."

David's mouth dropped open.

Angelica walked back up to him, her face frighteningly hard. "I don't care if whatever that little fast girl has been giving you is the best you've ever had..."

"But we haven't..."

Angelica gave his face a little slap. "...If you've told her anything about me, you're both not safe. I don't know what's happened to you since we came to this little raggedy town, but you're not the same. Don't think I haven't noticed. You've gone soft! I been watching you, David. If you're thinking you can get over on me, get it out your mind. You can't. You're no match for me. Bring the drinks downstairs. My wine glass is the one with the flowers on it. Make sure to give Dean the other one."

She picked up both plates and headed downstairs.

Reeling, David had to get himself together. Tonight was going badly and undoubtedly was about to get worse. He couldn't believe Angelica had just threatened him--and Eve. It became obvious that his mother was indeed capable of killing him if she felt there was enough of a threat. His head clouded by revelation, David patted his waistband to make sure the gun was still secure and headed into the basement.

Dean and Angelica were seated on the couch in front of the television, eating calmly, and looked up when David appeared. Wordlessly, he set the plain wine glass down on the table in front of Dean and the flower-etched one in front of his mother. Then he sat in the armchair and watched as both of them went back to their food and drink.

"Are you eating, David?" Dean asked.

"Nah, my stomach has been messed up today." David looked at his mother out of the corner of his eye. Her face didn't change at all. "That and Mom didn't fix me anything."

"I only bought two steaks since you haven't been eating at home, David," Angelica said brightly, as though she hadn't just threatened him upstairs.

Watching their every bite and sip, David nodded slowly. He waited until they both had consumed the majority of their meal.

"Yeah," David said listlessly. "That's okay. I don't want you to poison me anymore anyway."

Angelica's face changed. Dean, who had been vigorously chewing his second to last piece of steak, slowed his mastication and looked blankly from mother to son, question marks in his eyes.

Angelica forced a laugh. "David, you're so dramatic. Go on back upstairs."

"You left your bedroom door open today. I read your little 'journals'. I know you've been poisoning me. You might want to stop eating that, Dean."

Dean rose to his feet slowly. "Wh-What in the world is going on here?"

Now it was David's turn to laugh. "Man, are you really this whipped?" he asked Dean bitterly. "It didn't ring a bell that every time you ate here you got sick? You too stupid to put two and two together?"

"Shut up, David!" Angelica lunged at David, only to be surprised when he swiftly pulled the gun from his waistband.

"What the-?" Dean yelled.

Now that David knew he was completely in control, an odd sense of tranquility washed over him. "I almost feel sorry for you," he told Dean flatly. "Mom's been poisoning you, man. She is trying to kill you so she can cash in that insurance policy that you were stupid enough to let her take out. You signed off on one amount, but she has a guy that does fake papers who altered your policy. When you die, she'll be rich."

"He's lying, Dean!" Angelica screamed. "He's lying! I'd never do that to you."

Dean stared at Angelica in disbelief. "Why would he say that?"

"Because he is angry that we've been spending so much time together," Angelica said in a rushed voice. "That's all. He's jealous. The two of you were hanging out, playing basketball, and then you and I got back together and you stopped doing those things. But it'll be okay. He just wants you to spend a little time with him too, right, David?" She looked at her son pleadingly.

David shook his head slowly.

"David," Dean said gently, "can you please put the gun away, so that we can talk?"

"We're talking right now just fine," David said with a shrug, "so if you don't mind, I'd like to hang on to the gun."

Dean gazed at Angelica, his eyes probing hers. Without a word, he started to lean over to the chair next to him, where his jacket lay.

"What are you doing?" David yelled, pointing the gun at Dean.

"I-I-I have to see if what you're saying is true," Dean stammered, putting his hands up. "I actually have an antifreeze test on me."

"You're lying," David said, steadying his grip on the gun.

Dean used one finger to retrieve the jacket and slid the jacket over to him. "I thought it was Grace…Check the right inside pocket," he told David. "You'll find it in there. I promise that's all I have on me. My gun is out in the car."

David patted the jacket and found no evidence of a gun. As Dean said, there was a little box in the inside right pocket of his jacket. David took it out and slid it across the room. Angelica looked on, fighting the urge to panic.

"I need water to do this."

Moving cautiously, David retrieved a little Dixie cup of water from the bathroom sink and slid it over to Dean. Dean chopped up some of his food and put it into one of the containers, which he then immersed with water. He broke the three little vial-looking things, then did the same thing using the other container and a sample of his wine. Then he waited. Within seconds, the contents of the first container turned bright blue. Dean didn't need to see if the second container's result was the same. He was enraged.

Dean lunged at Angelica and wrapped his hands around her throat. "You were trying to kill me?" he screamed as he shook her.

Yelping, Angelica pawed and scratched at Dean's hands, trying to get him to release his powerful grip. "David!" she managed to squeal.

David looked at her and shook his head "no."

He watched, just as placid as a person watching a rain shower through a window, as Dean and Angelica tousled. Angelica may have thought herself to be a physically strong woman, but she was no match for Dean. As he continued to depress her airway, tears formed in her eyes as she sputtered and fought for breath. The look in Dean's eyes was absolutely demonic. Not only was he watching the life escape from her body, he was enjoying it.

When David saw the look of almost trance-like bliss in Dean's eyes, he wondered if Dean got the same feeling when he was beating Eve and Miss Grace. Angelica's will and ability to struggle was diminishing rapidly as her oxygen levels depleted. David could see that she didn't have much left in her. He panicked. Yes, she was a monster, but he couldn't let her go out at the hands of another monster--a wife-and-

175

child-beating monster at that. And what would Dean do to him if he killed her?? "Mom!" David shouted suddenly. "Here. Take this!"

He slid the gun across the floor. Relieved, Angelica grabbed it, pressed it into Dean's abdomen, and pulled the trigger.

BANG! BANG!

Dean's grip on Angelica's throat loosened; his body slumped down on top of her. David's breath caught in his throat and the room grew quiet. Dean was laying on top of Angelica. David could not tell if Dean was dead or not. Angelica, zapped of all of her strength, loosened her grip on the gun and lay there, breathing heavily.

An eerie silence filled the room. Holding his breath, David timidly approached Dean and used his foot to roll him over. There was no doubt about it. Dean Hardaway was dead.

Angelica was still wheezing a little, but when she realized that she had won the fight, she smiled weakly to herself. "What took you so long?"

David didn't respond.

Suddenly, Angelica raised the gun and pointed it at her son. "You were thinking about letting him get me for a minute, weren't you, you little bastard? As if I'd ever let that happen. Maybe if you go to heaven you'll get the father you've always wanted, and when you're gone I can get the daughter I always wanted."

She struggled to pull herself up into a sitting position, pointed the gun right at David's head, pulled the trigger and… the gun clicked. Angelica pulled the trigger again. It clicked again. Only then did she realize that there were no more bullets. Suddenly her head began to spin uncontrollably and her stomach felt unsettled. Just as soon as she identified the nausea, her entire meal came up violently. This was followed by the worst bout of abdominal cramps she had ever suffered in her entire life.

"Were you really going to kill me, Mom?"

Angelica looked at him, her eyes wide. Her hands felt strange, causing her to lose her grip on the gun. Looking oddly detached, David plucked the gun from her hands. Only then did she notice he was wearing gloves.

"David, what..?"

He shook his head, tears in his eyes. "Up until right now I was really hoping you loved me more than money, but now I see."

Another powerful bout of emesis left Angelica with nothing to do but curl herself into the fetal position. "What have you done?" she managed weakly.

"Like mother like son," David said casually. "I seasoned your food and drinks with some of your special brew."

Earlier while David was emptying his mother's guns, he spiked all of the liquid contents in the kitchen with some of his mother's beloved potion, including the wine and the steak sauce that Dean and Angelica had just used. While Angelica had been stealthily giving Dean small amounts over time so he'd think he had just caught a stomach virus, David hadn't taken the same precaution. If he discovered that his mother was in fact trying to kill him, he was done. If she had shown some remorse, he had planned to get her medical help and tell the police that Dean attacked her and she shot him in self-defense. But as soon as his mother raised that gun and pulled the trigger, David had his answer. His mom was a monster, and he had just fed her a fatal dose of ethylene glycol. Without rapid medical intervention, she would surely die.

She gasped. "David...You gotta get your mama some help."

David shook his head. Tears flowed freely down his face. "Nah, I can't even do that, Mom."

Her lips turned blue. "I'm sorry, David."

Looking at her face, David began to hyperventilate. A part of him wanted to believe that she was sorry, quickly call 911, and get her some help so she could possibly survive. The smell of blood and vomit assaulted his nostrils and he began to gag. He had to decide whether he was going to leave his mother there to die or stay.

"David...you need me..."

David cocked his head to the side in thought. Needed her for what? To use him as bait to lure in more prey? To help her kill more innocent men? What kind of life was he living? If he called the police and they were able to save Angelica, then what? Undoubtedly she would tell them that David was the one who poisoned her, and she would probably blame Dean's murder on him as well. The narrative of David's life ran through his head. All of Angelica's acts of evil, and all of the times when she could have been caught and wasn't...

David pulled himself to his feet and headed for the steps. Angelica gasped as she watched her son, knowing he was leaving her to die, and that her time was measured. As she watched David ascend the basement stairs, Angelica's body went into convulsions. Willing himself not to look back, David continued up the stairs and out the back door. He had to go meet Eve. He rehearsed a story as he made his way to the park. Some of the truth was okay. As much as he hated to hide things from her, Eve couldn't know everything.

David arrived at the park at eight-thirty on the dot. Eve was there on their bench with a hoodie pulled up to mask her bruised face. When David saw her appearance, some of the consternation he felt about Dean being dead disappeared. The entire left side of Eve's face was purple and swollen. David held her and took her tender face into his hands, shaking his head quietly.

"What happened tonight, Eve?"

She managed a bitter laugh. "Dean is mad at the world because he's been sick. Somehow he managed to come to the ridiculous conclusion that Mom has been poisoning his food, so he jumped on her. I got in the way and ended up like this." She motioned to her face and shook her head. "I'm just hoping that was the last straw for Mom. After Dean hit me, she unloaded on him. I've never seen her fight him back before. Tim that lives next door heard the fight and called the cops and finally, Mom told them everything, so now it's all out there. All of the other neighbors saw the police car at our house, so I'm sure wherever that coward is, he is scared and hiding.

When they find him, he's going to get arrested. Tim changed the locks so he can't get in. He can't hide for long."

David swallowed. "Call the cops and give them my address. Bet money that's where he is. And if he's not there, my mom knows where he is."

Eve frowned.

"You still have your phone?"

Eve nodded.

"Call them right now and send them over there. Let's get that piece of garbage locked up tonight so y'all can rest."

Eve obligingly called the police station and asked for the cops who had visited her home earlier. Dispatch agreed to relay them a message, as they were currently out looking for Dean. "He is probably at 1435 Sunrise Court. His girlfriend Angelica Billups lives there."

David knew what was about to happen. The police would go there and see Dean's car. David strategically left the front and back door unlocked so they would hopefully go in and discover the grisly scene he'd left behind. In the meantime, Eve needed to take care of herself.

"Does your mom know you're here?"

Eve shook her head. "I told her I didn't want to go to the hospital because I was too embarrassed and didn't want to get her in trouble, and that I just wanted to lay down."

"You need to be at home, Eve."

"Mom's going to be mad that I snuck out."

"She'll get over it. You need to put something on your face. I can tell it hurts." He touched it gently, and she winced and pulled back.

Eve nodded miserably. Hand in hand, they walked back to her home.

Grace was still reeling from having her head bounced up against the wall and the floor as Dean threw her back and forth and punched her only an hour prior. In the kitchen, she sat with an ice pack to her head surrounded by the other girls, and was surprised when Eve and David walked into the house.

"Wha-?"

"I'm sorry, Mom," Eve said sheepishly. "I wanted to get out of here for a minute. I'm sorry I lied. David made me come back."

Grace looked back and forth between the two. Under different circumstances she'd have had several questions, as it was obvious that her daughter and David were involved in more than just friendship. She'd become aware of them crushing on each other but up until that moment wasn't sure as to their level of involvement. The fact that Eve had reached out to David and had followed his advice to come home illustrated a deeper connection. Grace decided to forego the conversation to when they both felt better. David was looking at her with wide eyes.

"I'm okay, David."

"Miss Grace…" He was struggling with emotion. She was probably the kindest person he'd ever known, and to see her bruised and banged up was difficult. "I--I don't know what to say."

"You don't have to say anything. Thanks for bringing Eve back."

"Why aren't you laying down?" he asked. "Why aren't both of you laying down? I can stay here for awhile. Why don't y'all go rest?"

Grace's head was pounding and she felt weak. Although she didn't want to admit it, Eve didn't feel so well either. Grace nodded wearily. "You come with me, Eve."

Eve didn't argue. The two of them went upstairs to Grace's bedroom, where they took aspirins for their aching heads and bodies and wasted no time falling asleep. David made popcorn for himself and the other girls and they went downstairs, where they entertained themselves and David with toys and Disney movies.

Only half an hour into their nap Grace was startled awake by a series of loud, incessant knocks on the front door. Shaking her fuzzy head, Grace got out of the bed gingerly so as to not wake Eve, who was still sleeping soundly. As soon as she got to the top of the stairs, Grace saw flashing police lights. She hurried downstairs and opened the door. The two cops that had been at her house earlier, Officers Delaney and Whitmore, stood on the porch, looking grim.

"Have you found Dean?"

"May we come in?" Officer Delaney asked.

Nodding, Grace stepped aside and let them both in. "I take it you found Dean?"

"As a matter of fact, we did," Officer Whitmore told her. "We found him at the home of a Ms. Angelica Billups."

Grace pursed her lips, disgusted but not surprised. "Is he now in custody?"

"We regret to inform you of this, Mrs. Hardaway, but there appears to have been some type of domestic incident at the Billups residence, and your husband was killed."

Grace's eyes widened. "Excuse me?" she said blankly.

"We're very sorry, ma'am. Dean Hardaway was dead from two gunshot wounds by the time we arrived."

Grace's breath caught in her throat and she stumbled backward. Officer Delaney reached out to steady her. "Let me help you to a seat, ma'am. Are you sure you don't need medical attention?"

In the kitchen, Grace sank into one of the chairs, shaking her head as vigorously as her pain would allow. "No, no, I'm not interested," she protested. "But what you just said makes no sense. What do you mean, 'some type of domestic incident'?"

"We are still investigating, but it looks like he was shot by Ms. Billups."

Grace's mouth dropped open. "Did she say what happened?"

"Unfortunately Ms. Billups was found deceased as well."

"Wha-WHAT?" Grace squawked. "What in the world is going on? What happened to her?"

"We don't know at this time. We're looking for her son, David. Do you know where he is?"

"Right here."

All three adults turned. David was standing in the doorway, and had been the entire time. The look on his face was unreadable.

Officer Whitmore carefully approached the teen. "I'm sorry you had to find out this way, David. But something happened at your house, and your mother has passed away."

David remained expressionless. To the others in the room, his lack of emotion appeared to be shock. Although David knew that his mother was near death when he left, hearing those words come out of the officer's mouth was more than he could bear at the moment. Everything went black. Just as Officer Delaney had done Grace, Officer Whitmore caught the boy as he slunk onto the floor.

When he woke up, David was on a gurney being loaded into an ambulance. He could make out the sullen faces of Grace and the girls, who looked on worriedly with clasped hands. Officer Delaney appeared from the side of the ambulance and told Grace, "They said they're taking him to Mott's."

"I can't let him be alone," Grace said tearfully. "We're going to follow them to the hospital."

And she did. Although she had just lost her husband and the girls had lost their father, Grace mustered all of the strength with which she had been operating for the last decade and headed to the C.S. Mott Children's Hospital at the University of Michigan. No one spoke during the ride. Only after they got to the hospital and into the emergency room where they watched as David was immediately wheeled to the back for evaluation did Sarah ask timidly, "Is Daddy really dead?"

Feeling as though she were in some type of nightmare, Grace had to think fast. This was a situation she'd never imagined being in. How would the girls react to this? Luckily, the ER was uncharacteristically empty, so Grace was able to find a relatively secluded area of the waiting room for she and the girls to occupy.

Once they were seated, Grace cleared her throat and closed her eyes. "To answer your question... Yes. Yes. I'm sorry, girls. Something happened tonight and your father was killed."

Grace waited for the tears and outbursts of emotion and was surprised when she got none. When she opened her eyes again, the girls were looking at each other blankly. Then came the questions.

"Somebody shot Daddy?" Rebekah asked.

"Yes," Grace said uncomfortably.

"Who?" Rebekah demanded. "Was it a burglar or a carjacker?"

"No," Grace said uneasily.

"Where was he when he got shot? Why would someone shoot him?"

Grace didn't know how much was appropriate to tell the young girls. "He was at a friend's house, and it looks like maybe him and the friend had a fight and the friend shot him."

Even Abby knew that was odd. "What 'friend'?"

Grace wasn't sure how to answer, but Eve was. "It was Angelica Billups, that big-boobed broad from church. Daddy was over there cheating on Mom with her," she replied witheringly.

Grace massaged her temples with her fingertips. "Eve…"

" 'Eve', what?? Was I wrong? Do I need to sugarcoat it because he got killed? Just because he's dead am I supposed to act like he wasn't an abusive, cheating bastard?"

"Eve!" Grace cried, dismayed. "Now is not the time!"

Eve stared at her mother, astonished. "Why isn't it?" she asked, befuddled. "I'm tired of denying the truth. I won't do it anymore. We are *free*. God finally answered my prayers."

CHAPTER FOURTEEN

"Remember not the former things, nor consider the things of old."
(Isaiah 43:18)

Dean's funeral was a sad affair. Not necessarily because he was dead, but because the paltry attendance at his service showed how utterly disliked he truly was. Of the people that did come, it was obvious they only did so to show support for Grace and the girls. Even Pamela, Denise and Diana were unemotional.

The funeral had been delayed for almost two weeks as Grace struggled to access enough money to get him buried. A number of surprising revelations about Dean and Angelica came to light during that time. When Grace started making calls about Dean's insurance policies, she was startled to find that the funds would not be disbursed because Dean was being investigated for insurance fraud. As it turns out, the policy documents he had signed with Angelica were the culprit. Grace was called into the police department to identify her husband's signature on a policy that awarded Angelica Billups half a million dollars. It wasn't until David handed over his mother's journals that the police figured out the complexity of the insurance scam and the policy was nullified. The insurance company awarded Grace the entire amount of money per their original, valid life insurance documents. Despite the fact that Angelica never referred to her insurance "guy" by name in any of her notebooks, authorities were still able to track him down. Surprisingly, Angelica's "guy" was a woman that she'd known from childhood who owned a life insurance franchise.

Angelica had victimized men in multiple states. With Angelica's murderous lifestyle completely actualized, news media pounced on the otherwise quiet little city. Grace found herself being hounded by reporters. Upon his release from the hospital David was taken in by Tyler and Samantha Ware. They wasted no time taking him and their children on an extended vacation for his protection. By the details made available in Angelica's journals, it was obvious he'd been living a far worse life than anyone had ever imagined.

A month after Dean's death, things were beginning to quiet down, allowing Grace time to finally process everything. It wasn't really a period of mourning; it was more like a period of readjustment. The money from Dean's death benefits in addition to donations she'd received from sympathetic strangers all around the nation had put her in a very good position financially. However, Grace still managed her money carefully and started looking for her first job in almost fifteen years.

The perfect job opportunity fell right into her lap. Out of the blue one day, she received an email from Cecile, encouraging her to get in contact with Duane Pleasant ASAP. Confused but eager to see what her old mentor was up to, Grace took down the phone number Cecile provided and called.

"Pleasant's Pleasantries, this is Duane speaking."

A huge smile crossed her face. "I can't tell you how good it is to hear that."

"Grace? Is this you?"

She laughed. "Yes, it's me, Duane."

"Sweet Jesus am I glad to hear from you! How in the world are ya?"

"I'm better than I have been in years," Grace told him. "How's business?"

"Interesting that you should ask. That's actually one of the reasons I wanted to get in touch with you. I heard that you might be looking to get back into cooking?"

"Cooking of course would be my preference, but right now I'll have to take whatever I can get," Grace told him. "I've been out of the workforce for years. A lot of these places don't seem to want to give me a chance."

"Well, don't you worry about that, because I've got something that is just for you."

Grace perked up. "Go on…"

Duane and his wife were both approaching seventy and were looking to unload several of their businesses. One of them was the very business Grace had just called, *Pleasant's Pleasantries,* a successful local banquet hall.

"If you'd be willing, we can work out a deal to where you can take this thing over."

Grace almost dropped the phone.

"If you're not interested, I understand completely…"

"I'd love to!" Grace almost screamed.

Duane laughed. "Well alrighty then. Let's meet up so we can figure everything out."

Grace hung up with Duane and screamed with happiness. Her daughters, alarmed, came running.

"Are you okay?" Eve asked frantically.

"I'm perfect!" Grace squealed. "Girls, it looks like I might have a job! My old mentor from Eastern is going to sell me his banquet hall!"

The girls erupted into screams, squeals, dances and hops of their own. They knew how much it meant to Grace to get back into the world as her own woman, and were happy to see her taking steps to do so.

Two days later she met with Duane, his wife, and a representative from the local small business administration office to get the plan together to transfer ownership of the banquet hall from the Pleasants to Grace. In order to prepare herself mentally for her first major career undertaking in over a decade, Grace spent hours studying her Bible, praying and fasting. However, an important piece of her relationship with God was lacking. As she read her Bible, Hebrews 10:25 kept popping into her mind: "…*not neglecting to meet together, as is the habit of some…*"

Going back to Christ First was out of the question, namely because Grace did not want to deal with their nosiness and judgment. The deacon board that had been crippled by Dean's divisiveness had lost all of its key members and the ones that remained were struggling to secure decent pastoral applicants. Some of the members who were loyal to Rev. Riley left when he did, and others, disgusted with the recent developments, had transferred their membership to other local churches. Grace knew Rev. Buckley was probably turning over in his grave. She was hurt that the church she had once loved and devoted herself to had fallen victim to religious people who desired to play church more than they did to have a bonafide relationship with Jesus, but she also knew that she needed to focus on getting herself and her daughters in a good spot mentally and physically.

Grace continued to ponder the Hebrews Scripture in order to decide whether or not she even wanted to bother with another church. The empty feeling in her heart was the final determinant. There were so many benefits of going to a church, the benefits that had helped her through her rough times when she first started going to Christ First: Not just the teaching she received, but also the opportunities for fellowship, friendship, and community outreach. The Christ First of old had truly been a blessing, and Grace was confident that there was a church out there that was actually preaching, teaching and trying its best to live out the vision of Christ.

Praying for God to give her a sign as to which house of worship was a good fit for her and her girls, the Hardaways started visiting churches, just as Grace had done during her first foray into Christianity. Each Sunday at dinner, she and the girls discussed the experience. If the girls had any objection to the church, that settled it. Not before long they found two churches that they all agreed they liked. Both had a good amount of children, had programs established that helped the surrounding community, and the people and pastor were extremely friendly.

Before committing to either of them, there was something Grace had to do.

After attending their second service at Mount Sinai Baptist Church, Grace told the girls to stay in their seats while she spoke to the pastor, Rev. Keenan Ricks. She approached him as he was greeting members and hesitantly tapped his shoulder. He greeted her with a broad smile.

"It's good to see you again. I hope you enjoyed yourself today."

"I did, thank you," Grace replied warmly. "Um, I was wondering if you have a minute?"

He looked confused, but nodded.

Grace waited until the other members cleared out. Clearing her throat, she said, "As I mentioned last week, I am looking for a new home church for myself and my girls, but we didn't have the best experience at our last one, so I was kind of wondering if you wouldn't mind me asking you a question or two."

His face melted into a smile. "No, go right ahead."

"What is your stance on abusive husbands?"

His posture changed.

Grace realized that her delivery was a tad blunt. Maybe she should have started with a disclaimer. "I apologize," she said. "I'm sure that's not a question you're accustomed to from a visitor. It's just that my late husband was abusive, and when I asked for help, I didn't get it. I just wondered what your take was on abusive marriages. Like, if me and my husband would have come to you for that, and he was a deacon, what would you have said or done." She waited hopefully for his response.

"It would depend on the situation," Rev. Ricks responded.

Grace's eyebrows furrowed. "How so?"

"I'd like to think I was a better judge of character than to promote someone to the office of deacon who was that type of person," Rev. Ricks told her. "I'd have to understand why he was being abusive."

"Do you think there's ever a good excuse?" Grace quizzed him.

"No, there are no excuses. But without understanding the why I'd have a difficult time just condemning the man altogether. Good Christian men don't just get abusive without reason."

Grace left dissatisfied.

The next week the girls went back to West Side Baptist Church where Rev. Johnny Milton was the pastor, the same reverend who had been the first to agree to participate in Rev. Riley's pastoral celebration several months back. After service, she approached him with the same question.

"Please, come into my office. Will your daughters be okay out here in the sanctuary for a few minutes?"

Grace nodded.

In Rev. Milton's cozy office, which was reminiscent of Rev. Buckley's--packed full of religious texts--he sat down at his desk and motioned for her to sit across from him.

"I've been doing this for years," he told her, "and although there is no one-size-fits-all approach to what you just described, what I tell members who have come to me in that situation is the same. First, I want to hear from the man that he has repented and he is willing to receive help. I need to hear from the man directly that he knows he has a problem, that he knows what he is doing is not okay. I want him to let me know that when he fails to conduct himself as a man should, he damages not only the wife, but the entire family. You see, Grace, I believe that although we may have different roles, men and women are equal in God's eyes, but I also believe that with increased responsibility comes increased accountability. A man who has been blessed with the opportunity to oversee a family is to be held to the utmost standard. I have daughters myself, and I would never advise them to stay with a man who is abusing them."

He started thumbing through the pages of the worn Bible in front of him and pushed one across the table to her. "As a matter of fact, can you call your daughters in here, Grace?"

Grace stood, went to the door, and motioned for the girls to come in. Shyly they came and flanked their mother as she sat back down across from Rev. Milton.

"If you will, turn to Ephesians chapter five, and read for me verse twenty-five."

Grace read, "For husbands, this means love your wives, just as Christ loved the church. He gave up his life for her."

"Exactly. Christ's sacrifice is the pinnacle of our faith, right? And if you think about what He did, that act was the pinnacle of love. That Scripture there is admonishing husbands to love their wives in the same manner. How is a man showing love for his wife if he is putting his hands on her? Is that how God would like for his daughters to be treated? When you took your marital vows, and you pledged to honor one another, is it safe to say that abuse is actually dishonoring your spouse?"

Grace nodded slowly.

"Colossians 3:19."

Grace read again, "Husbands, love your wives, and do not be harsh with them."

"Good. Now 1 Corinthians 10:13."

"No temptation has overtaken you that is not common to man. God is faithful, and he will not let you be tempted beyond your ability, but with the temptation he will also provide the way of escape, that you may be able to endure it."

"I have been married for 52 years," Rev. Milton told her, "and best you believe me and my wife have had our share of ups and downs. I've made her angry; she's made me angry. But at the end of the day, the Word tells me as a husband, as a man, how to respond when I am angry. I'll admit the temptation has been there to say something I shouldn't--never thought to hit her though--and each time I had to remove myself from the situation, pray, and come back to her later. None of us are going to go through life with a partner and never get angry. There's going to be friction when two people become one. But if we are faithful we can get through those times without alienating our spouse."

Grace felt so happy she could cry. "So when a couple has this type of problem you counsel them in this manner?"

"I do. But I also refer them to Safe Haven as well. They have professional counselors who have spent years studying the very issue."

"Do you advocate getting the police involved or do you tell the wife to be quiet?"

"I have told women to do whatever they needed to do to keep themselves and their children safe, and yes, that involves getting the authorities involved."

"How long do you counsel them?"

"Until it's no longer required."

Grace was impressed. "If you have an abusive deacon..."

"He would be sat down immediately. I'm not saying he would never be reinstated, but until he has taken steps to address his problem, he will not be standing before my congregation."

Grace and the girls exchanged glances. With tears in her eyes, Grace stood to her feet. "Thank you."

He stood as well and offered her his hand. "You are worthy of being loved. I wanted your girls to come in here so they could hear that as well. Love does not hurt. Love is patient, kind, sacrificial, long-suffering. I cannot believe that our loving God would be content to see one of his own be used as a human punching bag."

Grace watched as a huge smile crossed Eve's face. "I think this is the one, Mom," she told Grace.

Grace laughed. "I think you're right."

With that part of her psyche being fulfilled, Grace was feeling better than ever. But there was still one more thing hanging over her head. Surprisingly, there were moments in her life during which she did mourn Dean. Somehow, Grace had managed to love some part of Dean even while he was oppressing her, and when she realized she was having a harder time dealing with her emotions than she expected, she called Safe Haven and made an appointment to speak to one of their counselors.

Adriana Willoughby was a lovely redhead with a soft voice. Grace took to her right away. In addition to the psychological expertise that she provided that helped Grace sort out her feelings, she also helped Grace come to a very important decision. It was one that would not only impact Grace but the girls as well, so she decided to discuss it with them one night over dinner.

"I'd like to sell the house."

The girls had been engaged in lively chatter--something that would never have happened before with Dean--but stopped immediately once they heard their mother's declaration.

"Good, I hate this place," Eve mumbled.

Grace wasn't surprised. There hadn't been many happy moments in that house. "So you wouldn't miss it... good. I know you all are still getting used to giving me your honest opinion, but I want it right now. I've seen a few beautiful houses that would be closer to my new job and your cousins, but that would mean you'd have to go to another school."

The girls exchanged glances.

"I don't care," Eve said flatly. "I'm sick of stuffy old Cornerstone anyway."

Grace wasn't surprised to hear this. "What about the rest of you? Tell me the truth. If you'd rather not leave your friends I understand."

All of them shrugged.

Grace turned to her youngest baby. Naomi had always been the one to have problems in school, but she had improved greatly since Dean passed. Grace didn't want to do anything to upend her academically. "Nay?" she asked gently. "Do you want to stay at Cornerstone?"

"No," she admitted. "Some of the kids were mean to me when I was having a hard time reading."

"What kids?" Eve barked.

Grace held up her hand. "Calm down Mama Bear, no need to beat up kindergartners," she said, chuckling. "It looks like I've gotten my answer. We're all in need of a fresh, brand new start, and I think a move is the best thing for all of us."

All of the girls leaped out of their seats to hug and cheer. After dinner they joined their mother in her bedroom as she went to Zillow and searched for houses. After oohing and aahing over several, they headed down to the basement for popcorn and a movie. As they huddled together on the couch, Grace couldn't stop herself from smiling. A new home, a new shot at a career doing what she loved, happy kids, and a happy, carefree her. *This* was the life she'd always wanted. And for the first time in years, she truly felt that she deserved it.